Queen Zenobia & the Brigade of Persistence

Emojis Book II

Evan Clouse

COVER IMAGE ILLUSTRATED BY

Gabe Perez

CONTENTS

This book is dedicated to every person who cares about our personal freedom. To every person who cares about our democracy. To every person who shuns the politics of hate and division. To every person who accepts and embraces others for who they are. Thank you for your voices. Thank you for your caring. Thank you for your kind hearts. I love you all.

ACKNOWLEDGMENTS

I would like to thank every person who has supported me and understands just how important this work is to me. Thank you for reading. Thank you for your input. Thank you for caring. You know who you are.

Chapter 1

Celestial Eyes

The fresh blood spatters were beginning to congeal and freeze on her enthralled freckled face on this Christmas Eve, 2023. She removed the black hood from her copper bangs and surveyed the carnage with her glimmering green eyes. Her thin mauve lips curled upwards in an evil smirk as her eyes scanned the frozen, snowy gravel that was saturated by her first victim's blood. *One down, a ton more to go,* she thought to herself while peering at the dismembered arm and leg that had been ruthlessly sawed from his body and haphazardly tossed to the side. She could no longer hide her excitement and began jumping and clapping like a schoolgirl as she glared at the decimated face and skull of a now former corrupt health insurance executive.

"This is so (expletive) cool," she admired to herself as her gleaming emerald eyes continued to survey the macabre destruction. "Oh, I feel soooo (expletive) alive!" she exclaimed. "Hey, how are *you* doin' buddy? Not so good? Well, can I interest you in our platinum plan? Sure, it costs a (expletive) ton more, but on the plus side, there's waaaay more shit that it won't cover. No? Not interested? Well, (expletive) you then. And (expletive) your worthless insurance."

She looked around at her unfamiliar surroundings and said to herself, "Now how the (expletive) do I get back to Morgan's? No way I'm driving that ugly (expletive) thing. Only assholes drive swasti-cars. I wouldn't be caught dead in one. This douchebag would though, heh, heh, heh. Guess I'm walkin'. (expletive), it's cold. Why couldn't Morgan have written me as being all hot blooded and shit? I'm gonna have to talk to her about that. And I don't want these (expletive) freckles, either. And I should get to eat ice cream in at least every other chapter. Oh, and I also want…"

"Oh, my dearest Sruja, just what have you done?" Agatha Cabot asked her ward as the pair looked down at the horrific scene on Earth from their subdivision in Eden. Everywhere throughout the lush landscape was a menagerie of female spirits laughing, talking, and splashing in a deep azure pond. The intoxicating aroma of exotic flowers filled the air while a brilliant star's warm beams enveloped their heavenly home in a brilliant yellow.

Sruja looked up at her mentor, shrugged, and said in her native Hindi, "What do you mean, Agatha? I only did what I was requested to do. It was you who told us all to look after your descendants, after all. I remember it quite clearly. You said, 'Whatever it is that my Sophia, Lori, or Morgan may need from us, we shall provide. They are my most special ones. My family. My mediums who will one day join us here in Eden to also protect the future female mediums of the Earth. So, anything that they may require, we shall provide to them.' Remember that, Agatha?"

"Yeah, toots, remember that?" an approaching Minnie Marples parroted in her high pitched, squeaky voice. The fringe on her short, white flapper dress swayed with each step. She leaned upon Agatha's firm shoulder and batted her long, black eyelashes before continuing in her cartoonish voice. "Remember Agatha? We were to fulfill any and all requests from your family. That's why I took care of all those assholes who were harassing your Lori. All she had to do was recite that incantation once, and I became connected to her. And from that point on, if any big lug bothered her with those dastardly machines, I acted on her behalf. Alls I needed was the incantation and then for Lori to respond with an 'Angry' emoki. Or, is it emoti? Oh, they're called emojis. Weird word, huh? Anyways, alls I needed was to be summoned and BANG, ZOOM, BAP! I took those bastards out using their own expressions. Yep, I 'Liked' that one guy up the ass until his innards came out. Remember that one? So funny. Or that guy that couldn't stop laughing and those young toughs beat the snot out of him? That was fun. Yeah, or that pious bitch that was undone by her own 'Praying Hands' emoki, um, I mean emoji. Guess her prayers didn't work. I heard she ended up with a one-way ticket to Flamesville, heh, heh, heh. Then, of course, there was her asshole husband who I had drool himself to death. Yep, he just kept on-a droolin' and a-droolin' until he looked like a deflated balloon! Oh, what fun I've had with Lori. I really do hope that some more men harass her. Good times. Good times. Anyways, toots, I did all of that for your family, just like Sruja. So, what's with all the hubbub-bub?"

"Ladies," Agatha began. "I do appreciate your efforts, and I thank you for watching over my girls. But, Sruja, I do believe you may have overstepped your bounds."

"Why?" a defiant Sruja countered. "I did *exactly* what was asked of me. Here, look! This is the incantation that she used. Ex corde meo et ex manibus meis nunc intelliget populus meus. Which means, 'From my heart and from my hands people will now understand my creations.' So, what's the problem?"

Agatha paused for a moment to collect her thoughts before responding. "Yes, that was the incantation that Morgan finally found and recited. But her intention was to bring to life only *one* of her creations. Larry the Leopard. Her animated, constantly rhyming character from her children's book. It was never her intention to bring to life, um, *her*. Her *dark* creation. This Maddy Sommers creature who Morgan created to be a freedom fighting serial killer. She is tenacious and violent and…"

"And whatta mouth on her!" Minnie shouted out as the trio watched Maddy trudging through the brush on the outskirts of Plymouth, Massachusetts. "Oh my (expletive) God! It's (expletive) cold out here! Why the (expletive) does Morgan live so far away from this construction site? I've been walking for hours! I'm gonna miss (expletive) Christmas morning! Ow! (expletive) tree branches! Hit me right in the (expletive) head! Oh, I'm *totally* using Morgan's sweet-ass ride from now on to get to and from my little murderous escapades. Ooooh, I'm gonna look soooo cool behind the wheel of that (expletive) 1968 Pontiac Tempest. And I need a cool theme song to crank as I'm driving around wearing my cool sunglasses and shit. I wonder how much trunk space there is? I'm gonna have a lot of bodies to haul around. Yep, I'm gonna have to measure that (expletive) trunk when I get back to Morgan's. If I ever *get* back to her (expletive) house! This (expletive) sucks!"

"Yes," Agatha continued. "She does have quite the vocabulary. But that isn't the biggest issue. The *biggest* issue is that she is a serial killer who has now murdered someone, and this may cause trouble for my Morgan. We really need to find a way to undo this."

"Listen, this isn't my fault," Sruja argued. "Look at the incantation again. It doesn't say 'creation.' It says *'creations.'* Plural. So, I took it literally and brought *both* of her creations to life. And as far as undoing it, well, Morgan will have to stumble upon the correct incantation for me to do that, and quite frankly, I'm not sure that she is going to want to. This Maddy character might just come in handy. Just think of having your own personal assassin at your disposal. All Morgan has to do is write a scene for Maddy to perform and it shall be done. And, Agatha, may I point out that I am *only* responsible for fulfilling a medium's request. How they choose to use my gift is up to them. So, if you want to guide Morgan, maybe you should whisper into her *grandmother's* ear, because there's no way to reverse this."

"Or we could consult the queen," Agatha replied. "Perhaps *she* knows of a way to undo this and send this foul-mouthed beast back into the pages where she belongs. Yes, I shall consult the queen. She is the wisest of us all. She has been connected to the female mediums and witches of the Earth since her arrival here in 274AD. She was a brilliant warrior on Earth and commanded a very large section of the Middle East which was then known as Palmyra of the Roman Empire. She then disconnected from Rome and declared independence for Palmyra, which did not sit well. She was defeated by the Roman forces and held in Rome until her passing. But her tenacity and wisdom lived on. It lived on here, in Eden, as she collected others like her. Others like *us*. Others who could connect with the gifted women of the Earth. The mediums and the witches. We would be the source of their power. And just like in her beloved Palmyra, she has been a strong, wise, and just leader of all of us here. She is a cultured monarch and fosters an intellectual environment. She welcomes the input of scholars and philosophers, like ourselves. She is accepting of everybody and protective of minorities. And just like in Palmyra, she has created a multicultural, multiethnic empire. But this time, it is an empire made up only of women who may be called upon to support and protect the gifted women of Earth. She says that women will one day rule the Earth. I simply do not see it. We are too fragmented, and most men are too brutal. They exploit our differences and use them to keep us divided. But perhaps I will be proven wrong one day. Yes, I shall summon our queen. Queen Zenobia. Has she returned from her holiday?"

"I dunno," Minnie's squeaky voice answered. "Let me check." Minnie sauntered over to a harvest gold rotary phone and dialed a number. "Jeez, you'd think we could update our technology around here. I mean…hey girl! It's Minnie! Whatcha doin'? You don't say. You *don't* say! Oh my God, *you don't say*! Turned his entire body inside out? That's so cool. Where's that medium at? Berlin? Cool. I've always wanted to be summoned by someone in Germany. Okay, we gotta catch up. Come over to my place tonight. Oh, I dunno. How about eight-ish? Listen, is Zens back yet? Yeah? Just arrived? Could you send her down to the pond? Oh, I dunno. Agatha has a stick up her ass about somethin' and wants to see if Zens knows how to undo an incantation. Well, that's what I *told* her, but she still wants to talk to Zens. Yeah, there's plenty of ale. Okay, cool. Thanks! See ya tonight!"

Minnie hung up the phone and turned around to a smiling Sruja and a scowling Agatha when a thick plume of red smoke appeared between them. Within the dense fog, an imposing woman wearing a pure white flowing robe levitated above her reverential subjects. She looked down upon them with her glowing red eyes and said in a deep, husky voice, "Who *dares* to summon Queen Zenobia? Who *dares* to disturb their queen? Who *dares* to…" she then broke out into laughter as her bare toes descended upon the soft green grass. "Oh, I can't do this shit with a straight face. Wazzup bitches? Oh, I've missed you so!"

Queen Zenobia was immediately embraced by a trio of laughing spirits. "Okay, okay, I love you too. Jeez. It's like a damned puppy when you get home," a joyful Zenobia stated. "What's going on? What didja need me for?"

"Well, Zens," Minnie began. "Before we get to that, how was your holiday? Where did you go? What did you see? We want all the details."

"Oh, that'll take a while," a chuckling Zenobia replied. "But I'll give you the quick version. Oh, ladies, the sights that I have seen. I heard through the grapevine that The Keepers in Enlightenment had created a new weapon. A new *female* weapon. And I just had to see it for myself. So, I've been hanging around in the Sirius system watching this unstoppable killing machine named Sin.D. take out every toxic man on that planet. Oh, ladies, you should see her. The ruthlessness. The brutality. The sexual perversion. The only thing I didn't like about her is that she has quite the mouth on her. Yes, I can't tell you how many F-Bombs that woman drops."

"Well, my queen," Agatha interjected. "Speaking of foul language, we have a bit of a problem on Earth. You see, my descendent Morgan Cabot requested for one of her creations to come to life. A delightful, animated leopard in fact. But Sruja, um, mistakenly brought another of Morgan's characters to life as well. Her name is Maddy, and she is, um, well she is, well, just come take a look."

"Okay, I'll take a look," Zenobia stated as she approached the viewing portal. "But Agatha, for the umpteenth time, you do *not* have to refer to me as your queen. Zenobia, Zens, Z-String, Z Bomb, are all acceptable. Please, Agatha. You are such a talented spirit. You have all that you could ever want in our paradise. Plenty of food.

Plenty of ale. Swimming. Tennis. Horseback riding. And, if we ever need anything, the new convenience store is just a few blocks away! Man, was *that* cloud a bitch to get re-zoned though. But we did it! And do you know why?"

The three women looked at each other with rolling eyes and answered in unified, bored voices, "Because we're women." "That's right!" Zenobia excitedly yelled back. "So, Agatha, it really wouldn't kill you to take that stick out of your ass and loosen up a bit. Okay, what am I looking at?" "Well, my que…um…Z Bomb," Agatha sheepishly answered. "You are looking at *that.*"

An enraged Maddy was climbing the trellis on the front of the home of the Ladies Cabot. "How many (expletive) miles have I had to walk and now I gotta (expletive) climb this (expletive) thing! And for what? Just so I can kill that insurance douchebag and…well, okay. That was (expletive) worth it. And that Poindexter bartender did make a nice gin and tonic. But still. I'm covered in (expletive) blood, and I'm (expletive) cold, and I'm (expletive) tired, and I'm (expletive) starving! There'd better be a hot meal in my future and Morgan had better not have closed that (expletive) window!"

"Oh, my," Zenobia replied as her face flushed red. "Yes, I see what you mean. She could give that Sin.D. a run for her money with that mouth. But what is the problem?"

"Well, my que…um, Z-String," Agatha answered. "You see, Larry the Leopard is quite harmless. Annoying? Yes. But harmless. But this Maddy was written by my Morgan to be a vigilante serial killer. If you think that her *mouth* is bad, you should see what she did to an insurance executive and I'm worried that my Morgan will be blamed for this. We need to find a way to reverse the incantation and send her back to just being a fictional character. Please, look at what she has done."

The scene suddenly changed, and the quartet of women were peering down upon the decimated body of Maddy's victim. Zenobia stared into Agatha's eyes, shrugged, and said, "And again I ask, what is the problem? A bad man has been sent to his death. In a really brutal way, at that. Your Morgan seems to have quite a bit of pent-up anger to have created a character so deliciously violent. And it seems to *me* that Morgan's creation may be useful. Hey! Who is it that Sophia's talking to on the phone?"

"Oh, that is her cousin," Sruja answered. "Her cousin Victoria Colombo."

"Victoria *Colombo?*" a shocked Zenobia asked. "Like, the leader of the Plymouth witch's coven? Why aren't they yelling at each other? Witches and mediums hate each other!"

"Not any longer," Agatha stated. "They used to hate one another, but Sophia and Victoria have buried the hatchet, so to speak, and are now on the best of terms. Yes, they genuinely love one another."

"And that's not all," Minnie's high-pitched squeak contributed. "Morgan and Naomi O'Sullivan, who is *also* a witch, love one another as well. Since you've been gone there are two sets of mediums and witches who have united."

"Oh my God, oh my God, oh my God," a nearly hyperventilating Zenobia yelled out as she began furiously pacing around the lush garden. "Are you *serious?* Are you telling me that two *mediums* and two *witches* have united? That they love and care for one another? Oh, I have waited *centuries* for this! Don't you see? Don't you ladies understand what this *means?* The one thing that has prevented women from overthrowing the brutish men of the Earth and taking their rightful place on the throne is their hatred for one another and their inability to unite against a common enemy. The gifted women, the mediums and witches, have *always* hated one another. And that hatred prevented them from focusing on breaking their shackles of servitude to men. Until now. If the mediums and witches can unite across the Earth, then they can help the *other* women to tap into *their* natural gifts. The Earth will be *filled* with women who are either mediums or witches! And *those* women can then overthrow the evil men of the world and create Eden on Earth! The curse of stupid Eve will finally be broken! It will no longer matter that she was tempted by evil and ate that stupid apple. All past sins shall be forgiven, and women will be free to evolve into their true, powerful selves. All that was needed was for mediums and witches to get past their pettiness and unite. And we now have that. Don't you see? We now have the opportunity to build our army! Our army of gifted women! We will now build our Brigade of Persistence! And this Maddy character may be just what we need to put us over the top. Oh, look. Maddy's at the window. And boy, is she pissed that it's closed. Come, come ladies. Let us watch how this plays out. This is going to be fun."

Chapter 2

(Expletive)

"Morgan!" Sophia yelled out later that evening. "Would you and Larry stop jumping on the bed? It sounds like the ceiling is about to crash in!" "Sorry Gramma!" Morgan replied followed by Larry. "Yes, we will stop causing such a commotion. Maybe we'll just look out the window quietly and stare at the ocean!" The tittering pair went over to the window and gazed at the majestic snowfall that glistened on the nearby branches and ground. Morgan had her arm around Larry's soft shoulders and was resting her head against his. She had never felt so safe, warm, and happy in her life. Her abusive father was gone. No one was bullying her. She had the love of a best friend and the love and security of her family. And now, she had her animated companion of her own creation. She shed a single tear of happiness as she stared at the tranquil landscape. Morgan was finally home.

Suddenly there was another pair of piercing eyes staring back at her from outside the window. The red-headed, green-eyed young woman that was sitting on the roof scowled at her and yelled out, "Hey! Are ya gonna open this fuckin' window or *what*? It's *cold* out here! Why didja think that I kept it open, anyway? Oh whatevs. I'll just do it myself." The young woman lifted the unlocked window open and crawled into Morgan's bedroom. She was dressed in black and covered from head to toe in blood. "Wh-who are *you*?" Morgan stuttered.

"Who am *I*?" the young woman roared back. "Well, isn't *this* just a fine how-do-ya-do? To not even be recognized by your own creator. That hurts, Morgan. It really hurts." "M-M-*Maddy*?" Morgan stammered. "Uh, yeah. Hi kid. Sorry about the mess, but that douchebag was *quite* a bleeder. And man, are my arms sore! All that sawing then bashing his stupid head in. It kinda takes a toll, y'know? Hey, you got a shower that I could use? And maybe a set of jammies?"

"Maddy!" Morgan yelled out. "What are you *doing* here? You aren't *real*!" "Oh!" Maddy bellowed. "But *this* come-to-life-cartoon *is*? Listen, kid. You really should be more careful with your incantations. You never know what you might bring into this world by being willy-nilly with that shit. Now, where are we at with the whole shower and jammies situation? Chop-chop, sister! I'm getting blood all over your floor."

"Whose blood *is* that?" a shocked Morgan asked as she looked at Maddy's spattered face and saturated black hoodie. "Well, you should know," Maddy responded. "You wrote it. Right after you said the incantation. You wanted me to find a corrupt insurance executive. You know, the type of dickhead that denies people critical care then laughs all the way to the bank when they die. And it was so easy! I found one leaving a local bar last night. All I had to do was flirt with him a little bit, then have him drive to that construction site. On man, was *he* surprised when I unzipped my hoodie. He thought that I was gonna show him my, um, well you know. But instead, I pulled out a big knife and slashed his throat! Then, as he was clutching his throat trying to stop the bleeding, I dragged him out of the car. He was still alive when I sawed off his right arm. And he was still kinda kickin', well, not exactly *kickin'*, heh, when I sawed off his left leg. He was dead by the time I took off his head and smashed it with a sledgehammer. Man did *that* feel good! I guess I have some repressed anger or somethin'. Maybe I should see somebody about that. Nah. I'm fine. Anywhoo, I kinda got lost coming back to the house. I've never been in this town before and it's not like you wrote much of a description. So, how's about that shower and jammies. And maybe a little ice cream, hmmmm?"

"Um, um, um," was all Morgan could manage to say as she heard her mother's footsteps coming up the stairs. Maddy placed her hand on Morgan's shoulder, looked at her with her glimmering emerald eyes and said, "Listen roomie. Whether you like it or not, you're stuck with me. You called me here. You wrote the incantation in the book. So, *you're* here and *I'm* here. And Morgan…we're gonna have a *lot* of fun together, heh, heh, heh."

"Yeah, well, maybe," Morgan blurted out. "But right now, I need you to hide under the bed."

Maddy defiantly folded her arms and tapped her left foot while glaring at her creator. "So, you're ashamed of me, huh?" Maddy stated in a hurt voice. "That's real nice, Morgan. Real (expletive) nice. To be ashamed of your own (expletive) creation. I mean, I'm like your (expletive) daughter or something! Do you know how it feels for your own parent to be ashamed of you? Well, it hurts, Morgan. It really (expletive) hurts."

"Oh my, oh my, your mother is very near!" Larry exclaimed. "And she will not like Maddy being here!" "Oh, shut the (expletive) up." Maddy replied to Larry. "What the (expletive) are you supposed to *be* anyway? What with your bright yellow fur, curly Q tail, and goo-goo-googly eyes. You're like a (expletive) cartoon come to life! And what's with the (expletive) rhyming? That shit's gonna get real (expletive) annoying, Morgan. You need to do something about that shit."

"Okay, I will!" Morgan yelled out as the handle on her bedroom door began to turn. "Just get your ass under the bed! Now!"

Morgan's mother, Lori, entered the room wearing a quizzical expression. She looked around the room and found her daughter and Larry sitting on the bed reading a book that was turned upside down. "What are you yelling about up here?" she inquired. "And, and what are all these red drops all over the floor? What are you two up to?"

"Nothing, Mom," Morgan replied in an innocent voice. "Um, Larry and I were just playing around and one of his claws got me and I bled a little bit. Sorry. I'll get it cleaned up. And we'll keep it down."

"But Morgan," Larry interjected. "That isn't true. Lying is not a very nice thing to do." Morgan's face turned beet red, as did Maddy's, who was seething from under the bed. *What a (expletive) narc,* she thought to herself. *I'm gonna be wearing that (expletive's) cartoon fur as a (expletive) coat if he doesn't shut his (expletive) mouth.*

"What's this, now?" Lori asked. "Oh, nothing Mom, nothing," Morgan replied through forced chuckles. "It's just something that I'm trying out. I'm trying to write Larry to have a sense of humor, that's all. Still needs some work though, don'tcha think? I'm sorry Larry, but that wasn't funny. It *really* was *not* funny, got it?" "Yes, yes, I understand," a quivering Larry sheepishly answered. "What I said was poorly planned."

"Okay," a content Lori replied. "Listen, I just wanted to tell you that I just heard from Connor. He's coming over and spending the night tonight." *Hell's yeah,* Maddy thought to herself as she stifled her giggles. *You go girl. Get yourself some, heh, heh, heh.* "He's really shook up. He said that they have just now cleaned up the murder scene and it is nothing like he's ever seen before. He just kept saying that it was absolute carnage, and they have to find who did it before they do this again. He said it was so bad that he vomited. It makes him wish he wasn't a detective.

Detective? Maddy screamed at herself. *There's a (expletive) detective coming over here? How the (expletive) is that gonna work? I need a shower! And some (expletive) ice cream! I can't be wandering all over the house with a detective here!*

"So," Lori continued. "I just wanted to let you know that Connor is spending the night, and he's really frazzled, so please no commotion from you two tonight, okay?" "No problem, Mom," Morgan dutifully answered. "We'll be quiet. And that sounds really awful. I'm sure Connor will catch whoever did this. Good night."

"Good night sweetie, and thanks for your understanding," Lori replied as she exited the room. "Yeah, I don't know this detective Connor," Maddy stated as she rolled from under the bed leaving a crimson streak on the carpet, "but there's *no way* this mother(expletive) is gonna catch lil' ol' *me*. Right? *Right* Morgan?"

Morgan looked up at the ceiling to avoid Maddy's glaring green eyes. She cleared her throat and responded in a shaking voice, "Well, you see Maddy, I created you as a fictional character. Your antics weren't supposed to be real. I don't really believe in people taking the law into their own hands. It's fiction. It's a fantasy. I'm sorry, Maddy, but I can't have Connor and the rest of the town going around thinking there's a psychotic serial killer running around. I'm going to have to tell them, Maddy. And I'm going to have to find some way to put you back into my pages. I'm sorry."

Maddy stood glaring at Morgan with her arms crossed while she furiously tapped her left foot. "Huh," she began. "So, you're gonna (expletive) narc on me, huh? Sure, sure, why wouldn't you? You just created me and then brought me to life. And for what? Oh, just to stab me in the back. Real nice, Morgan. But I suppose I should be used to it. I guess I was created to do nothing but suffer in this world. No shower. No jammies. No ice cream. And now being forsaken by my creator. I guess I now know what Jesus felt like when they hung him on that cross. He was put on this Earth to be a martyr, and I guess I was too. That's okay, Morgan. I understand."

"*Really?*" a shocked Morgan asked. "You're comparing yourself to Jesus Christ? Are you *insane*? Jesus died for our sins. You...you...are a killing machine! You cuss and lie and have an inflated ego and murder people! I did not write you to resemble Jesus in any way, shape, or form! That's just ridiculous!"

"Oh, *is* it now?" a slightly grinning Maddy retorted. "Sure, sure, maybe on the *surface* we don't have a lot in common. I mean, we *would* make a pretty unlikely couple. But let's just think about this for a moment. We were *both* risen from the dead, now, weren't we? We *both* hate sinners, now, don't we? And we *both* have suffered greatly at the hands of our creator, now haven't we? *He* was forsaken by his father and crucified! *I* have been forsaken by *you* and denied a (expletive) hot shower, jammies, and ice cream! So, it seems to be that me and JC are two peas in a pod."

"Wow," Morgan replied. "Just wow. I really shouldn't have written you to be able to rationalize so well. Whatever. Believe whatever grandiose shit you want. The point is that I can't have it on my conscience knowing that I've created a monster who is freaking out the whole town. I need for you to go back into the pages. Please understand. You won't be gone. You'll live forever in my pages. But until I find a way to do that, you have to stop killing people and you have to clean up your language."

"What the (expletive) are you talking about?" an annoyed Maddy countered. "There's nothin' wrong with my (expletive) language. Maybe I can refrain from killing people as long as I don't see injustice being committed, but nobody is gonna tell me that there's something wrong with my (expletive) language!"

"Nothing wrong with your language?" Morgan roared back. "Are you serious? Every other word you use is the F-Bomb! Do you see how many times this author has typed (expletive)? Do you know why? Because every time there is an (expletive) it's you using the F-Bomb! There must be fifty of them so far just in this chapter! So, yes, you are going to clean up your language. Or else."

(Expletive) you, Morgan," a defiant Maddy replied. "Or else *what*, bitch?" Morgan casually reached over to her bedside table and picked up her notepad and a pencil. She flashed a wicked little smile before saying, "Or else I'm going to write that you contract some sort of thyroid condition that makes you gain weight. A *lot* of weight. See how easy it is to go through windows or run down your victims while carrying three-hundred pounds."

Maddy gasped in horror and clutched her be-freckled face with her shaking hands. "Okay, Morgan, okay. Let's just calm down. No need to be rash about this. Morgan, please just place the paper and pencil down and slowly walk away. Don't think about it. Just calmly put the paper and pencil down and walk away. What you are saying is quite serious. I hear you. We're all calm now. Just put the paper and pencil down and everything will be alright."

"So, you'll watch your language?" a grinning Morgan asked. The pair stared at one another with blazing intensity before a nervous Larry interjected. "Oh, please Maddy, won't you agree? All of this tension is overwhelming to me." "Shut up, Larry," Morgan and Maddy said in terse unison while continuing their stare down.

Finally, after four long minutes of icy silence, Maddy said, "Oh, fine! Can I say *'fine'*? It's a four-letter word that starts with 'F', after all. Is that *fine* with you, your highness? Okay, I won't say that word throughout this f-f-f, UGH! This is hard! That's what she said! Fine! I'll watch my language. Are you happy now?"

"Yes, thank you," a satisfied Morgan answered as she placed the paper and pencil back on the nightstand. "Good," Maddy replied. "I need to go for a walk and clear my head before that f-f-f, UGH! Damned cop gets here. But I'll be back. And when I return, I expect a hot shower, some comfy jammies, and a huge bowl of ice cream. Got it, sister? Okay, cool. Lata Gatas!"

Before Morgan could protest, Maddy's lithe frame had bolted out the window. Larry and Morgan watched her silhouette disappear down the darkened street. Morgan could only nod her head after Larry said, "Oh dear. This could be bad. I'm afraid that Maddy is stark raving mad."

"I'm so f-f-f, UGH! Damned stark raving mad right now." Maddy muttered to herself as she trudged down Plymouth's frosty streets. "Stupid Morgan with her stupid rules and no stupid shower or stupid jammies. Stupid Larry with his stupid goo-goo-googly eyes and stupid rhyming. Stupid Lori and her stupid cop boyfriend. This whole thing is stupid. Why couldn't I have been written by somebody cool? Like, some cool chick bass player in a cool punk band or something? We'd hang out, rock out, have a few drinks, cuss all we want, and then I'd slash some wannabe date rapist in the back alley of the club. Yeah, those would be good times. But *nooooo*. I had to be written by little miss goody-goody. Watch your language, Maddy. Don't eat ice cream, Maddy. Don't kill anybody, Maddy."

She was then distracted by a muffled scream coming from a nearby house. She ran to a lit living room window. A tiny ember of rage began growing as she looked at a scruffy man towering over a bleeding and bruised woman. Her rage intensified and her face turned beet red before she said, "Oh, hell no. Not on *my* watch. And I don't recall actually promising not to *kill* anybody, heh, heh, heh."

"Sorry for the mess, sister," Maddy stated to the shocked woman who was recoiled in fear on the couch. She cackled with glee as she looked down at the man's skull that had a hammer protruding out of it. Streaks of blood covered the floor, walls, and dripped down the television screen. "You know, you really should get better at picking men," She stated. "I know, I know. I've been there. It's easy to get sucked in by these abusive assholes. And once you figure out who they really are, it's too late. They have their hooks in you. One minute they're nice and sweet, the next they're knocking you around. It's totally confusing, and you live your life in complete fear of what he might do if you displease him. If you stay, he'll keep beating you. If you leave, he might hurt you worse. Or those that you care about. It happens all the time. It's not your fault. It's his and every asshole like him. But, hey! Silver lining here! This little f-f-f-UGH! Asshole is now dead, and he can't hurt you or anybody else anymore. So, you're welcome. Just do me a little favor. Um, just tell the cops that it was some male intruder or something okay? And give me a few minutes before you call the cops. Okay, well, gotta go. It's been really fun. We should get a coffee sometime! See ya!"

Maddy somersaulted out the broken living room window and began jogging down the street and into a wooded area. "Well, shit," she said to herself as she navigated the slumbering foliage. "This is probably gonna piss Morgan off. But it's not my fault! What could I do? Just allow that dick to beat that woman? Nope. Something had to be done. I was in the right place at the right time. Maybe it was divine intervention or some shit. Maybe..." Her thoughts trailed off and she stopped in her tracks while looking around the eerie surroundings. "W-Who's there?" she said as her heart began pounding.

"Hello, Maddy," a voice whispered from within the biting December breeze. "My name is Queen Zenobia. I have been watching you. I believe that you can help me. Help *us*. Help all of the women of Earth join together in a Brigade of Persistence to overthrow the evil men of this world. I am here to offer you a deal. I will ensure that Morgan never finds a way to put you back into her pages. And *you* will agree to abide by Morgan's rules, get along with Larry, and not kill anybody until we are ready to strike. I know that this goes against your nature, but I need you to be obedient, Maddy. I need for you to be patient. I need to hold you back until our time has come. You will be our secret weapon. But this will only work if you keep a low profile and not speak a word of our agreement to anyone. Oh, and do please watch your language. The ladies Cabot certainly aren't prudes, but they do disapprove of such gratuitous use of profanity. Do we have a deal?"

"So, let me get this straight," Maddy said to the disembodied voice as she stroked her chin with her bloody fingers. "You want me to be a good little girl and follow Morgan's rules and in exchange I get to stay alive on the Earth and join some bad-ass bitches to overthrow the patriarchy? Did I get that right? Well sister, to *that* I have only one response. Where the (expletive) do I sign?"

Chapter 3

Put On A Happy Face

Maddy was climbing the trellis towards Morgan's second-story bedroom window when she heard Detective Connor O'Sullivan's voice from the front porch. "I'm sorry again, Lori. I don't know what the hell's going on in this town. Another murder. This one at least kinda makes sense though. He's a guy that has a reputation for beating on women. Especially his wife. We've had him down at the station a hundred times, but the women never press charges out of fear. Fear that the criminal justice system, including me, won't do our jobs and will release this piece of crud right back into their home. It absolutely breaks my heart when women don't trust us. But who can blame them? There are so many men out there who are all too happy to be a member of the good ol' boys club and protect their own. Men who are sexist pigs and look down upon women. And yes, a lot of male cops are that way too. It's disgusting that women mistrust us so and it's even *more* disgusting that they are right to do so. But I don't think this is connected to the insurance guy. The battered wife said some short, red-headed woman crashed through their living room window, picked up a hammer, and beat this guy to a pulp."

Sonofabitch! Maddy thought to herself while her frozen fingers clung onto the trellis. *I told her not to say that! That's the thanks you get for being a good samaritan, I suppose.*

"Anyway, I've gotta go. Deputy Gigi Holloway is at the crime scene now conducting the interview. I've gotta go and make sure everything's secured. I'm so sorry that I've ruined your Christmas, Lori." Lori looked into her beau's eyes, tussled her blonde locks, and suggestively whispered, "You haven't ruined anything. Just come over whenever you're done. And save some energy." Connor's eyes widened and his pasty white skin flushed red as he nervously nodded and hastily retreated to his car.

"What the hell did you say to that boy?" Lori's mother, Sophia Cabot asked while wearing a knowing grin. "I haven't seen a man blush like that since I was in high school." "Never you mind, mother," Lori replied while mirroring her mother's grin. "I'm all wound up. Why don't we make some popcorn and watch a movie?" "Sure, why the hell not? I'll make two bags if Morgan's gonna join us," Sophia replied. "Let's run upstairs and see what she's up to. It might be nice for the ladies Cabot to have a nice evening together. Oh, and Larry, I suppose. That damned cartoon leopard better keep his mouth shut. I don't like being interrupted when I'm watching my stories."

Maddy lifted the bedroom window and catapulted into the room. "Hiya roomie!" she declared as she landed on her feet and spread her arms as though she were a gold medal gymnast who had just stuck a perfect landing. "Listen, all kidding aside, I really need that shower, some jammies, and something to eat. So how aboutcha just go ahead and arrange that, alright? Chop, chop sister! My poor lil' bod needs some relief."

"Hello Maddy, how are you," Larry interrupted. "We were just wondering what you've been up to." Maddy looked at Larry, rolled her eyes dismissively, and silently shook her head in disgust. Morgan then said, "Yes, actually we *were* just talking about that. It seems as though there has been another murder. Please, Maddy, please. *Please* tell me you weren't involved. I'm in enough trouble as it is."

Maddy began lightly chuckling before responding. "Well, kid, see this is kind of a funny story. Seriously. Now, you may not *think* it's funny right away, but I'm *sure* the humor will grow on ya. You see, I was just strolling along thinking about how *wise* you were to tell me to watch my language. You see, I would *never* want to offend someone by using any sort of crass vocabulary, so you making me promise not to use that one word was very wise of you. Anyhooo, I was just strolling along when I heard the scream of a damsel in distress. Well, I rushed over to a window and what did my little green eyes see? Why, it was a *very big, bad man* who was hurting this helpless woman. Now, *you* never wrote that I have a cell phone, so this is *kinda* your fault. You see, if I *had* been written to have a cell phone, I *most certainly* would have called the cops and allowed the proper authorities to take care of the situation. But, seeing as how *you* never wrote about me having a cell phone, I was left with two options. Option Numero-Uno; Ignore the situation and allow that *big, bad man* to continue to hurt that woman, or Option Numero Two-O; to intervene in *whatever* way that lil' ol' me could. Now *certainly* Morgan, you would *agree* that leaving that woman to be harmed would be *awful* of me, *right*? So, what I did was, okay... get ready for this. Here comes the funny part."

Maddy's demeanor suddenly changed from faux sincerity to frenzied excitement. "I smashed through the living room window, landed on my feet, saw a hammer laying on a table, picked it up and went SMASH, SMASH, SMASH into that bastard's face. The final blow lodged the hammer in the back of his skull, and it got stuck there, and I had to stop smashing him, but that's okay. He was already dead. Anyhooo, you shoulda seen this guy's shocked face when I started beating the f-f-f-um-hell out of him! See? I don't use that word anymore. Pretty cool, huh? Anyway, as I was saying, you shoulda heard him screaming like a little girl as I pummeled him with that hammer. It was like, POW! WAAAA! POW! WAAAA! POW! WAAAA! He even pissed himself! Seriously! His pants were totally soaked! See? Isn't that funny? And, as I said, if I *only* had a cell phone to call the proper authorities, then none of this would have happened. Pretty funny, huh?"

Morgan and Larry silently stared at her with their mouths agape. The silence was broken when Lori and Sophia opened the door and unexpectedly entered the room. Lori looked at the petite blood-soaked stranger standing in the middle of her daughter's room and her mind immediately flashed to what Connor had just told her. *The battered wife said some short, red-headed woman crashed through their living room window, picked up a hammer, and beat this guy to a pulp.* She cleared her throat and said in a shaking voice, "M-Morgan. Who is *this* then? Who is this that is covered in…in…is that *blood*?"

"Sure is, Mrs. C! And howdy Grams!" Maddy exclaimed as she extended her hand. "Hiya Lori and Sophia! My name is Maddy! Maddy Sommers. And yes, this is blood, and I am *so sorry* to be tracking it on your lovely floors, but *somebody* who shall remain *nameless* but whose name starts with an '*M*' and ends with an '*organ*' has been a wee bit cinchy with a shower and jammies. Oh, and ice cream. You got any ice cream in this joint? Okay, not important at the moment. Anyhooo, I'm your daughter's creation. You see, when she used the incantation to bring this asshole animated furball to life, it also brought me. Yep, right out of Morgan's mind and into the real world. And let me just say what an *honor* it is to be created by such a *gifted* young lady who comes from such a *lovely* family. So, that pretty much explains it. Who's up for some ice cream?"

"Huh. Suddenly Larry doesn't seem so bad," Sophia muttered under her breath before saying to the group, "Yes, we are quite aware of our Morgan's, um, *creation*. And we are *quite aware* of what Morgan's imagination has you do. So, I just have one question. Maddy, are *you* the one that is responsible for the two murders in our town?"

"Aw shit," Morgan sobbed while hiding her sorrowful face in her hands. "Oh yes! Oh yes! She is the one!" Larry blurted out while his goo-goo-googly eyes rolled around in their bright white sockets. "Tell them Maddy about all you have done!"

"Would you shut the fu-um-would you please be quiet, Larry?" Maddy replied. "I do not need your assistance. Thank you for your cooperation in this matter. Now, Sophia, it is okay to call you

Sophia, isn't it? Or should I call you Grams? We *are* kinda like family. And did I mention what a *wonderful* family you have? Yes, you *certainly* have done a *fine job* raising these two. Why, just earlier tonight, I was thinking…"

Maddy was cut off by Sophia's impatient voice. "Yeah, yeah, they're real peaches. You want to answer my question?" Maddy forced a chuckle and replied, "Oh, you're a no-nonsense, straight to the point type of gal, aren'tcha Sophia? I admire that. Yes, I can certainly see why these ladies turned out to be the *fine, strong* women that they are. You really have done a *wonderful* job with them, Sophia. You should take a bow. Y'know, I was just thinking earlier that…"

She was once again cut off by an increasingly irritated Sophia. "Maddy! Answer the damned question!" "Fine, I will," Maddy responded in her 'hurt' voice. "Sheesh. You don't hafta get your panties all in wad about it. Hey, quick question. Do old broads wear sexy panties? I mean, you've still got the figure for it. I mean, Va-Va-Voom, Sophia. I bet you get *a lot* of attention walkin' down the street. Am I right? It's okay. You can tell us. It's just us girls. Except for… Larry! Get out of here! Girl talk time!"

"Oh my God!" a guilt-ridden Morgan yelled out. "I'll answer the damned question! Yes! Yes, I accidentally brought her to life and yes, she's the one responsible for the deaths of the insurance guy and the wife beater! I'm so sorry. I didn't mean to. Please forgive me."

"Well, that was boring," Maddy stated while blood continued to drip off of her copper strands of hair. "Jeez, Morgan. And you call yourself a writer? I guess I hafta do everything around here. Here let me show ya how to tell a story."

Following a half-hour of a very descriptive and animated retelling of the two murders which included many POWS! WHACKS! and SPLATS!, Lori and Sophia stared at one another in bewildered silence. Lori started to cry as she realized the trouble that her beloved daughter was in and said to her mother, "Oh my lord, what are we going to do Mom? As crazy as this is, Morgan's going to be blamed for this. She's ultimately responsible for the murder of two innocent people."

"Innocent?" Sophia countered. "No, these were not innocent people. This character was not written to murder innocent people. She was written to provide some semblance of justice in an unjust world. These two had it coming. Just like all of *ours* had it coming. We don't really have a high moral ground when it comes to this, now *do we* dear? Or should we ask your ex-husband? Oh right. We can't. He was 'Drooled' to death. By the vengeful spirit that *you* summoned. No, these men were far from innocent."

"I likes the cut of your jib, Sophia," Maddy stated. "You know, I think we're going to get along splendidly. Why just earlier I was thinkin'..." "Maddy, please be quiet," Sophia interrupted. "Morgan, go get our book. I think I know a way out of this. And then, Maddy, I am sorry to say this, but it will be best if we say our good-byes."

Maddy started to reply when she heard a queen's voice in her head. *Not one word, Maddy. Not yet. Remember our deal.* Maddy let out a deep breath and said, "Yeah, I kinda figured that was coming. I understand. At least it'll be fun seeing what Morgan writes about me. Which reminds me, Morgan. You think you could get rid of these freckles? And about my daughter, Josie. She's really fun as a young child but becomes kind of a smartass when she hits her teens. Why don't you do something about that? Cool? Thanks. Anyhooo, it's been really lovely getting to meet you all. Yes, I certainly understand. Morgan's safety is the most important thing here. So, let's just get Morgan out of this trouble that I've caused her. And then, I'll say my good-byes."

"Um, thank you for being so understanding, Maddy," a surprised Lori stated. "Yeah," a suspicious Morgan contributed. "That was *really selfless and understanding* of you. Not exactly characteristics that you are known for." Maddy smiled innocently and shrugged as Morgan left the room to retrieve her family's book of incantations.

The room turned to any eerie red the moment the book was placed into Sophia's waiting hands. "Whooooa! Cool!" Maddy exclaimed while a fearful Larry scurried under the bed. "Oh dear! Oh dear! This is scary! This is not the place for sweet, loving Larry!"

"What are you going to do, Mom?" Lori asked. "It is not what *I* am going to do, my dear," Sophia answered. "It is what *we* are going to do. Come. Hold the book with me. We will turn each page until the right incantation appears to us. We will then recite the incantation, and our vengeful spirit will be summoned. And, to answer your question, what we are going to do is frame some sleezy man for these crimes. Now, which spirit shall it be?"

Sophia turned each page as the room continued to be encased in a dark red glow. She turned to page twenty-three and an incantation began glowing. "Ah, here it is, my dear," Sophia stated. "And it seems to be an incantation that will summon your favorite spirit, Lori. Yes, we shall see what Minnie Marples can do about our little situation."

"Minnie! Phone's for ya!" one of the spirits in Eden yelled out. She handed the harvest gold receiver to Minnie who said in her high-pitched voice, "Thanks toots. Who is it?" "It's that Lori Cabot," the spirit answered before splashing into the warm pond waters. "Oh, cool. Lori. Haven't heard from her for a while. What's she asking for?" She placed the receiver up to her ear and heard Lori's voice say over and over, "Pinge imaginem in tabula et fac malum hominem abire" (Paint a picture in a frame and make a bad man go away).

"Oh, cool!" Minnie squealed as the fringe on her short, black, flapper dress swayed to each strut towards the observation portal. "I get ta take care of some big lug by framin' him for Maddy's moiders. I was kinda wonderin' how they would handle that. Hmmmm, let's see here. Who shall it be? No, not him. Nor him. And not...hey! He's kinda cute! But no. Oh, *there* he is. Connected to the mob. Lotsa extortion and moiders. Plus, a really bad dresser. And what's with the combover, mista? Oh! And he's the brother of Maddy's first victim to boot! Alrightythen, time to get to woik. Hmmmm. I wonder what else I can do with these fun lil' emokis...I mean, emojis."

The brother of the murdered insurance executive sat at his

computer and re-read the news report of his sibling's ghastly demise. "Whatta dumbass," he said to himself while flattening his thin streak of combed over hair. "I told him he'd wind up dead in some construction site someday if he didn't stop his whoring around. Probably some broad's jealous husband. Or maybe it *was* the broad. Now I gotta find a new way to launder my money. That insurance scam was perfect. What a waste. Hey! What the hell is wrong with this thing?" he yelled to his computer whose screen had suddenly turned bright red.

"Whaaaat the heeeell?" he said as a blurry, bright yellow dot appeared in the center of the fiery red background. The yellow dot grew larger and began to come into focus until a harmless smiling emoji filled the screen. "Is this some kinda joke?" he bellowed. A high-pitched woman's voice came out of the computer and said, "Nope. This is your time to die, you big palooka!" The smiling emoji winked at him then jumped out of the screen and attached itself to the man's face. He frantically pulled at the elastic, rubbery substance that was burrowing into his flesh, skull, and brain. He let out an anguished scream as he could feel another presence penetrating the deepest recesses of his thoughts and memories. His screaming stopped once the smiling emoji was firmly attached to his face and the intruder had complete control over his faculties.

"Alrightythen!" the smiling emoji face gleefully stated in a woman's high-pitched squeal. "This is fun! I can actually bring these emojis into the real world and control 'em! Now, Mista Mob Guy, let's just see what you got here in your balding noggin that I can put into a confession letter. Oh yes, this should woik." The man's hands turned bright yellow and began typing while a woman's voice giggled.

Dear cops, It was me. I admit it. I killed my brother. He was about to spill the beans about my money laundering operation through his insurance company. I couldn't have that, so I went with him to that construction site, and I cut off his arms and legs and bashed his face in. I've been filled with remorse and rage ever since. I had so much rage that when I went for a walk, I saw some jerk slapping his broad around. I busted through the window and beat the hell out of him with a hammer. That was me too. But I can't live with this guilt any longer. I murdered my brother and there is no coming back from that. To my family, alls I can say is I'm sorry. See you all in that big cannoli in the sky.

"And now, press 'send' to the coppers, and viola! Maddy and Morgan are off da hook!" a delighted Minnie squealed. The smiling emoji's grin widened as Minnie marched the man's body to his garage. She took his bright yellow hands and placed a hose into his car's exhaust pipe with the other end going in a slightly opened window. She sat his body in the driver's seat and started the ignition. Plumes of deadly exhaust poured into the cabin of the car. Minnie stretched his arms wide, and the emoji face let out a big yawn. "Welp, nap time," Minnie said. Just before she sent the man into his final slumber she thought, "But I really gotta get into the head of that abused wife. She saw Maddy. Gave her description to the coppers. Shouldn't be too difficult. She was traumatized. I'll just sneak into her dreams once this big lug is dead and have her dream about him. I'll change her memories. Then, she'll give the coppers a different story and alls well that ends well, heh, heh, heh."

"Well, alls well that ends well, heh, heh, heh!" Maddy exclaimed after hearing Lori's description of Minnie's actions. "Now, can I *finally* have that shower, jammies, and ice cream? I've had a busy day!"

"Aren't you forgetting something?" Sophia asked while handing the book of incantations to her granddaughter. "Oh, right!" Maddy replied. "Silly me. Time for me to say my good-byes!" She began going around the room and shaking everybody's hands while saying, "Yep, it's been a pleasure to get to meet ya, but I suppose I need to go now. I wouldn't want to overstay my welcome. But you know where to find me if ya ever need me. Yep, you can find me right in

Morgan's funny pages, heh, heh, heh. Okay, Morgan. Send me home. Oh! Do I need to tap my heels three times or some stupid shit?"

"No, I just need to read an incantation in reverse," a solemn Morgan answered. "*This* incantation that I created to bring you here. I just need to make sure I say *creation* instead of *creations* so that Larry doesn't get taken away too. Goodbye Maddy. I'm going to miss you. But you will always be a part of me. I promise you that." She turned to the last page of the book and stared at the glowing green letters. She opened her mouth and prepared to utter the first syllable. Suddenly, flashing bright red capital letters appeared over the incantation. "Blocked?" Morgan yelled out. "I've been *blocked* from this incantation? It won't let me read it! What the hell, Gramma? Has this ever happened to you before?"

"No, it certainly has *not*," a mystified Sophia answered as she stroked her weathered chin. "It would seem as though our other-worldly friends do not want Maddy to go away just yet. Which means, they have something in mind for her. Do you know anything about this, Maddy?"

Maddy stroked her bloody chin for a moment while wearing a perplexed expression upon her freckled face before responding. "Nope, I'm as blank as a republican at a science fair. But, huh. What a strange turn of events, right gang? Well, I guess I'm bunking with *you* for a while kid. Which reminds me, you got an air mattress or couch or somethin' that you can sleep on? I tend to toss and turn, and I wouldn't want to disturb your rest. Anyhooo, until you folks get this whole blocked from sending me away thing straightened out, I'll be in the shower. Oh, and could someone lay out some jammies for me? And a big ol' bowl of ice cream *sure would* hit the spot right about now!"

CHAPTER 4

THIS ISN'T FAIR

The morning sun was beaming through the kitchen picture window as Sophia Cabot poured a steaming cup of coffee for her recently discovered long-lost cousin and unlikely ally. Victoria Colombo picked up her cup and blew the billowing steam away before taking a bitterly satisfying sip. "Thank you, Cousin Sophia. You do make the best coffee," she said while a smiling, pajama-clad Sophia sat back at the table. "But this is so weird. Never in a million lifetimes would I have ever dreamed that a witch and a medium would be sitting together in peace," she stated while brushing her blonde hair away from her thirty-year-old attractive face.

"I mean, who would have ever thought it? Witches and mediums have hated each other for, um, well, forever. We were all *indoctrinated* to hate each other. I mean, I know *I* was. I was told what horrible bitches mediums were, and I'm sure you were told the same about us. And why? Because we evolved differently? Because we witches have the ability to connect with and manipulate the forces of nature and mediums have the ability to connect with the spiritual world and ask them to do your bidding? I mean, if we were to combine forces rather than be at each other's throats, there's *no telling* how we might be able to make this world a better place. A more under-standing and accepting place. A more peaceful place."

"Yes," a reflective Sophia answered. "Yes, our ability to join one another would be quite revolutionary and shocking to the powers-that-be. And I believe that is the point. I believe that there are people in this world who know of our existence and understand quite well what our unification would mean for their consolidation of personal power. And by *people*, I mean *men*. There are men who are obsessed with power and control. *Especially* over women and the thought of our solidarity scares the hell out of them. So, they have spread false-hoods throughout our ranks through their manipulation of the media to keep us at odds. Newspapers. Books. Films. And now the internet. Subtle little messages about women not being able to trust one another spread throughout the world for generation after generation until we become brainwashed by it. It is how all bigotry works. Spread lies about a particular group of people. Make it seem as though that group is a threat to you. This then, instills fear amongst the dullard masses. And that fear becomes anger. And that anger becomes hatred. Until finally, the hatred spills over into suppression and violence against those that have actually done nothing to us. These influential male forces know about us. They know how powerful we are and just how powerful we can become if we are united. And, my dearest cousin, I believe that perhaps it is high time we showed them just how powerful of a threat we can be."

Victoria began kicking her feet as she exploded into laughter. "Yeah, I bet these assholes never saw *us* coming! Which is why I really want you to go to our witches' retreat this weekend in Salem. Please, Sophia. This is our opportunity to show everybody that witches and mediums can not only get along but can truly care about one another. That we can battle alongside one another. That we can sacrifice together. That we can persist together. I know it makes you feel uncomfortable, but Naomi and Morgan have set the example, and *they* are going together. The loving friendship that those two have for one another is what allowed *us* to break through our icy wall. And all of us, including Lori, can set that example for this entire group. This could be the first step towards complete unity between witches and mediums. And when *that* happens, the damned sky's the limit for all of womankind. Plus, we always get really drunk and make S'mores and shit. And Papa Doc is going to DJ at the dance. It really is fun. Please, Sophia? Won't you come with me?"

Sophia sat in contemplative silence as she stared into the black liquid nothingness swirling in her cup when her front door was suddenly kicked open. An anxious Detective Connor O'Sullivan was rapidly darting his eyes around the home while waving his drawn revolver. "Morning Connor," Sophia stated flatly as she got up from her kitchen chair. "You want to tell me why you just kicked my door in?"

"Shhhhhh," Connor replied quietly. "Where's Morgan? Where's Lori?" "Upstairs sleeping," Sophia answered. "Why? Just what are you doing? And are *you* going to pay for my new door or will it be the police department?"

"Listen, Sophia," Connor replied while continuing his frantic surveillance of the home. "You and Victoria need to get outside. Quietly. I'll check the upstairs. There's bloody boot prints in the snow outside under Morgan's window. And there appears to be bloody fingerprints on the trellis. Now, don't panic Sophia, but I think that killer we're looking for may have broken into your home. Oh God, if something has happened to Lori and Morgan…no. They're fine. They have to be fine. Please, Sophia. Just go outside and let me handle this."

"Aw shit," Sophia muttered before yelling out, "Morgan! Maddy! Get your little asses down here! We've got company!"

Connor lowered his weapon and stood with a dumbfounded expression on his face as Lori was the first to descend the stairs. "What the hell is going on, Mom? I told you I wanted to sleep in this morn… Oh! Hi Connor. When did you get here? Oh, I bet you had an awfully long night, didn't you? Come in. Let me fix you some breakfast. Why do you have your gun drawn?"

Connor's perplexed expression continued as a yawning Morgan

came shuffling down the stairs while rubbing her weary eyes. "What is going on, Gramma? Man, I didn't hardly get any sleep last night. I had to sleep on a stupid air mattress on the floor because…"

Her sentence was interrupted by Maddy whose pajama-clad body came bounding down the stairs. "Morning all! Man, I slept like a fu…um…a log last night. That bed sure is comfy, Morgan. But, hey. Could I get a different blankie? That blue one is kinda scratchy. Thanks. Appreciate it. So, what's for eats around here? Man, I sure could go for some eggs. Over easy, please. And bacon. And sausage. And toast with strawberry jam. And, oh! Hey, you got any of those cute little breakfast potatoes? Maybe fry some of those up with some onions? Yeah, that sounds good. Chop, chop, people. I'm starvin' here!"

"So, this is Maddy, huh?" Victoria asked to a silently nodding Sophia. "Yep, she's spunky alright. And a bit overbearing, just like you said."

"Overbearing?" a furious Maddy began to retort. "Who the *hell* says I'm overbearing? Why that's just hurtful. Yeah, real nice. Invite somebody into your home then insult them. Real nice, folks."

"You weren't invited!" Sophia, Lori, and Victoria answered in unison just before Larry the Leopard bounced down the stairs and playfully flung himself onto Connor's back. "Why howdy there Connor, nice to see you! Are you here to play some games with me too?"

"No, no," a confused Connor stated. "Please, Larry, get off my back. Literally. Okay. What is going on around here? Why are there bloody boot prints in the snow outside? And bloody fingerprints on the trellis? And who is this…this…young woman. A young woman who perfectly fits the description given to us by the wife of one of our victims?"

"Oh, yeah," Maddy replied. "I probably should have cleaned that shit up." She then looked at five pairs of glaring eyes staring at her. And one pair of goo-goo-googly eyes. "Hey! Why is everybody staring at me? You know, you people really could use some lessons in hospitality and where's my breakfast? You know, I'm starting to think…"

She was cut off by Lori's stern voice. "Maddy, please be quiet for a moment. This is Connor. Detective Connor O'Sullivan. He also just happens to be my boyfriend. And he knows about our, um, special abilities. So please just tell him who you are and what you have done. You won't be in any trouble. We've already framed another bad man for your murders, so please just explain everything to him."

Maddy began nervously chuckling while looking down at her shuffling feet. "Weeeeelll," she began in a sing-song voice. "You see, I'm Morgan's creation, you know from her book she wrote. And weeeeelll, you see, when she recited an incantation to bring this cartoon dumbass to life, it also brought *me* to life and weeeell, sooooo, I kinda…" Her voice trailed off and she lifted her copper head until she was staring at Connor with her glimmering emerald eyes while wearing a wicked grin.

Following twenty minutes of her animated retelling of her murders complete with many ZAPS! SCRUNCHES! And SPLATS! Connor was sitting on the couch, holding his head in his hands. "Here, Connor, drink this coffee," Lori said as she handed him a cup. "Um, thanks Lori," he replied. "Yeah, thanks. Thanks a lot. Thanks for bringing a serial killer into my town. This is just great. Yeah, I've read all about this Maddy. Remember? I had to look through all of Morgan's notebooks and writings. I know all about this character. I know all about her viciousness and tenacity and thirst for blood in the supposed name of justice. And now, she's real. And in my town. Committing murders. So, yeah. Thanks. Thanks for that. Just what the hell am I supposed to *do* with this, Lori? Arrest her? She's a fictional character! She doesn't exist! Oh, now you've done it. Now, you've gone and done it. I'm going to lose my job over this. I just know it."

Lori sat next to him and delicately placed her hand on his shoulder. "No, you won't, Connor. Please don't worry. Morgan is going to write Maddy as a peaceful character, so we won't have any more murders, right Morgan? Maddy?"

Morgan and Maddy looked at one another and then said in unison. "Yes, We promise. There will be no more murders." Sophia noticed Maddy's crossed fingers behind her back and could not help but let out a slight, knowing smile.

"Good," Lori continued. "And Connor, about these murders. You see, we've taken care of that. You should be receiving word any moment that…" She was cut off by the voice of Deputy Gigi Holloway coming through his police radio. "Hey Detective, pick up." "Yes, what is it deputy?" Connor answered. "Okay, well, this is just weird," Deputy Holloway replied over the staticky speaker. "We can call off the manhunt. Or the womanhunt. It's solved. We received an email confession from the insurance exec's brother. He murdered his brother, then took his own life. We found him dead in his running car in his garage. Died of asphyxiation. And not only that, but he also copped to killing that wife beater. So, I guess we can relax now."

An unblinking Connor was staring at a smiling Maddy as he said, "Yeah? Well that might solve the construction site scene, but the wife of the other victim had a detailed description of her husband's assailant. Short, petite Caucasian woman. Around 5'4". Dressed all in black. Red, shoulder length hair with bangs. Green eyes. Late 20's or early 30's. What about that?"

"Yeah, the wife actually just left," the deputy responded. "She's totally changed her story. She said that she was in shock and had just read a book about someone fitting that description, so that was what she recalled. But after sleeping on it, she had another description. And *that* description perfectly fits the brother. The brother who confessed and who is now dead. I know it's weird detective, but I think both of our murders are solved."

"Yeah, it would seem so," Connor replied while wiping sweat from his brow. "Okay. If you could please type up the report. I'll be in to look it over in a little while, okay? Thank you, deputy. Nice work." He looked into the eyes of his love and said, "Well, I guess you ladies thought of everything. So, here's what I'm going to do. I'm going to the office and wrap this up. I'm going home. I'm taking a shower. Then, I'm going to sleep for two days and try to forget all of this. But Lori, no more murders. Understand? Please. No more murders."

"Why the hell is everybody looking at *me*?" Maddy lashed out. "SHEESH! I already *said* I wouldn't kill anybody else. What's it take for a girl to be trusted around here anyway? SHEESH! Although, I don't know what I'm gonna do with myself. It's gonna be pretty boring just hanging around the house while I just *know* that there's assholes running around. But whatevs. A deal's a deal, I suppose. So, where are we at with that whole breakfast situation?"

Sophia went over to Maddy and placed her hands on her shoulders while wearing a mischievous grin. "Oh, you won't be bored, my dear. No, I'm going to keep you *quite busy*. And I'm going to keep my eye on you. No, you won't be lounging around the house. You're going to come to work with me in the diner. Congratulations on becoming my new waitress. Now, why don't you run upstairs and jump in the shower and get dressed? We need to get going. It's the day after Christmas and we're going to be wicked slammed."

"Aw sonofabitch," Maddy lamented as she trudged her disappointed body up the stairs. "This isn't fair."

"That's a great idea, Gramma," Morgan stated as she rested her head on Larry's bright yellow furry shoulder. "Come on Larry. Let's start packing for witch camp."

"Not so fast young lady," a crossed-armed Lori stated to her daughter. "You are grounded. You are soooo grounded."

"What? Why? I've promised Naomi! Why can't I go to witch camp?" Morgan yelled back. "Why?" Lori retorted. "Why do you *think*? Gee, could it be that you brought a vigilante serial killer to life? And could it be that your creation is responsible for two murders that we had to cover up? No, my decision is final. And I don't want to hear any lip from you, young lady. You are grounded for the entire winter break. And not one word. Now go upstairs, get the cleaning supplies, and clean up all of the blood from the trellis.

And the carpet. And the bedding. And the bathroom. And every place else your creation may have dripped on. I don't want to see one drop when I get home tonight. I have a big catering job for New Year's, and I don't have time for this. Now, march young lady."

"This isn't fair," Morgan stated as her drooping body ascended the stairs.

"No, this isn't fair," an observing Queen Zenobia said to her sisters. "Not fair at all. This gathering of witches was to include mediums for the first time. This is the event that will begin their sisterhood. A sisterhood which will expand to all women of the Earth. And that will take quite a while, and I sense that our window of opportunity is short. This cannot stand. Morgan must be allowed to attend this gathering. Agatha. Whisper to your granddaughter, Sophia. This union must take place."

Sophia stood as though she were in a trance as she heard the voice of her deceased grandmother whispering to her. She shook her grey head and said to her daughter, "Lori. I believe that you may be acting too hastily. This witch camp is an opportunity to bury a hatchet that is long overdue. Did Morgan screw up? Sure. But look at the bigger picture. This is an opportunity for witches and mediums to come together. There are other ways to punish Morgan for her error. But please. Not this. Allow her to go." She then smiled and looked at her cousin, Victoria. "Just as *I* am attending. Yes, Cousin Victoria, thank you for the invitation. I will graciously accept. As does my daughter. And granddaughter. Right, Lori?"

"Oh, man," an exasperated Lori muttered. "This isn't fair."

Chapter 5

Meets and Greets

"Morgan! Would you *please* slow down!" Lori yelled at her giggling daughter as she slid back and forth on the red vinyl backseat of Morgan's 1968 Pontiac Tempest. "It's okay Mom!" a thrilled Morgan shouted back. "I have a spirit guiding my steering. Don't worry about it!" She continued to giggle as her black beast effortlessly glided around yet another sharp corner on the icy highway headed to Salem.

"Just, just be careful, okay? The roads are snowy," a white-knuckled Lori replied as a relaxed Sophia sat smiling in the front passenger seat. "I don't know why I needed to come to this witch camp, anyway," a frustrated Lori continued. "I mean, who's going to watch over Gabriel? He may be sweet to *us*, but that giant Doberman is very protective of his house and freaks everybody else out." "Oh, that dog is just fine," Sophia countered. "I'm having Vince come over and feed him and walk him. Plus, he's frightened of Larry the Leopard for some weird reason, so it will be fine. He'll probably just cower under the bed until we get home."

"Well, well," Lori continued as she struggled to find the words appropriate for her contrarian, pouty mood. "Well, that just brings up yet *another* point! I'm not worried about Larry. All he'll do is bounce around the house and rhyme and shit. But what about Morgan's *other* creation? What about Maddy? Isn't it a bit irresponsible of us to leave a vigilante serial killer unattended? I swear Morgan, if we get back from this weekend and there's blood all over the house because she's murdered people all over town, grounding will be the *least* of your worries, young lady."

"It's fine, Mom. GAAAAWD. Lighten up!" Morgan answered while guiding the Tempest around yet another sharp corner. "I already told you. I've added a chapter at the end of my book where Maddy realizes that vigilante justice is wrong, and she becomes a sweet, docile person. She *can't* murder anyone anymore, because *I* changed her character. You're welcome. I think I need to take a left up here. Hang on."

"Well, that might work for a *while*," a suspicious Sophia contributed. "But I'm not sure that your final chapter is going to last forever. She is *your* creation, Morgan. And you have a lot of rage in you. Well intentioned rage, sure, but rage all the same. You created her as an outlet for your rage. It had to go somewhere, and you placed it into her. And just as *your* rage cannot be extinguished by simply writing some new characteristics, neither can *hers*. You may have written that she is peaceful, Morgan, but you did not *believe* it. You did not *feel* it. What you wrote goes against your nature. And it goes against hers. Eventually, her rage will be unleashed once again. Probably sooner rather than later. I can see it boiling just under the surface. Why, just the other day some asshole at the diner slapped her on the ass as she walked by. She glared at him for a moment, then gave him a sweet smile before entering the kitchen. She calmly picked up his order and spit in his mashed potatoes. Oh, then she went on a break, went outside, and slashed his tires. I have to admit, it was pretty funny, but that's not the point. My point is, she, like you, is filled with rage. And that will be uncorked again at some point. But not this weekend. I have given her so many tasks to do at the diner under the watchful eye of my manager, Taylor, that she'll be too exhausted to pick up a knife and slice somebody open. Yes, I have been meaning to do some deep cleaning there. It's rather nice to have such an energetic creature to get that done for me. She does bitch a lot though. So, Lori, don't worry. Everything will be fine. Besides, you aren't worried about any of that. You're just pissy because you can't spend the weekend with Connor. Am I right?"

"No, you are not right," a blushing and defiant Lori replied as she folded her arms and watched the blur of bare trees through the frosted glass. "Yes, I am very fond of Connor, but we are taking things slow. We are both over forty and have been through a lot and want to make sure before we commit to anything long term. So, we are just dating. Taking it slow, as I said."

Morgan and Sophia looked at one another with their jaws agape and burst out laughing. "Taking it *slow*?" Sophia roared through her hysterical chortles. "Yeah, tell that to the poor bedsprings! That bed is an antique, you know! Passed down from my Great Grandmother Agatha. So, maybe you and Connor need to take it easy on it!"

"Oh my God, Mother!" an embarrassed Lori exclaimed. "My daughter is sitting right there! How about a little tact?"

Morgan continued laughing and rolled her eyes. "It's okay, Mom. I think I kinda know about the birds and the bees. I really don't get how anybody could be attracted to a penis, because, BLECH! But whatevs. I guess I'm just not wired that way. And Gramma, you're not exactly one to talk. What about you and Vince?"

"What about us," an amused Sophia answered. "I'm not embarrassed by my relationship with him. My lord, I'm over seventy years old, so if I want to get laid, then I'm going to get laid. And that Vince is, um, well, he's a damned good lay. Oh, that man has stamina. And the size of his…"

Sophia was cut off by her daughter and granddaughter yelling out in unison, "Shut up! Shut up! Shut up! Lalalalalaaaa! We're not listening!" Sophia giggled like a mischievous schoolgirl and said, "Fine. I'll spare you the details. Let's just say I enjoy my time with him. And that is all that I care to say on the subject." She paused for a dramatic moment before adding, "and I really enjoy his eleven-inch dick." She knew that she had hit the right nerve when she heard her beloved family respond with "EEEEEEEWWWWW!"

The Tempest pulled into an unmarked dirt trail that was surrounded by bare, contorted trees. Their thick, black branches twisted and bent over the nearly impassable frozen, dirt trail. The brilliant sun was suddenly blotted out by thick clouds that hung from the sky like a foreboding black cloak. The tree limbs let out heavy creaks as the ancient appendages swayed in a brisk, frigid wind.

"Well, *this* doesn't look good," Morgan stated. "No, it does not," Sophia replied. "But certainly not unexpected. This is a witches' retreat after all. I'm sure they are controlling nature and making this look all spooky and shit to dissuade any curious looky-loos from interrupting their festival. Like us. Oh, how I hope Victoria and Naomi and the rest of the Plymouth coven have arrived on their broomsticks. Otherwise, we are going to be in the middle of a whole lot of pissed off bitches. Um, I mean, witches. There was a time not so long ago that I didn't think there was a difference. Oh, how I hated witches. All of them. And they hated me, and everyone like me. But the caring between you and Naomi taught me that mediums and witches can co-exist peacefully in this world. And once I found out that Victoria was in fact my cousin, I learned that not only can we co-exist, but we can be unified. Unified by a common cause and unified by a common love and caring for one another. I just hope that Victoria is here, because our presence will not be welcome without her. That's why I brought this. Just in case." Sophia pulled her family's ancient book of incantations out of her crocheted shoulder bag and began flipping through the pages. Her eyes glowed as she looked upon incantation after incantation that had been handwritten in her family's blood. Each incantation would summon a different protective spirit. And each spirit would have her own personal flair for protecting the ladies Cabot.

"Oooohhh, she's pulled out the book," Sruja stated in her native Hindi as she watched the ladies Cabot from their observation portal. "Yes, I suggested it last night in her dream," a smiling Agatha Cabot replied. "Yeah, nice job, Aggie," Queen Zenobia stated. "They need that book if this is going to work. I can see it all playing out in my mind. Step One: Get the mediums and witches together. Step Two: Get them to get along. Step Three: Have them combine their spells and incantations to open our portal to Earth. Step Four: Myself, Agatha, Sruja, and Minnie come through the portal and freak them all out. That'll be funny. They'll all be cowering and confused and not knowing what to do. Step Five: Get drunk and dance and shit. Step Six: We shall lead our Brigade of Persistence to enhance the evolution of all women of the Earth. And finally, Step Seven: Take over the levers of power from evil men and replace them with women. And maybe a few decent men. I dunno about that yet. We'll play that part by ear."

"Ohhhh, this is gonna be such a grand time!" Minnie Marples squealed. "I just can't wait to drink and dance on Earth! I haven't shaken my tail down there since 1926!" "Yes, it shall be a blast," Queen Zenobia replied. "We have waited for far too long for this moment. But now, once the witches and mediums join forces, we will be able to overcome, and our centuries-long persistence shall finally bear fruit. But, until we are called to go down there, anybody up for a pizza and some ale?"

The Tempest parked in front of a towering, grey-stoned mansion. Morgan's jet-black hair was tussled by the violent wind as she got out of her car and made her way to the trunk. "Oh, dear Enlightenment, give me strength," Sophia muttered as she and Lori exited the vehicle. The trio gazed in wonder at the ominous stone behemoth that stood in front of them while streaks of lightning crashed all around them. Chills ran down their spines as the brisk wind cut them to the bone. The dozens of glaring eyes peering out the mansion's windows did little to ease their feelings of dread.

"Well, we're definitely in the right place," Sophia stated as she pointed out the plethora of broomsticks that were carefully lined up in the vast, arched stone entryway. The broomsticks began to twitch as the watchful eyes disappeared from the windows. The heavy wooden front door of the estate flew open and nearly one hundred black-clad women of all shapes, sizes, and skin tones came rushing out and jumped upon their broomsticks. Before the ladies Cabot could react, they were surrounded by a swarm of flying, cackling witches. An elderly witch with pale green skin and a long, crooked nose yelled at them as she buzzed by Sophia and took her shoulder bag. "You are not welcome here! You are mediums! You are not one of us! And for this blatant trespass against us, I shall relieve you of your silly little book. I shall relieve you of your ability to connect with your protective spirits. You are now at our mercy, bitches! And you shall rue the day that you intruded upon our sacred land!"

"I do not need the book. I *am* the book," Sophia snarled before saying, "Fortitudo inimicorum meorum erit mea (My enemies' strength shall be mine)." "Well, this isn't off to a very good start, now, is it?" Agatha Cabot stated as she hung up the phone receiver. "Definitely not why I wanted to be called." "Hey! Let me go down and help them!" Minnie squeaked. "I have an idea! The witches' strength seems to be their numbers and flight. I think I know how to counter that without harming anyone. Stand back ladies and watch this!"

Lori's laptop computer tumbled out of her leather attaché case. She picked it up and looked at the screen. A bright yellow smiling emoji winked at her. Lori instinctively hovered her cursor over the smiling symbol and clicked the mouse. The smiling emoji winked once again before turning bright red and angry. Thousands of emojis began flying out of the screen toward the menacing witches. The tornadic clusters of emojis swirled around the confused and blinded witches until they were forced to land their brooms on the cold ground.

Several witches jumped off of their brooms, held hands, and began reciting a spell. Through the storm of brightly colored emojis, tree limbs extended and wrapped around the ladies Cabot and lifted them into the air. Sophia, Lori, and Morgan screamed while they strained against their wooden restraints. The swirling mob of brightly colored emojis turned to a dark brown and began a merciless assault upon the faces of the witches. A chorus of "Oh Gross!" "Stop it!" and "Eeeeewww!" rang out as the witches' faces were pelted by a flying army of poo emojis. The rapid-fire sounds of splats by the pungent insurgents were heard along with pleas for mercy from the besieged women. Sophia, Lori, and Morgan continued to fight for their release from the barked tentacles from ten feet in the air before the entire scene was silenced by a woman's demanding voice.

"Stop this immediately!" The poo emojis instantly disintegrated and the ladies Cabot were returned to the ground. All of the confused women looked down the dark lane and saw thirteen shapely women wearing tight, black party dresses and pointed hats emerge from a dense fog. "Stop this, my friends," Victoria Colombo stated again as she and the entire Plymouth coven strutted into the battle zone. "Please, stop this. I know that this may be quite a shock to you, my witchy sisters, but these three ladies are not our enemy. I understand that we have been told for centuries that mediums could not be trusted. And they, in turn, have been told that they cannot trust us. For generation after generation, we have allowed ourselves to be indoctrinated by scurrilous men to hate one another. These men understand who we are and our abilities. And it was thought that if we were divided and turned our anger upon each other, then they would be free to greedily and brutally rule the Earth. And they have been successful. Until now.

"These ladies are not our enemies. They are our friends. In fact, these three ladies are my family. My blood. My cousins. Which makes them *your* cousins, my sisters. Think about it. Why do we hate each other? Because we evolved differently? Because we have different special abilities? Because we can control the forces of nature, and they can connect with vengeful spirits? Why would we hate one another for that? It is nothing but ridiculous bigotry. It is no different than hating someone simply because of their skin color, or culture, or sexual orientation, or gender identity. We all scoff at less evolved humans for hating one another for ridiculous reasons. Hell, they even hate people because they like a rival sports team. The underdeveloped, less evolved humans hate each other for a myriad of insignificant and asinine reasons. And we all ridicule them for their stupidity. But we are no better. We have allowed ourselves to be just as pitifully ridiculous. We have allowed ourselves to be manipulated by men who understand what our unification would mean for their control over us. We should all be ashamed of ourselves."

Within the dense forest a pair of onlookers listened intently. "You know what?" a werewolf said in an inspired tone. "They're right. I just jumped out and attacked you for no reason. I mean, we have so much more in common than differences. Why are we fighting each other?" "Yes, it does seem quite silly, doesn't it," a vampire answered. "For generations, we vampires and werewolves have been at each other's throats. Quite literally. Why, if witches and mediums can find common ground, perhaps there is hope for us all." "Yeah," the werewolf agreed. "I mean, who woulda bet that there would ever be a truce between witches and mediums? If there's anybody on this Earth that carry grudges, it would be those two groups of strong-willed women. Wow. Look at them not trying to kill one another. This is just beautiful. And inspiring. I'm really sorry about slashing your arm open with my claws. Come on. Let me make it up to you. Why don't you come back to my place for a steak?"

The vampire looked horrified at the suggestion and bared his fangs and hissed before the werewolf realized his error. "Hey, hey, no. I didn't mean 'stake' like stake through the heart. I meant, I got a couple sirloins in my fridge, and I'll cook them however you'd like." "Well, I like mine a bit, um, raw." the vampire replied. "Oh, yeah? Me too," the werewolf countered before the pair burst out into laughter and embraced.

"Does anybody else hear that? It sounds like laughter coming from the woods," Morgan asked as her eyes strained to see into the dense forest. "Oh, that," Victoria answered bluntly. "Probably just some vampires or werewolves. They're thick around here. Anyway, where was I? Oh, yeah. Please allow me to introduce the Ladies Cabot. Sisters, this is Sophia, Lori, and Morgan. They are my family. Just as much as you are all my family. And yes, they are mediums. Which means that if we embrace them, and they embrace us, then we can finally remove the shackles of patriarchy. We will be unified by our love and caring for one another and we can combine our forces to free all of womankind from the oppressive thumbs of their male overlords. I think. Um, Sophia and I haven't exactly figured out how we're going to do that yet, but we were hoping everybody could help us brainstorm. Maybe tonight, after the dance? Which reminds me, is Papa Doc here yet? I think he's planning on an 80's night."

"Um," Morgan interjected. "A better question is where is Naomi?" At that moment a loud crashing sound was heard in a tree above them followed by a young woman's voice. "Ow! Who put this stupid tree here? Man, of all the places to put a tree. Right where I was wanting to park my broom. Hey guys! I'll be down in a minute!"

"There she is," Victoria stated flatly. The entire group of women burst into laughter before a moving exchange of names, handshakes, hugs, and tears between the witches and mediums. Morgan began uncontrollably sobbing with joy as she embraced welcoming witch after welcoming witch. Sophia and Victoria looked upon the scene wearing identical joyful smiles. "Thank you, cousin," Sophia stated. "I have never felt more at home. I love you. Now, where is the restroom in this joint? I have to piss like a racehorse. And then, I'll be ready to boogie."

CHAPTER 6

ONE TIME, AT WITCHES CAMP

"Who out there is *ready* to *boogie?*" Papa Doc announced from his position behind a large DJ stand. A voodoo priest by day and dancing enthusiast by night, his bent-over, crippled one-hundred-three-year-old black leather clad body was drenched in kaleidoscopic disco lights. As were the writhing and sweating bodies of nearly one hundred ecstatic witches. And three mediums.

"Do you know what this reminds me of?" Naomi yelled to her best friend over the thundering beats of 80's synth pop. "This reminds me of summer camp. Like, one time, at summer camp..." She was interrupted by a question from Morgan. "You're not going to tell me you did something perverted with a flute are you?"

Naomi tilted her ebony head and looked at her friend with a quizzical expression before responding. "Um, no. What would I do with a flu...oh! Like that girl said she did in that movie! No, nothing like that, Morgan, but that was pretty funny. Good one. Anyway, as I was saying, one time, at summer camp, there was this dance, and they played really cool songs. Like, every song was really good, and I really wanted to dance, but I was really shy back then and just sat in the corner by myself and..."

She was once again cut off by Morgan. "Wait, *what? You* were *shy?*

Like, a wallflower who didn't talk to anybody? What the hell happened? You're like most talk...um, you're the most outgoing and friendly person I've ever known."

The seventeen-year-old Haitian adoptee of the O'Sullivan family and newly minted witch burst into laughter. "I know right? I'm totally outgoing now! And it's all because of that summer camp. So, like I was saying, one time at summer camp, there was this really cute boy who I wanted to dance with. He was a year older, like in eighth grade, and he was a total jock. He totally won all of the athletic competitions at the camp, and I just thought he was like, the dreamiest thing ever! So, at the dance, I totally wanted to dance with him, but I was too shy to talk to him and then some mean girl shoved me right into his back! She didn't like me at all and called me the N-word the entire time. Why do people have to be that way, Morgan? Why do people hate each other for no reason? Anyway, not important. He totally spilled his drink all over his camp shirt, and I was so embarrassed that I just kept apologizing over and over. I don't know what got into me, but I just couldn't stop talking. Until he smiled at me and kissed me. Then, we danced together all night long. And ever since then, I've found it easy to talk to people. I figured if it worked on him, it would work on others too. And it has. I totally have tons of friends. But nobody as important as you, Morgan. You are my BFF. And I do mean forever."

Morgan looked at Naomi, then turned her blushing face away to wipe a tear of gratitude from her eye. She then rolled her eyes and smiled as Naomi's verbal engine revved up once again. "I really am so lucky that you moved here, Morgan. I wish it wasn't because your dad was such a verbally abusive dickhead who couldn't accept that he couldn't control who you were, but your mom took care of that, didn't she? Yep, totally used her connections with the spirit world to drool his ass to death. That was pretty funny. And I'm so lucky to have been adopted by my parents, the O'Sullivans, after my real mom died when I was a baby. I couldn't have dreamed of having a more supportive family. And all the activities they keep me involved in. That seemed to start right after I got home from that summer camp. We would all be in the living room or whatever and I'd be talking to them, and they'd suggest a new activity for me to do by myself. Like games, or gardening, or cooking, or tennis, or learning guitar, or journaling. All kinds of stuff they've suggested to keep me busy. And my Uncle Connor and your mom sure are hitting it off. Oh! Morgan! I just thought of something! What if my Uncle Connor and your mom get married? We'd be like sisters or something! Or, well, I'm not sure what we'd be. Let's see here. I'm his niece and if they got married your mom would be my aunt, right? And you're her daughter so, that would make you my..."

Morgan strategically cut her off. "You know what, Naomi? It really doesn't matter. Sure, we'd be family. But we're *already* family. We are besties, sure, but we're also bonded by our special abilities. So, it doesn't matter. Although that would make you my, um, oh shit. I don't know. Cousin-in-law once removed or some shit. Who cares. Come on, let's just dance."

The pair of friends made their way onto the dance floor and were immediately pelted by strands of flying, sweaty hair from the other gyrating revelers. In the far corner of the ballroom, three dark figures watched the celebration of freedom, unity, and power with anticipation. "Are you sure this will work?" Lori asked the smiling pair of Sophia and Victoria. "Yes, I'm sure it will," Victoria confidently answered. "If we combine our power over nature with one of your incantations to the spirit world, then I believe that witches and mediums will finally be joined together. And then, our combined forces can work toward educating all women of the Earth about their great, untapped potential. And then, well, there sure are a bunch of asshole men who will be in for a shock."

"Yes, but how to do that last part is a bit of an issue," Sophia contributed. "I think that combining our forces may be the easy part, but how to spread our message of unconditional love and unity to all womankind on the Earth is another matter. That is why I have chosen a specific incantation for tonight when we combine our power. As you and your sister witches are casting a spell upon nature, Lori, Morgan, and I shall hold hands with you and shall recite an incantation for guidance from our spirits. That is the part that I'm not sure about. And time is fleeting, I'm afraid. I can feel demonic male forces growing in strength all over the world. The fear and resentment and hatred of women is spreading throughout the ranks of the less evolved men. They are becoming more powerful and influential. Our time to strike is now. And we must succeed. Otherwise, I fear for the future of our Earthy sisters for all generations to come. Victoria dear, just when will our unification ceremony take place? When will the combination of your power of nature and our connection to the spiritual world be consummated?"

Victoria looked at her elder cousin while wearing a devilish grin and replied, "Tonight. During the sacrifice." "The *what?*" Lori exclaimed. Before Victoria could respond, Papa Doc approached the trio. He supported his bent-over frame by walking on hand-held crutches as he scurried toward them.

"Ladies, ladies, ladies. What are you three doing over here all by yourselves? Don't you feel the beat? The rhythm of the night? The… oh! That reminds me. I must play some DeBarge. Nothing more '80's than that. Come on, Sophia! Let's get out there and boogie! I'm all revved up and ready to go! Oh, perhaps some 80's Ramones would be in order."

Sophia wore a sly smile upon her lightly wrinkled face and said, "Papa Doc. As you can see, you have *plenty* of willing participants out on the dance floor that you can boogie with, so my services really aren't needed. Besides, I'm a bit, um, spoken for."

"Spoken for?" Lori asked. "What do you mean *spoken for?*" "Well," Sophia replied while wearing an uncharacteristically blushing face. "It really isn't a big deal, dear. It's just that Vince and I are contemplating thinking about talking about a possible, um, merger. You know, more than just our current physical merger."

Victoria and Lori stared at one another in disbelief before Lori exclaimed, "Are you talking about *marriage?* Are you going to marry *Vince?* Oh, my lord! I never thought that I'd see the day! Well, when's the date? Where are you going to have it? Is Papa Doc going to DJ? Oh, have you found a caterer yet? Please, mom. Let me do it. I would be honored. Oh, and we need to have flowers and a photographer and…what about your dress? Have you picked out a dress yet? White doesn't really seem appropriate in *your* case, but how about a nice teal? Oh, we must go dress shopping together. Without Morgan. Everything that she'll pick out will be black and depressing. Oh, and…"

Lori was silenced by the index finger of her mother pressing against her lips. "Lori, shut the hell up. This is *exactly* why I didn't mention anything. I knew you'd jump to conclusions and begin planning everything. That's what's going through your mind right now, isn't it? All of the little details swirling around until they come together like pieces in a puzzle. No, I did *not* say that we were getting married. What I *said* was that Vince and I were *contemplating thinking* about *talking* about it. That is all. But, out of respect for Vince, I am sorry that I must decline your invitation, Papa Doc. But thank you all the same."

Papa Doc shrugged and said, "Whatever. Your loss. How about you Victoria? Let's get out there and spin 'round like a record, baby! Oh. That gives me another idea."

"Sorry, Papa Doc," Victoria replied as she got off her wooden folding chair. "I'm running late. It's almost midnight and I've got to get our sacrifice ready. Oh, I do love the years when I'm assigned to bring the sacrifice. Although, you also have to bring the stuff to make the S'mores, and that's kind of a pain in the ass. I never know how many marshmallows to bring. But the *sacrifice* part? Yeah, that's pretty fun. I'll see you all in a bit. Sophia, get that incantation ready."

As Victoria sauntered out of the room, she could hear Lori's voice once again say, "What does she mean, 'sacrifice'?"

"Welcome to the Winter Witch Camp 2023 sacrifice, ladies!" Victoria announced to thunderous applause, whistles, and laughter. Nearly one hundred women, and Papa Doc, stood around a large red satin covered mass in the middle of the frozen field behind the grand stone manor. "It's freezing outside, but why is it so warm here?" Morgan asked Naomi. "Oh, because all of us witches are controlling the temperature within our circle. It's really cool. Like, we can just think about warming the air and poof! A perfect seventy-two degrees all around our bodies. But I'm kinda warm. Are you warm, Morgan? Here, I'll lower it to sixty-eight."

At that moment, Victoria looked down from her stone altar and yelled out, "Okay! Who's screwing with the thermostat? Listen ladies, we are *not* discussing this again. We are *not* having a repeat of the Witch Camp Sacrifice of 2019. Temperature goes up, temperature goes down. Up, down. Up, down. All damned night. It took over an *hour* to complete the sacrifice because we'd lose our focus while putting on a sweatshirt. Then taking it off. On, off. On, off. That is why the Great Council has decreed that the temperature during all outside sacrifices shall be set at seventy-two degrees. Got it?"

"Um, sorry," Naomi's sheepish voice answered. "Way to go, newbie," One of the witches stated as she sharply elbowed Naomi's ribs. "You almost got us all into trouble. And do you know what that *means*? Do you know what type of horrific punishment we must all endure when we get into trouble? Well, let me enlighten you there, rookie. No S'mores. That's *right*, there won't be *any* S'mores if you keep jerking around with the thermostat. So, knock it off."

"Um, okay, yeah, sorry," Naomi answered while hanging her head in embarrassment. Victoria rolled her eyes and scolded, "Naomi, it's okay. Just keep it at seventy-two degrees. And read your new employee handbook again, alright? This is covered in Section III, Subsection H, Part twelve. And I quote, 'All outdoor sacrifices shall be performed in a temperature of seventy-two degrees. Failure to adhere to this provision shall result in serious sanctions including, but not limited to, denial of post-sacrifice S'mores.' End quote. Alright, now back to business, ladies. Are you getting fired up?" The crowd roared while Lori's anxious blue eyes darted around the scene. "I can't hear you! I said, are you getting fired up?" Victoria yelled out again to a crescendo of witches' cheers. "Are you *ready*? Is your blood boiling yet? Are you ready to meet our sacrifice? Well, everybody, let's all get *fired up* and give a very *warm* welcome to our Witch Camp Sacrifice of 2023…Herb Jacobson!"

"Oh, shit, yep, that's a sacrifice, all right," Lori muttered under the roaring crowd as the red satin cloak was lifted, revealing a pudgy, naked White man who was tied to a post in the middle of a wooden pyre. "Hey! Couldn't you have found one with a longer wick?" one of the witches yelled out from the hysterical crowd. "He looks like he should have an apple in his mouth!" another yelled out with glee. "Alright, ladies, alright," a chuckling Victoria said as she stroked the stubbled chin of the gagged, quivering man. "Well, let's get to know our contestant, shall we? Herb Jacobson. Thank you so much for joining us. Now, it says here on my card that you are forty-two years old, never married, from Portland, Maine. Good for you. Beautiful country up there. And the lobsters are to die for. But I don't have to tell *you* that, now do I Herb? Stock broker. Enjoys camping, fishing, boating. Oh, and a scout leader. How sweet. Teaching young boys to grow up to be fine men like you. Yes, fine men who do horrible things to fine boys, right Herb? You really made those innocent lads earn their badges now, didn't you? Well, ladies, do we have a winner here? Doesn't he just get you all fired up?"

The crowd let out another unbridled round of cheers before becoming silent. They closed their circle tightly around the pyre and held hands. Their glowing red eyes stared at the bound man who was frantically trying to free himself from his scratchy rope restraints. Victoria took her place in the middle of the circle and invited Sophia, Lori, and Morgan to join in the handheld ceremony. The women began softly chanting, "fire, fire, fire." Their chanting increased in volume. "Fire, fire, fire." They opened their mouths wide and screamed out, "Fire, fire, fire!"

The man shrieked as the pyre burst into flames. His skin snapped, crackled, and popped as the licking flames began scorching his fatty tissue. Steam was releasing from his sizzling pores while his blackened toes fell off into the white-hot embers. Finally, he succumbed to the merciless torture just as his seared eyes exploded out of their sockets. "Now, Sophia," Victoria whispered to her cousin.

Sophia, Lori, and Morgan looked up into the starry night and chanted, "O, Magni qui super nos spectatis. Quaeso, duc nos in nostra nova unitate. Partire sapientiam tuam nobiscum. Duc nos ut alios ducamus. Iunge nos ut simus tua Brigada Persistance. Em, gratias tibi. (Oh, Great Ones who watch over us. Please guide us in our newfound unity. Share your wisdom with us. Lead us so that we may lead others. Join us so that we may become your Brigade of Persistence. Um, thank you)."

"Zens! Hurry up! It's happening!" Minnie squealed as Sruja and Agatha Cabot were hastily collecting their belongings. "They're doing it! The witches are burning some fat asshole, and the mediums are inviting us to come to them. At the same time! And they're all holding hands! They're unified! Hurry up before the portal closes!" "What?" Queen Zenobia yelled back. "It's happening *now*? Ah shit, I really tied one on last night. Damn near slept through this shit. Alright, alright. Just let me get my helmet. I wanna make a good first impression. Hey! Where's my shield? I told you guys not to move my…oh. Here it is. Sorry. Okay, ladies. Let's go to Earth and introduce ourselves, shall we?"

"Okay, ladies," a triumphant Victoria announced as her glowing face flickered from the burning remains of the incinerated corpse. "Now, who wants some S'mores?" "We do," came a dark female voice out of the mouth of the smoldering carcass. His charred body cracked wide open, and the silhouettes of four females emerged from the dissected body and into the thick, black smoke of rightful sacrifice. The four figures elevated above the flames and looked down upon their confused and cowering congregation. The witches and mediums gasped in disbelief as they stared at the features of the four women floating above them. A brown-skinned woman wore her black hair tied back in a bun while her body was covered in a red, decorated Ghagra choli. Another woman had pale skin, black, wavy cropped hair and wore a short, fringed white dress. A third woman clutched at her flowered handbag and wore a dowdy, ankle-length beige dress. She also had facial features that closely resembled those of the three mediums in attendance. The final woman wore a gladiator's helmet and metal armor under her flowing, crimson cape. She held a shield in one hand and a broadsword in the other.

She smiled at her new subjects and opened her mouth to speak. The gathering of women beneath them held their breath in anticipation before forceful words came out of the warrior's mouth.

"Well, how the hell are ya? Sorry for all the hubbub, but we do like to make an entrance. Hey, thanks so much for inviting us. We've been wanting to come to one of these shindigs for a long time, but we could never get you ladies together. Until now. So, thank you Morgan, Naomi, Sophia, and Victoria. You all are peaches in my book. Anyway, how's about some introductions? This lovely Hindu woman is Sruja. Morgan, she's the one who brought Larry the Leopard to life. And, um, the *other* one. Hey. We aren't perfect. Mistakes happen. Anyway, enough about that. Water under the bridge. Now, *this* little flapper over here is Minnie Marples. Lori, you might recognize her. She's been having an awful lot of fun with your emojis. Now Sophia, you might recognize *this* handsome lady. I am so pleased to introduce you to your Great Grandmother, Agatha Cabot. And me? Well, I'm the *leader* of this ragtag group. Amongst many others. And now, I am the leader of all of *you*. My name is Queen Zenobia, but please. Formalities aren't necessary. You do *not* have to refer to me as your queen. Zenobia, Zens, Z-String, Z Bomb, are all acceptable. And together, we shall create a unified front for all women of the Earth now, and for all future generations. All of us. Witches. Mediums. Spirits. All of us marching together in our Brigade of Persistence. And ladies, do we have a plan for you. It's gonna be really cool. But first, let's deal with some important business. Didn't somebody mention S'mores?"

"Can you believe how many S'mores those spirits ate?" an exhausted Morgan asked her mother and grandmother as the trio trudged toward the front door of their Plymouth home. "And I wish they were staying with us, but I suppose they have some work to do before they get us all together again. They said it would take months of preparation before we're ready to launch our plan. January 2025 is the target date."

"Yes," Sophia contributed. "Plus, they want to party for a while. They haven't been on Earth for decades, if not centuries. Boston,

New York, LA, Paris, Tokyo. They really want to live it up for a bit. Good for them. Now, where did I put my key?" "Here, mother," Lori answered. "I have it right here. You left it in your dirty jeans. Again. How many times do I have to tell you? Everything has its place. I swear, you'd lose your head if it wasn't attached."

The trio let out a weary laugh as the front door opened. There was a light 'click' of the light switch. Then dead silence. The Ladies Cabot stood with their mouths agape as they looked upon the trembling, blood-soaked bodies of Connor O'Sullivan and Larry the Leopard holding each other on a saturated couch. Gabriel the Doberman was gorging himself on the internal organs of a torn apart corpse. Blood streaked across the walls, ceiling, and disheveled pictures. And in the middle of this psychotic mayhem was a blood-covered Maddy who was feverishly shoveling limbs into an overflowing wheelbarrow. She looked up with a shocked expression and said, "Heeeeey! You're home! How was your trip? I hope you had fun. Didja have some S'mores? I love S'mores. Now, I know how this must look, but it *really* wasn't my fault. I can explain everything." A kidney fell from the ceiling fan and splatted upon her head. She removed the organ from her copper hair, shrugged, and tossed it into the wheelbarrow before saying, "And Sophia, don't you worry. Everything at the diner is *just fine*."

CHAPTER 7

WELL, ISN'T THIS JUST A PILE OF SHIT

"But first we have to kill Morgan. And her mother and grandmother too," Jasmine said in a sadistic voice to her maniacally cackling co-conspirator, Hermes. "Those three will cause us trouble. They will try to foil our plans. And besides, look at what that little bitch has done to us. You were the king of the school, Hermes. President of the Student Council. Straight-A student. Everybody loved you. Except Morgan. All you did was steal her story. Big deal. And what did she do to you in return? Cast a spell or some shit on you so that you can never communicate with another person ever again. Everything you say or write comes out a damned word salad. Even your expressions of emotion are all screwed up. If you want to hug somebody, you punch them in the face. Like you did to me."

"Temper gonads calculator stop sign smoothie!" a remorseful Hermes blurted out. "I know, I know," an understanding Jasmine replied. "I know you're sorry. And I know it's not your fault. Wearing that jaw brace sucked though. But no need to apologize ever again. You and I shall get our revenge. And you don't have just *that* to get revenge for, do you, my friend? No, if stripping away your ability to communicate wasn't bad enough, she also blew up your, um, eggplant. Oh, the pain you experienced while it just kept growing and growing until it finally exploded on the way to the hospital. All over the EMT's. I heard it was really gross."

"Picture frame phone booth caterpillar licking nun!" an increasingly agitated Hermes responded. "Yeah, Morgan *is* such a little bitch," Jasmine agreed. "A little, vindictive, dyke *bitch* who has ruined your life. And *mine*. I ruled that damned high school. Me and my posse of mean girls who have now disappeared. No one knows what has happened to them, but I'm damned sure that little bitch Morgan had something to do with it. We could get away with anything just by bullying the other kids or threatening the teachers with accusations. 'Oh, Mister Peters, why if I don't get an 'A' on my final exam, I just might have to tell the principal that you touched me. *There*.' It was so damned funny. The teachers, male or female, would just blush and do my bidding. And the other kids would cower in fear as I strutted down the hallway. Yes, you were the king, and I was the queen. And we ruled that place. Until *Morgan* came along.

"I don't know how she did it, but she somehow made my ankles snap. Then I kept falling down on my face. I had to have painful, extensive surgery to get me back to my gorgeous self. But the *worst* thing that little bitch has done to me? The *worst* thing?" Her voice trailed off as streams of tears cascaded down her perfectly reconstructed cheeks. She placed her hand on the wall of the plastic bubble that she was now confined to and seethed. "The *worst* thing that she has done is making me smell like shit. Constantly and forever. No doctor can figure it out. No matter how hard I scrub, this rancid smell just oozes out of my pores and causes people to vomit or pass out. I'll never be in a real romantic relationship. I'll never go to college or get a great job. I'll never be able to travel, or go to the movies, or anything else that normal people do. Because I smell like shit. And neither will you, my friend."

"Scrap paper scissors pillow asswipe!" Hermes yelled out as he frantically paced around in his confinement cage. "Exactly," Jasmine responded. "Our lives are ruined. We've been shunned from society. Our best case scenario is that we'll be looked down upon as freaks. And our worst case? We're living it. Locked away from the world in my bedroom with only each other to depend upon. But now, my sweet Hermes, we have an opportunity. An opportunity to turn the tables on this cruel world. My parents have had a plastic suit invented for me that will allow me to go out in the world. Sure, I'll look like some geek at some cosplay convention, but at least I'll be free from this damned bubble. And once I'm free, I can free *you* from *your* cage. And then, my friend, our march toward world domination shall begin. We'll start by raising some cash. We'll just walk into bank after bank after bank. I'll unzip my suit, and everybody will start passing out and hurling. You can then hug everybody. And by hug them, I mean beat the hell out of them. Mercilessly. It won't take long before we'll be rich from our stolen loot. Then, we'll need to get an evil lair. Someplace hidden and dark. But in a town that has great pizza. That's non-negotiable.

"And from our evil lair, we'll collect other like-minded rejects. A bunch of violent, simple-minded oafs who we can easily manipulate into doing our bidding. They are everywhere in this country, and they'll be easy to find. They'll be wearing those stupid red hats. Once we have our army, we can take over town after town. We'll have property and money and will be able to pay off politicians and judges at every level of government. We will call the shots in this country by being the wealthy and lethal power behind the throne. Then, once we have conquered America, we can use our puppets in government to conquer the world. Country by country. Region by region. And the best part? Then, we'll have all the power and money that we'll need to have the best evil lair in the world! A really huge one! Like, maybe all of Greenland! Um, depending on their pizza."

Jasmine's cadence grew faster, and her voice grew louder as she continued her psychotic rambling. "Yeah, it's going to be so easy! *Everything's* easy when you're rich! We can do anything that we want because we can *pay off* anybody we want! And if they don't cooperate? Then they get to spend a day with *me* vomiting their guts out while you beat the hell out of them. I don't care who they are, they will succumb to us. Or they will die. Just like Morgan and her entire family. Tomorrow night, my friend, they will die. It will be Sunday.

We'll wait until the diner closes, so that Sophia will be home too. Then, we'll pay them a little visit, heh, heh, heh."

"Scuttlebutt origami sushi reach around hand job!" a concerned Hermes asked. "So what if he *is* there?" Jasmine answered. "If Lori's cop boyfriend happens to be over, then we'll take care of him *too*. It might actually be better that way. Yeah, that will *really* make a statement. A statement that we are capable of *anything*. That we have no fear of *anyone* or *anything*. We will murder those three Cabot bitches and a cop and announce that there will soon be a new world order! A new world order that will cause the masses to bow in reverence and tremble with fear! A new world order that shall be ruled by us! Tomorrow night my friend, will be our coming out party! Tomorrow night we shall announce the arrival of Stinkbomb and Babbles!"

"Thanks for the ride home, Taylor," a weary Maddy stated as Sophia's manager pulled his car into the driveway of the Ladies Cabot. "Man, what a day. Is it always that busy on a Sunday? My dogs are barkin', let me tell ya. I need to soak in a nice, hot bath. Oh, and I suppose I should clean up a little. They're supposed to be home from their camp thing tonight, so I guess I should do the dishes, or they'll be all up in my ass. I can hear Lori's whiney voice now. 'Don't make a mess, Maddy. Don't throw any parties, Maddy. Don't leave your clothes all over the floor, Maddy. Don't kill anybody, Maddy. Don't leave empty pizza boxes all over the living room and pieces of crust all over the floor, Maddy. Don't smear chip dip on the arms of the couch, Maddy.' Jesus, do they have a lot of rules."

"Um, what was that middle thing you said?" Taylor asked as he placed his car into 'Park'. "What middle thing?" Maddy replied while wearing a sly smile. "Um," Talor responded. "Something about *killing* people?" "What the hell are you talkin'about?" Maddy roared back. "I didn't say anything about killing people. You might wanna get your hearing checked there, kid. I think you've been going to too many loud raves or some shit. Kill somebody. Oh, silly kids these days. Anyhoo, thanks again for the ride."

"Um, Maddy?" an anxious Taylor began asking with trepidation.

"Um, before you get out of the car, could I ask you something?" "Sure, I suppose," a curious Maddy replied. "Why are you so nervous? Are you wanting to come in and fool around or somethin'? Huh. I didn't think you swung that way, but I guess I can't blame ya. I *am* pretty adorable. But listen, kid. You're a bit too young for me. Plus, I don't like to get involved with co-workers. Oh, and I'm married. My husband isn't here right now, 'cause Morgan didn't bring him to life, but I'm married just the same. But thanks for asking, kid. It's very flattering."

"Wait, what?" a confused Taylor replied. "What do you mean Morgan didn't bring your…and no, that wasn't what I wanted to ask and…um…what?" "Oh, never mind," a chuckling Maddy answered as she zipped up her coat. "I'm just joking around. What do ya wanna ask me? Chop, chop, junior. I've got a hot bath waitin' for me."

"Okay, yeah, your humor is an acquired taste, I suppose," Taylor fumbled before getting to his main point. "No, what I wanted to tell you is that, um, listen. I think you're doing a *really great* job at the diner. You're friendly and you haven't made any mistakes with the orders and you're really good at making sure the customers' glasses are full. Especially when they order tea, I've noticed. But there is one *teeny, tiny* thing that I think you could improve on, just a little bit."

Maddy defiantly folded her arms and stared at Taylor while asking, "Oh yeah? And just what would *that* be Mister Manager?" Taylor wiped sweat from his forehead and said, "Um, well, if you could just stop spitting in the customers' food, that would be great."

"Hey!" Maddy roared back. "That's not my fault! If you wanna come into a peaceful diner and wear those stupid red anti-christ hats, then you deserve what you get! I've just arrived here and I'm *already* sick and tired of these assholes strutting around like they own the world! They're all a bunch of misogynistic, bigoted assholes who think that their savior has arrived! They are so fu-um-damned stupid that they can't see that he's gonna fu-um-screw them over along with everybody else! It pisses me off every time I see one of these stupid, gullible dickheads. Gee, Jonestown much? So, yeah, go ahead and advertise that you're in some fascist cult. Go ahead. In return, you're gonna get a big fu-um-damned loogy in your cheeseburger. And salad dressing. And soup. And pie. Listen, kid. There is a war coming. I can feel it. And we've all got do our part to show these assholes that their screwed up oppressive regime will not triumph. We have to fight back. All of us. I'm just trying to do my part."

"Well, yeah, you do have a point, I guess," an understanding Taylor nervously answered. "And I guess *that's* okay, but what about that pastor who came in this afternoon? Why did you spit in *his* grilled cheese?"

"Well," Maddy explained. "That would be because he stared at my tits the entire time I took his order, and I felt that was unbecoming of a so-called man of God. Plus, he left me a lousy tip on Thursday."

"Uh, huh. Uh, huh," Taylor replied while thinking of a response. "Well, okay, if you could just keep the spitting on the food to a minimum, I'd really appreciate it." "Will do, boss!" Maddy exclaimed. "Um, but just to clarify, where do we stand on the whole pissing into somebody's iced tea situation. Okay, I can see by the look on your face that it is slightly frowned upon. Message sent and received, boss. I promise I won't piss in anybody's iced tea. Anymore. Okay! Good talk! I'm looking forward to your glowing performance evaluation of me. See ya tomorrow!"

Maddy was whistling as she entered the home of the Ladies Cabot until she was assaulted by a frenzied, yellow blur. "Hello again, Maddy! Welcome back! Would you like to play a game before hitting the sack?" Larry the Leopard excitedly inquired while Gabriel cowered from the bouncing animated furball. "No, I don't want to play a stupid game, Larry," Maddy dismissively answered while rolling her eyes. "I'm exhausted. So quit being so annoying and happy and draw me a hot bath. Chop, chop, Larry! My poor aching bones need a soak!"

"Now, Maddy," Larry replied. "I need to tell you; I'm not your slave. Ordering others around is quite depraved." Maddy folded her arms and stared directly into Larry's goo-goo-googly eyes. The pair glared at one another in an icy silence before Larry finally succumbed to the pressure. "Okay, Maddy, I'll do this for you. But I can't help but think that Larry's getting screwed."

"Whatever," Maddy answered. "Just draw my bath. And nice and hot this time! And, hey! Didn't I tell you to pick up my clothes, and vacuum up the pizza crusts, and wipe the dip off the couch? And chair? And that other chair? I've been busting my hump all day! You could at least lift your paw and help out once in a while! SHEESH!"

Larry trudged up the stairs and muttered under his breath, "Oh, certainly, in will Larry pitch. I'll pitch a claw in your eyes you ungrateful little bitch." "What was that?" Maddy roared after him. "Nothing, Maddy, nothing," a fearful Larry answered. "I'm just drawing your bath. Yes, very soon you shall have a nice clean ass."

"It's so hard to find good help nowadays," an irritated Maddy said to herself as she rummaged around in the refrigerator. "Oh, just great. No more dip. What kind of joint are they running around here? I swear, I'm gonna have to have a little chat with those ladies when they get home and…" Her thought was interrupted by a knock at the front door. "GAAAAAWD! Now what?" she bellowed as she stomped towards the door before opening it. "Yeah, what do *you* want?"

"Hello. Are the ladies home?" the figure at the door asked. "Well, what the hell do you think *I* am? Chopped liver? Now, what do you want? I'm about to take a piping hot bath."

The figure entered the home and said, "What I want is to know if the ladies are home." "Um, no, obviously not. Why don'tcha just march right in like you own the place there constable," an irritated Maddy replied. "Oh, I bet I know why you're here. While the cat's away, the mice are gonna play, huh? Listen, Connor. You're a, um, fine lookin' guy, I guess. If you're into middle-aged dad bods. But if you think we're gonna have a side thing, you've got another thing comin'. I know that Lori can be an anal retentive, needy, overbearing bitch. And she really could do something different with her hair. Kinda stringy, don'tcha think? But having a little fling with me isn't the answer. Talk it out with her. Go to couples therapy. But having an affair is never the answer. Plus, I'm no homewrecker. But thanks for the offer. It's very flattering."

"Wait, what?" a confused and blushing Connor replied. "No, no, that isn't *at all* why I'm here. Why I wouldn't...I couldn't. No, that isn't why I'm here. I'm here to just check up on you. And no, you are *not* a lady. You are a serial killer that I feel a need to keep tabs on. *That's* why I'm here. To make sure you haven't flown off the handle and killed someone. Happy now?"

"Well, no I am *not* happy, thanks for askin'!" Maddy yelled back. "So, you don't trust me? Did I, or did I *not*, promise to not kill anybody? Gee, let me think here. Why, yes! Yes, I did! I promised to not kill anybody! But you kill one, or um, two people and all of a sudden you are branded a murderer! A serial killer! Well, if *this* just isn't a fine how-do-ya-do. You know what this is Connor? This is discrimination! Yeah, you're discriminating against me for being murder-impaired! Well, I won't stand for it! This is a violation of my civil rights! I'll call the mayor! I'll call the Governor! I'll call my Senator! I'll call..."

She was abruptly cut off by an infuriated Connor. "Go ahead! Call whoever you want! You don't have anybody to call because you're a fictional character who isn't real! So, how do you like *those* apples, little missy? And one *other* thing! If you're so innocent, what is all that stuff in the corner? Why do you have a baseball bat. And golf club. And machete. And axe?"

"Well, there's a perfectly good explanation for that Mister Cop Who Notices Everything!" Maddy screamed back. "In case you haven't noticed, I am a petite, helpless, cute, young woman living all alone in this violent world! So, I have that stuff for my personal protection, if you must know! Oh, and I'm gonna call the UN! I know my rights! This travesty of justice *shall not stand* sir!"

The pair's pointless argument ended when the front door swung open. Standing in the doorway was an ominous-looking pair. A young woman was wrapped in a black, plastic body suit and clear plastic helmet. A young man wore a bright purple athletic suit and a spiked collar.

"Who the hell are *you* two?" Maddy yelled. "Jumping jacks marshmallow anal beads!" the young man exclaimed through his gas mask as the pair entered the home. "Um, Jasmine? Hermes?" Connor asked. "What are you two doing here? I mean, it's great that you're out of your, um, cage and bubble, but what are you doing *here*?"

"Oh, one question at a time, Detective O'Sullivan," Jasmine dramatically responded. "First, to answer *this* little bitch's question, we are Stinkbomb and Babbles! And this is the first night of our new world order!" Connor and Maddy looked at each other with confused expressions and shrugged. "And as for why we're here," Jasmine continued. "Well, we're here to murder *everyone* in this God-forsaken house. Including you two." There was the sound of a plastic suit being unzipped as pungent dark green clouds began encasing the home. Connor bent over and began vomiting from the rancid onslaught on his olfactory nerves. Maddy nearly passed out and fell backwards, causing her foot to inadvertently kick Babbles in what remained of his balls.

While Babbles laughed uncontrollably while grasping his pained eggplant region, Maddy picked up one of her dirty, discarded T-shirts from the floor and tied it firmly around her nose and mouth. Out of her watering emerald eyes she saw the axe leaning against the corner wall. She instinctively ran towards the axe, picked it up, and swung it at Stinkbomb.

A trembling Connor continued to cling to an equally trembling Larry the Leopard on the blood-soaked couch as Maddy explained herself to the newly arrived and astonished Ladies Cabot. "So, like I was saying, this *really* isn't my fault. These two assholes barged into the house and interrupted the nice conversation that Connor and I were having. We were like, 'Hey! Who the hell are you? Get the hell out! We're, like, trying to have a nice conversation and shit! So, get out!' Then, *this* guy, um, well he *used* to be a guy. You can't really tell now, but he was a guy. Anyhoo, *this* guy blabbered out a bunch of non-sense and this bitch, um, well there was a girl too. I'll explain that in a bit.

"Anyhoo, this girl said something about a new world order, and they were going to murder everybody in the house, and they were like, we're 'Shambles' and 'Poogirl' or something. I don't know. I didn't really catch it. You'd have to ask them. Well, I guess you can't now. Oh, well. Anyway, she unzipped her plastic, space man costume and all of a sudden, the whole place totally reeked! So, that's what you're smelling! She totally made the whole place smell like a septic tank! Which *really* pissed me off, because I worked *so hard* all weekend to keep this place all tidy and ship-shape. Okay, that's not important right now. So, realizing that they were going to kill us, and with Connor bent over vomiting and totally useless, I instinctively did a super-duper quadruple somersault and kicked this asshole in the nuts! (Author's note: As you have read previously, Maddy did *not* do a super-duper quadruple somersault. She has a tendency to exaggerate from time to time).

"So, he's bent over, holding his balls in pain. But he's laughing! Why the hell was he laughing? I really think these two were a bit coo-coo if ya ask me. I then reached into the laundry basket that I had brought upstairs because I had just done my laundry because Lori said not to leave my clothes lying around, so, you're welcome, Lori. (Author's note: This is also not true. Maddy did not do any laundry). I reached in the basket and retrieved a perfectly folded shirt (Author's note: The shirt was dirty and wadded up on the floor) and wrapped it around my mouth and nose to protect me from the stench. Then, I saw the axe in the corner. Okay, okay, I know you must be thinking, 'Why did I have an axe in the corner?' Well, it's because I was planning on chopping some firewood and have a nice, warm fire built for you for when you got home. But *that* plan was ruined now, wasn't it? (Author's note: She had no intention of building a fire and…oh screw it. You figure it out. I'm going to take a nap. Let me know when she's done, and we'll get on with the book).

"Anyhoo, I picked up the axe and lopped this bitches head off with it. But do you know what happened? Instead of *blood* flying around, it was *poo*! Seriously, as soon as her head came off her entire body turned into a giant pile of poo! It was like a slow-moving lava flow, except it wasn't lava! It was poo! So, that's not just drying blood on the walls and floor. It's also poo. I thought I'd mention that so that you can figure out what type of cleaners you wanna use.

"Now, by that time, Stammers or whatever his stupid name was, lunges at me. But it was weird. It was almost like he was trying to hug me at first, but then it became a violent attack. So, I was like, screw this, and I swung the axe, and his right arm came off. Only this time, it was actually blood that came squirting out. It wasn't poo. So, *that* was a relief. Well, then, I have to admit, my excitement kinda got the best of me and I may have gotten just a *little* carried away and I just started going WHACK! SPLAT! BASH! with the axe, until he was all cut up into little pieces. Then Gabriel came upstairs from the basement and started eating his intestines, and these two worthless cowards just held each other on the couch. So then, I looked at the clock and was like, 'Oh man. The ladies are going to be home soon. Well, Maddy, even though this mess wasn't *your* fault, you should do a good deed and just clean it up so that my weary traveler friends can come home to a nice, clean home.' You're welcome. And so, I went to the shed and got this shovel and wheelbarrow and was just tidying up a little when you came home. Which reminds me. Could one of you possibly help me dig a hole in the back yard? We really need to bury these body parts.

"But enough about me and my silly rambling. Tell me all about witch camp! Didja have fun? Cast a bunch of spells and shit? Let me guess! Pointy hats? Bubbling cauldrons? Broomsticks? Didja have S'mores? Didja maybe bring me some, hmmmm? Oh, and that reminds me. Sophia, we're out of dip. Couldja maybe pick some up the next time you're at the store? Or maybe tomorrow? 'Cause we're out of dip *now*, so tomorrow would be really great. Or just whenever. I don't want to inconvenience you. But I think that tomorrow would be best for all concerned. Don't you? Tomorrow then? Cool. I'm glad we could come to an understanding about the whole out of dip thing."

CHAPTER 8

UNNATURAL DISASTERS

"Oh, dear Enlightenment, I think I'm going to vomit," Sruja stated to her equally hurting comrades. "Yeah, maybe we shoudn'ta went to that last bar. Or the one before. Or the one before that," Minnie stated as she sipped a cup of steaming black coffee. "Yes," Agatha Cabot agreed. "We did overdo it a bit last night, didn't we? But it was our first night in Paris, and there was just so much to see and do. Besides, we haven't much time to enjoy ourselves on this Earth. We must get to work soon. Speaking of which, where is Queen Zenobia?"

As if she had just heard her cue, a sweaty Queen Zenobia came bursting into the luxury hotel suite grinning from ear to ear. Her powder blue jogging suit clung to her muscular frame as she shouted out, "Well, it's about time you lollygaggers got up! Hell, it's damned near eight-thirty! I've just ran five miles, done a half-hour of pilates, and had breakfast. Mmmmm, that was good. You girls really need to try the restaurant downstairs. Nice, gooey buns. Runny eggs. Greasy sausage. It's just wonderful."

Sruja held her hand over her mouth and ran into the bathroom. The women were then greeted to the delightful sound of violent vomiting. "What's her problem? Huh, what a lightweight," Zenobia stated. "Hey! Sruja! While you're in there, jump in the shower and get ready! We have a whole day of museums to hit. And shops. Oh, I do hope to find another nice sword. Then, a little dinner and drinking and dancing until dawn!" Sruja's only response was a continuation of projectile vomiting.

"Poor thing," Zenobia said. "Can't hold her liquor. Ah, well. I'll get her shaped up in no time. Someone make her some dry toast. That'll help. But before we get going, why don't we check up on our girls in Plymouth. They should be back from witch camp by now. Now, to call up our handy-dandy viewing portal and adjust the settings to Sophia's house and…this is so much easier to do in Eden. Too much static electricity and pollution down here. Adjust the horizontal roll and…no. Still black and white and grainy."

"Here! Let *me* show ya!" Minne exclaimed as a pale green Sruja slowly re-entered the room. "All's ya gotta do is give it a little kick! Like this! See? Perfect picture! Or, well, maybe not. What in the hell happened to Sophia's house? And what is that smell? It's so strong that it's coming through the portal from thousands of miles away!" Sruja immediately retreated back to the bathroom. While the sound of her upheaval was coming from down the hall, Agatha said, "I don't know. Why do I have a feeling that our Maddy is responsible for this destruction? Let's rewind and see what has occurred. I'm not sure that I trust whatever her explanation might be."

A reluctant Sruja re-joined the group as they began watching Maddy's violent exploits. All the women could say was, "Oh, my." Oh, dear." "Oh, *that* musta hurt," while watching Maddy chopping off the limbs of her male marauder and gleefully dancing around in the spraying blood. "Okay, well I certainly hope she has a good explanation for this, or Morgan is going to be grounded until she's thirty," a shocked Agatha stated. "Here, let's fast forward to when the Ladies Cabot arrive home. Yes, there's Maddy trying to, um, clean up. She's going to need more than that shovel and wheelbarrow. And there's Connor and Larry the Leopard frozen in fear on the couch. And now, here come my darling descendants. Well, they certainly do look shocked. As does Maddy. Here comes her explanation. Let's listen.

And she had better make it good. Just look at all of that blood on my portrait. And…and…is that *poo* smeared in my hair?"

While the bemused female spirits of vengeance listened to Maddy's exaggerated explanation of the previous evening's events, Minnie would provide an occasional commentary. "Hey! She didn't do a super-duper quadruple somersault! She just fell backwards and accidently kicked that big palooka in the nuts!" "Hey! She didn't keep the house clean! It was a disaster even before this!" "Hey! She didn't do any laundry!" "Hey! She wasn't going to use that axe for firewood! Ya know, I'm startin' to think that this Maddy character might be a bit of a fibber."

"Yes, and a bit of a loose cannon," Zenobia contributed. "Although she was certainly justified in protecting herself, she did not need to do it in such a, um, graphic fashion. No, that was certainly overkill. Overkill? Hell, *overkill* doesn't even *touch* this depravity. And I don't believe that Morgan is going to be able to write this out of her. Maddy is Morgan and Morgan is Maddy. This is what Morgan has within *her*, so this is what her *character* possesses as well. Unbridled rage. I'm still convinced, however, that Maddy can be more of an asset than a liability to us in our endeavor to place women of Earth in the seats of power. But she is too violent. Too unpredictable. She needs a moderating force in her life. Sruja, do you know what you must do?" Sruja nodded her pounding head in understanding while munching on a piece of plain toast.

"Good. Now, let's go back to live action, shall we ladies? Oh, good. Victoria has arrived. Let's listen in. And then jump in the shower. We have museums to hit. And then a night of wine and spirits! Get it, gals? 'Cause we're spirits?" The very mention of alcohol sent Sruja back to her porcelain throne.

"I don't know if I have a spell to clean this mess up, Sophia," Victoria stated as she held her nose from the overpowering stench. "I mean, I'm one of the most powerful witches on Earth and can control all sorts of natural things but this…this…this is *unnatural*. You got insurance on this joint? It might be easier to just light a match and cut your losses."

"Oh, what a great idea, Victoria!" Maddy exclaimed as she bounded down the stairs. "Hey, Sophia! If you need a little help with that whole burning down your house thing just let me know. Just put a little bug in my ear, go on a little day trip somewhere, and I'll take care of the rest." She then gave Sophia an exaggerated wink and smile.

"Oh Maddy!" Larry excitedly chimed in. "For once we agree! Let me help you burn this place down! I'll do it for free!" "Larry!" Morgan exclaimed. "Why would you say that? You're sweet and peace loving. You don't have a violent bone in your body. What has gotten into you?" "I'm sorry, Morgan," Larry softly replied as his goo-goo-googly eyes stared awkwardly at the floor. "I don't know why I said that you see. Perhaps you-know-who is becoming a bad influence on me."

"No one is burning my house down," Sophia firmly stated. "Do you two understand? *Nobody* is burning my house down." Larry and Maddy stared at one another and shrugged. "Oh, Maddy. We do appreciate your protecting yourself and the others. But my lord, look at this mess. I mean, I suppose there was nothing that you could do about Jasmine turning into a pile of poo, but did you have to chop Hermes into so many pieces? Couldn't you have just whacked him on the head with a baseball bat a few times? Sure, there still would have been some blood, but it would have been in a small spot that we could probably just steam clean out. But this. This is just...just...well, it was a little extreme."

"So, *this* is the thanks I get, huh?" Maddy roared back. "I save Lori's stupid cop boyfriend and Morgan's stupid, um, whatever the hell *he* is, and this is the gratitude? Well, Sophia, if it was your intention to hurt my feelings, then well done. Mission accomplished. I know when I'm not wanted. I don't have to listen to such ungratefulness. I'm leaving! And I'm serious! I'm going to *walk* down to the diner! All by my lonesome, unwanted self! My shift starts soon and nobody can stop me! I'm serious. I'll do it. Here I am at the door. Anybody wanna apologize to me? Maybe give me a lift? I'm now opening the door. BRRRRRRR. Sure is cold out there. And once I'm outside in the freezing cold, there's no turning back. I'm going to walk. All the way. By myself. In the freezing cold. So, how 'bout that apology and lift, huh?" Maddy waited for a moment for the response she desired. All that she received was a chilled silence. Her freckled face turned beet red, and she yelled, "No? No apology? No ride? You're just going to let me walk the entire four blocks *by myself* in this freezing cold? Well, screw *all* of you then!" Maddy slammed the door of the home allowing Victoria, Morgan, Lori, Sophia, and Larry to let out a sigh of relief. Their respite lasted only a moment as the front door flew open once again. "And just one more thing!" Maddy screamed. "Sophia, what's the lunch special today so I can get it started!"

Sophia smiled slightly and said, "Well Maddy, our special today is lobster bisque." "Lobster bisque?" Maddy exclaimed. "Who in the hell eats that? I'm not cooking that smelly shit. So, today's lunch special is gonna be cheeseburger and fries! I'll go start cutting up the 'tatoes. And that's my final word! Screw all of you ungrateful bastards! Maddy out!"

The door slammed once again, and the women all began chuckling. "Well, Morgan," Lori stated. "I really do not like her and she is a calamity on two feet, but I must admit, she *is* entertaining. And it sounds like she's doing a good job at the diner, so there's that. Alright Mom. What in the hell are we going to do? We have a house that smells and looks like an exploded septic tank. Even Victoria can't help us clean this up. Any thoughts?"

"Um, I have a thought, Mom," Morgan answered. "I was thinking that maybe if I could find an appropriate incantation in our book and Victoria could maybe control the wind or something that we could combine forces. I mean, we need to practice that stuff together anyway, so why not get started. That's why Naomi will be here soon. So she and I can practice together, and we can show the mediums and witches of the entire world just how strong we can be as a united front."

"And that is why *I* am here," Victoria stated. "Naomi is very talented and very powerful and very, um, we'll say enthusiastic. But my lord, that girl's mind whirls around like a tornado and it's very difficult to get her to focus. Hey. Tornado. That gives me an idea. Morgan, go get your book."

The piles of poo and congealed pools of blood glowed in an eerie green as Morgan opened her family's ancient book of incantations that they used to summon assistance from the spirit world. "Oh, good idea ladies," an observing Queen Zenobia stated. "Yes, practice makes perfect. And no time like the present. Keep looking in the book, Morgan. I'm sure you'll find what you are seeking."

Morgan turned page after page searching for the perfect incantation. Her seventeen-year-old fingers lightly swept over the Latin words that had been written in her ancestor's blood. Her search continued through passage after passage until one began glowing upon her touching it. "I think I may have found it, Gramma. Here, take a look. Do you think this might work?" Sophia smiled at her granddaughter and nodded while tussling her jet-black hair.

Morgan touched the glowing incantation and held hands with her third cousin. She closed her eyes and said, "Laborare cum natura et videbis mundum tuum se purgans ab immunditia et fieri purum. Laborare cum natura et videbis mundum tuum se purgans ab immunditia et fieri purum. Laborare cum natura et videbis mundum tuum se purgans ab immunditia et fieri purum (Work alongside nature and you shall see your world ridding itself of filth and become clean)."

From the blood-stained walls several black silhouettes emerged and floated above the calamitous scene. Victoria smiled, gripped Morgan's hand tightly, closed her eyes, and concentrated. The dark figures suddenly began spinning faster and faster. The wind in the home increased causing the curtains to fly around and the pictures to shake. "Oh, shit!" Morgan exclaimed. "What have we done?"

"It's okay!" Victoria yelled over the howling winds. "Let's just get to the basement and watch! Hell, they can't make this mess any worse!" Gabriel yelped and galloped down the basement staircase immediately followed by Larry, Victoria, and the Ladies Cabot. They peered at the chaotic scene from a crack in the basement door and gasped as they witnessed the dark silhouettes transform into pitch-black tornadoes. The tornadoes twisted their way into the kitchen and rummaged around in the utility closet and cabinets before re-entering the living room and going to work. The intense winds whirled around the room with their sponges, brooms, and mops. The wheelbarrow that was filled with assorted limbs, internal organs, and a pair of heads was whisked out of the home, flown away, and dropped deep into the salty and predatory waters of the Atlantic Ocean. Poo and blood were scrubbed away from every surface by the ferocious cyclonic winds until the living room gleamed. The tornadoes hovered in the middle of the room and surveyed their handywork. The twirling funnel in the middle of the group extended a rotating hand that wore a white glove and swirled around the room looking for any remaining dust particles. There was a light giggling as the satisfied tornadic spirits shook hands. And then, the funnels dissipated as quickly as they had arrived.

"Well, I guess *that* worked," Sophia stated as she emerged from the basement while fixing her disheveled white hair. "Gee, maybe I could save a few bucks and lay off my cleaning crew. Naw. They need the work. Plus, we aren't supposed to use the spirits for personal gain. That'll just piss them off and...oh dammit. One of those assholes chipped my little cat figurine. And that was my favorite one. Oh well. Just an excuse to hit some tag sales this spring. Listen, I gotta get to the diner. I don't care *what* that little bitch says, today's special is lobster bisque. And she'd better not spit in it. Again."

A relaxed Sophia whistled as she left her pristine home. She started her car and carefully began backing out of the driveway. She then jumped from the sudden, loud sound of shattering glass as a broomstick came jutting through her back windshield. "Oh my God, Sophia!" an embarrassed Naomi exclaimed as she pulled her broomstick away from the splintered glass and stepped off of the trunk of the car. "I'm so sorry! But this is where I usually park my broomstick and you're usually gone to work by now and I didn't expect your car to be here and plus I was distracted by this fluke tornado that was dropping things over the ocean. Did you see that? Pretty wild, huh? Anyway, you're not going to tell my parents or my Uncle Connor about this, are you? Oh, please don't. They already took away my Miata. I'd just die if they took away my broomstick. Well, my parents don't know I'm a witch yet, so they don't know I drive a broomstick, but please don't tell them, okay? I promise I'll fix it. I'm really good at fixing stuff. Do you have any glue? Or maybe I can get insurance to pay for it. Victoria said that I could get broomstick liability insurance in case I have an accident. She said most witches don't get it, but she strongly recommended that I do for some reason. But I haven't done that yet. Maybe I should. Hey! Is Victoria here yet? She and Lori are going to supervise me and Morgan combining our powers and stuff. Oh, that's going to be so much fun! Me and Morgan joining forces. We'll be like superheroes or something. So, is Victoria here yet? Is she still mad that I messed with the thermostat at witch camp? I hope she's not. She's super nice to me. Even let me have S'mores and…"

"Oh, dear lord," Sophia muttered to herself as she surveyed her shattered back window. "From a tornado into a hurricane. Naomi, I will not tell your parents or Uncle Connor. It will be okay. Maybe Vince can fix it. Please just go in the house. Naomi, please be quiet and go into the house. Naomi, for the love of God! I'm already late for work! Please, I beg of you, just go into the house!"

"Hiya everybody!" Naomi gleefully stated as she entered the home. "Sorry I'm late but Sophia parked her car in the wrong spot and…wow! This place is spotless! Maddy sure did a good job of house cleaning while you were gone!"

"Yeah, *that's* what happened," Lori sarcastically replied. "Okay, girls, let's get started and…Naomi. Please listen. Naomi, yes, we saw the tornado and…would you please…no I don't know who carries broomstick insurance but…no, Connor isn't here. He's at work and…Naomi! Please! Just sit on the couch next to Morgan and be quiet!"

CHAPTER 9

THROWING SOME SHADE

"Okay, ladies, let's get started," Victoria stated to her two young pupils. "Hold on a second, Victoria," Lori said while staring at her black-clad daughter. "Morgan, take off the sunglasses." "But *whyyyy?*" Morgan asked in a whiney voice. "Because," her mother answered, "you look stupid wearing them indoors. Now take them off." "But Mom!" Morgan angrily countered. "My sunglasses are my trademark! Me and Naomi are going to do some really cool things together! We're the linchpin in the entire plan to get all the mediums and witches of the Earth together! And then, we're going to expand *other* women's abilities! We're going to help them evolve and develop their supernatural skills so that we can all rise up and unseat evil men from positions of power!"

"Yeah, so what does that have to do with sunglasses?" an irritated Lori inquired while Naomi looked up at the ceiling and Victoria tried to restrain her laughter. "Well, because what we're going to do will be cool!" Morgan shot back. "And I need to *look* cool! I need to look the part of a leader in the Brigade of Persistence! Plus, my cool nickname is gonna be 'Shades'! *That's* what it has to do with it!"

"Okay, Morgan," Lori answered calmly. "I have listened to your argument. I have thought about and processed what you have told me. And my decision is…take off your sunglasses. You look stupid. Now, can we get to work?" Morgan seethed as she slowly removed her sunglasses revealing her gothic, black-lined eyes and placed them on the side table. "I'm all ears, Mother," she said through gritted teeth as she picked up her family's ancient book of incantations.

"Well, I think Morgan's shades look cool, Lori," Naomi chimed in. "I could wear them too and we'd call ourselves Sister Shade. Wouldn't that be cool. Now, I can certainly understand why you may not want Morgan to wear them during class. We need to be focused on our studies and not our image right now. Yep, we need to be totally concentrating on learning our skills and working together and…OMG, Morgan! I just thought of something! What if we *also* wear matching outfits! Like all slinky and black that'll catch the guys' attention! Or, well, the girls' attention in your case. Or no! How 'bout a tailored black dress that's all lacey and stuff for me and a kick-ass tailored pants suit for you! Yours could be dark green and be like cool bell-bottomed slacks, boots, a T-Shirt that says 'FAFO' with a cool, short blazer over the top. And what would make it cohesive? Why, the shades of course! We'd look so cool strutting into some big meeting with a bunch of stupid old rich white men wearing our kick-ass outfits and our shades. I know somebody who's a fashion designer. Victoria, may I please have my phone so that I can call them? We need to get measurements, then the sketches, then pick out the materials. That's very important. We don't want anything too confining and definitely not itchy. I just hate wearing itchy clothes, don't you, Morgan? I swear, it's one of the things that…"

Naomi's most recent diatribe was mercifully ended by a zipper suddenly appearing over her mouth. She let out a muted chuckle, unzipped her mouth and began again. "That was a pretty good one, Victoria. That was pretty funny. So, like I was saying, could I please have my phone and…" Victoria waved her hand and there was a loud zipping sound. And then, tranquil silence.

"Naomi," a slightly frustrated Victoria began. "You are such a wonderful young lady. And you are capable of developing into a very powerful witch. But, for the love of God, Naomi! You have to be quiet and…don't you *dare* touch that zipper. Oh, give me strength. Listen, Naomi, the one thing you must work on is your concentration. You cannot allow your mind to venture off in a hundred different directions. You must focus on just one thing at a time. This is true for us witches and it is also true of mediums. Mediums must focus on their incantations and the purpose for contacting their guardian spirits in order for them to be summoned and complete their work. Concentration is the key to the success for mediums, witches and…women in general. And now, ladies, we shall begin today's lesson. Naomi. Do *not* touch that zipper. And Morgan. Just leave your sunglasses on the table. There will be plenty of time for dress-up later. And I already know an incredible designer in Boston, so don't sweat it. She does all the outfits for me and my coven, and you can *obviously* see how fabulous *we* always look. Okay, let's begin.

"And we shall begin with a bit of a history lesson. Naomi, I know that you already have heard some of this, but Lori and Morgan haven't, so we're going to catch them up. As all developed human beings know, gender is a bit fluid. Yes, there are biological men and biological women. But there are also people who, because of their personal biology and chemical make-up, may be born one gender but naturally identify as another. I'm not going to get too far into the weeds on this. Suffice to say, females are special. Regardless of whether it is someone who was born biologically female, or male but identify as female, or a biological female who identifies as male. It doesn't matter. We are *all* special. Due to our biological hormonal make-up and the construction of our brains, we are further evolved than men.

"All men. About half the men on this planet are decent people. A bit developmentally challenged, sure, but they are decent people who genuinely care about the welfare of others. They are not bigoted. They are not self-centered. They believe that our existence on this planet is enhanced by different people with different abilities working together. And they embrace those differences. They're real sweethearts. Usually. Kinda stingy with the remote, but whatever.

"But that is only *half* the men. The *other* half are not much different, evolutionarily speaking, than their caveman ancestors. They are self-centered. They believe that if they want something, they have the right to just take it without regard to how that may impact others. They are bigoted, narcissistic, bullying knuckle-draggers. And that's on their *best* days. And it is *these* types of men, generally speaking, who have controlled society's institutions over the ages. Whether it be business, political, religious, or any other type of institution, these types of men have ruled.

"Which begs the question, if women are so evolved, then how have the underdeveloped, as we witches refer to them, been able to wield such oppressive power for so long? And the simple answer to *that* ladies is, and Naomi, pay close attention to this. The answer is concentration. I'll expand on that in a moment. But first, let us talk about the special abilities that all women have.

"Again, due to our biological make-up and the construction of our brains, women have an intuitive connection to nature. But there is one final piece to this puzzle. Women *also* have a natural *spiritual* connection. To put it simply, our souls are also more evolved, and the purer the soul, the deeper the connection to everything in the natural universe. And that connection has led us to evolve in one of two ways. Either a connection with the powers of nature which we can enhance with various crystals or herbs. Those women are known as witches. Or women who have a connection with the spiritual world which can be enhanced through certain incantations that have been passed down for generations. Those women are known as mediums. Every woman on this Earth has the ability to develop their soul and evolve into one of those two entities.

"So, why have we in this room evolved faster than most others? Our families have simply evolved more rapidly. Don't know why, we just have. Just like some families have a genealogy for a propensity in mathematics or athletics or musical ability and others don't. All mediums and witches come from families whose souls have developed to the point of being able to tap into their natural abilities as witches or mediums. Yes, Morgan, you have a question?"

"Um, yeah, thanks," Morgan replied. "So, has there ever been a woman who has been both? Like, could a woman be both a witch *and* a medium?"

Victoria pondered the question for a moment then said, "Nope. It has never happened. We're wired to only be one of those two things. That would be cool though. Shit, a woman who could be *that* could rule the world all on her own. There is a mythological creature that *is* both, but that is just a myth. She is known as a 'Fabula', which means legend. And like *all* legends, she doesn't exist. Never has, never will. But, a good question, Morgan. Now, back to the lesson. There are some of us who have naturally evolved to tap into our predestined abilities. The vast majority of women haven't, but they all have a feeling that they are special. Women's intuition is a good example of all females tapping into the natural energy of the world and feeling what may come to pass. But most have not fully developed their souls because they have not been allowed to *concentrate* on that. The underdeveloped men know how special we women are and they enact laws and societal norms to keep us down. To keep us focused on our day-to-day survival rather than focusing on developing *ourselves*. To focus on their dependence upon men, rather than focusing on how to be a strong, independent woman. The men keep us oppressed because they know the power we shall wield should we ever reach our full potential. And it totally scares the shit out of them to think about millions, if not billions, of independent women banding together. They know what that would mean. It would mean the end to their dominant, ruthless, male patriarchy.

"Which, ladies, is exactly what we are about to embark upon. Which leads us to today and our first attempts at combining the spiritual forces of mediums with the natural forces of witches. Once we all get good at that, it will be easier to bring together all of the witches and mediums from around the world. And then, ladies, we shall work together to enhance the souls of every *other* woman upon the Earth. And we shall do so by uncluttering their minds from the shackles of their oppressive patriarchy. We shall open their minds. We shall open their souls. And then, they shall be connected with their special abilities and there will be billions of strong, independent mediums and witches covering every corner of the world. And then, well, let's just say Queen Zenobia is going to have one hell of a brigade to commandeer, heh, heh, heh.

"Okay, everybody up to speed? Got it? No, Naomi, don't answer that. Naomi, let's start with you. And *don't* touch that zipper. Let's start very basic. Concentrate on that vase on the shelf. The blue one. Concentrate on the winds of the Earth. Have the winds gently, and I do mean *gently*, lift the vase and place it into your hands."

Naomi squinted her eyes and focused on the air circulating in the room. Then came thoughts about pizza toppings. And what she wanted to wear to dinner with her family that evening. And the cute boy in her algebra class. And the cute boy in her chemistry class. And the cute boy in her history class. The vase shook, lifted into the air, and immediately plummeted to the floor.

"Ah, shit, I'll go get the broom," Lori lamented. "Mom's going to be pissed about that." "Sorry," Naomi attempted to say through her zipped lips. "Okay, let's try again," Victoria stated. "See that houseplant in the corner? Focus on its essence and have it extend its branches until its leaves are wrapping you in a big hug. Got it? Now, concentrate."

Naomi focused on the plant and could feel her soul connecting with its energy. The branches began to expand. Naomi's mind became bombarded by a flurry of thoughts about her high score at Pac Man. And where her missing pink sock might be. And how she was craving caramel corn. The more chaotic her thoughts, the more chaotic the plant's behavior until the leaves of the plant were thrashing around the living room in a frenzy. Pictures were knocked from the walls, curtains were torn down, and Gabriel's cold, wet nose was repeatedly slapped until he retreated to the basement. The potted plant lifted off the carpet and flew in a circle around the room several times before crashing through the living room picture window. Naomi's eyes began welling up in tears as she hid her embarrassed face in her shaking hands.

"Okay, well, *that* was cool," an increasingly annoyed Lori stated as she went back into the kitchen to retrieve the broom once again. "I don't know, Victoria. Are you sure that *these* two are the key to this? It seems to me that they are going to be a bit of a project. I have no doubt that Naomi will get it at, um, *some* point. But wouldn't it maybe be better if you and I or you and my mom worked on it?"

"Yes, and we will," Victoria answered while hanging a painting back on the wall. "But these two are the key. They are the original medium and original witch to have real love and regard for one another. It is through their love that we shall unite everyone else. The rest of us, including you and I and Sophia, are merely foot soldiers in this. As much as I regret saying this, it is Naomi and Morgan who are our generals. So, we get back to work. Okay, Naomi. Please, just concentrate. You can do this. Let's try something a bit less, um, dangerous, I guess. Here. The seat cushion on that chair. Just focus on the wind, lift the cushion into the air and into your arms. It's very easy, dear. Just focus now."

Naomi wiped the tears from her eyes and stared at the seat cushion. The cushion lifted into the air and began gliding effortlessly towards her. She then began thinking about the fireworks display on New Year's. And the cushion exploded. A blizzard of tiny bits of fabric and feathers floated down and covered every surface of the living room. Naomi unzipped her mouth and yelled out, "I'm so sorry! I can't do this! I can't clear my mind! I want to concentrate on the plant or whatever and it starts working but then I just start thinking about all sorts of other stuff and my mind gets all confused and then…and then…everything gets messed up! It's all messed up because of me! Because my stupid brain won't keep stupid thoughts away! I'm so sorry, but I'm not the one who should be doing this. I can't. I just can't. I'm just going to put my broomstick away forever and forget I was ever a witch. Because I'm *not* a witch! I'm a failure!"

Naomi sobbed as her best friend wrapped a caring arm around her heaving shoulders. "Shhhh, it's okay, Naomi," Morgan whispered to her hurting friend. "It's all okay. You're not perfect. Neither am I. I mean, look at what *I* brought into the world. A vigilante serial killer. I've got four deaths on my hands. All you have is a shattered window. Well, and a destroyed cushion and vase, but at least they aren't dead *people*. You can do this. I know you can. It may not be perfect for a while, or like, ever, but you can do this. You are smart. You are caring. In fact, you might be the most caring soul in this entire world. Don't you see? It's *because* you are so caring that your mind goes in a million different directions. You care about everything and everyone all at once. You care about your studies, and dinner, and cute boys. But you also care about people. Strangers on the street. People in other countries. And certainly, people in your own life. Your Uncle Connor. Your parents. My family. And me. You are the most caring person in the world. Let me help you. Let me help you focus your caring on cleaning this mess up. We are both going to focus on the wind and the natural energy of the world and make this right. We're going to clean this room up. We're going to clean this world up. You and me. Together. Let's just shut our eyes and focus. Take my hand and feel my concentration. Let me be your guide."

The dear friends clung to one another and the potted plant flew back into the living room and took its place in the corner. The pieces of the vase flew around and reattached themselves before landing back on the shelf. The light sound of clinking glass could be heard as the picture window reconstructed itself. And the seat cushion was reassembled in mid-air before coming to a rest back on its chair.

"Oh my God! Morgan!" a thrilled Naomi exclaimed. "I did it! With your help, I did it! We did it! Together! It was like I could feel your calm and love in my soul, and I just let myself be absorbed by it. All that I could think about was righting my wrongs. I thought about the vase and the plant, and the window and it all just happened! Because of you! Because you were leading me! Oh, Morgan! Maybe we truly *are* sisters!"

"Yes, maybe you are, of a sort," a shocked, unblinking Victoria stated. "This should *never* have happened. It's impossible. An average woman cannot have such influence over a witch's power. And a medium, no matter *how* strong of a spirit they might summon, cannot have that influence, either. The only being that can guide a witch in such a way is another witch. A very *powerful* witch who can connect with another witch's soul. I'm sorry, Morgan. It seems as though I may have lied to you. You are not only a medium. You are also a witch. You are a legendary Fabula. You are...probably the most powerful force in our world."

"Uh, huh," Morgan arrogantly stated as she flashed a haughty grin at her mother and put her sunglasses back on. "So, Mother, you were saying about my cool shades?"

Lori thought about what she had just witnessed her beloved daughter do. Her scrambled mind contemplated the sheer power that her daughter now possessed and the enormous responsibility that came with it. She stared at her smirking daughter, marched over to her, grabbed the sunglasses off of her face and tersely said, "I *said* that they make you look stupid. Don't be a smartass. And your grandmother and your *creation* will be home soon and it's your turn to fix dinner. So, into the kitchen with you."

"But Mom!" Morgan yelled back. "Didn't you hear what Victoria said? I'm a Fabula! I'm a medium *and* a witch! I'm totally like royalty or something! You wouldn't see Queen Zenobia cooking dinner, would you? So, why should *I* have to?"

"Because," Lori answered. "You are *my* daughter. You are a member of *this* household. And in *this* household, there are rules and everybody contributes. With no exceptions. So, get your little ass into the kitchen...your *highness*."

"Oh my God! This is so unfair!" Morgan yelled as she stomped into the kitchen followed by an uncharacteristically silent Naomi. The sound of clanging pots and pans and slamming cabinet doors could be heard while Victoria said, "Nicely played, cousin. We're going to need to keep her in check. She is in danger of flying a little too close to the sun and that will not just endanger *her*, but *all* of us. She has an arrogant streak. Just like her creation."

At that moment, the front door opened. "Well, I'm *sorry*, but I can't help it, Sophia! That dick was an asshole!" an irritated Maddy was saying. "I *know* he is," an irate Sophia retorted. "But he is *still* a paying customer, and he did *not* to pay for the added piss in his iced tea! Or saliva in his soup!" "Yeah, whatevs," Maddy replied. "Just let me know when supper's ready. My poor tired bones need to soak in a hot bath. Hey Morgan! Dinner ready yet? Chop, chop, sister! I'm starvin'! Oh, hey. Cool shades. Hey Morgan! Can I have these cool shades? I think I'd look really cool wearing them while I'm hacking some douchebag up. I mean, if I am ever *forced* into such an *unfortunate* situation. So, can I have them? I'll take your non-response as a 'yes'! Thanks Morgan! Now, how are we doin' on the whole dinner in my belly situation, hmmmm?"

CHAPTER 10

GOOD GAME!

"Good game, Sophia!" Maddy exclaimed as she firmly slapped her on the ass. "Good game, Vince!" "Ow!" Vince yelled out. "That really hurt!" "Good game, Morgan! Nice commencement speech!" She screamed out as she continued to make her rounds. "Ow! Maddy! Would you *please* stop slapping everybody on the ass?" Morgan scolded.

"Well, hell," Maddy began explaining. "If I can't congratulate people on a day like *this*, then when can I? I'm really proud of ya, Morgan. All the hard work that you've put into high school. And to be the Valedictorian! It's really quite the honor, Morgan. Ya know, if *I* had actually gone to high school, I woulda been a Valedictorian too. Probably with even *better* grades. But today isn't about me. It probably *should* be, but it's not. It's about *you* and everything that you've accomplished. Man, that speech was awesome. You really are a good writer. All that stuff about people having the power, and each individual can accomplish anything that he, she, or they want as long as they have a supportive community around them. Oh! And all the shit about battling against bigoted forces of division. That was spot on, sister.

"But the thing that you should be most proud of? How hard you and Naomi have worked to unite your powers. I mean, you're kinda cheating since you're a Fabula or whatever, but still, the way you have guided Naomi has been really cool to watch. You have guided her through your spiritual connection and love. And that shit's pretty cool! Now she can totally focus on what she's doing and connect with nature and shit as effortlessly as breathing. She's still a bit of a talker and she can't fly her broomstick worth a shit, but her progress has been quite remarkable. And now, the two of you and the rest of the Plymouth coven and mediums are ready for their world debut with all the other witches and mediums of the Earth! So, kudos to you, kid."

Naomi came up to the pair and opened her mouth to begin talking. Before she could get a word in, Maddy yelled out, "Good game, Naomi!" and slapped her ass. "Now, where's my next victim? Heh, heh, heh. Oh yeah, there she is." "What's with all the 'good game' ass slapping, Morgan?" Naomi asked. "Did you write her to ever do that?" "No, I didn't," Morgan answered while rubbing her throbbing bottom. "But she just has so much pent-up mischievousness and violence that it has to go *someplace*, I guess. Since she can't kill anybody, she's bored. She started doing *this* shit about a month ago. And for the dumbest things. Finish doing the dishes? Good game with a slap. Take out the trash? Good game! Bring in the mail? Good game! Even at the diner. The cooks will announce that an order's up, and then immediately tuck their ass into a corner away from her. So, she'll see that she doesn't have an obvious target, pick up the order, and take it to her customer. The cooks go back to work, and then suddenly she yells out 'Good game on that last order!' and slaps them as hard as she can. I don't know how many hamburger patties have been dropped on the floor and wasted because of it. Hell, my Gramma actually has started wearing a cushion in her pants for protection. I've talked to her a million times about it. And do you know what her response is? Yep, you guessed it. 'Good game, Morgan!' Then she slaps my ass. It's getting *really* annoying."

"Good game, Sruja!" SLAP! "Good game, Minnie!" SLAP! "Good game, Agatha!" SLAP! "Good game, Queen Zenobia!" SLAP! "Oh,

Maddy!" Zenobia stated. "I must say, that was a bit, um, firm. Yes, *quite* firm. I haven't been spanked like that since, well, last Thursday in Sydney, actually. Wow. That was an adventurous couple, I must say."

"You sure are a *kinky* old broad, Z-Bomb!" Maddy stated through her giggles. "Okay, who's next, heh, heh, heh." Maddy departed the four spirits to look for her next victim before Zenobia said, "Oh, dear. That one certainly has a lot of energy. And spirit. But I guess it is better that she's just going around spanking people than murdering them. But still, the rage is there, just under the surface. It is only a matter of time before that bottle gets uncorked and all the bubbly comes pouring out. We have to keep that bottled up until we can put it to use, ladies. Sruja, where are you at with our little distraction?"

"I'm still working on it," Sruja replied. "It's a bit difficult. I have to work from the last time Morgan recited that incantation and that was five months ago. So, I have to piece together the remnants of that incantation that are still floating around in the universe and focus them on our distraction. But I'm getting there. I think it will be complete by the time we arrive back from Berlin." "Well, it can't come a moment too soon," Zenobia stated as she listened to Maddy yell out, "Good game, Victoria!"

The beaming couple of Lori and Connor were sauntering around the high school stadium where the commencement ceremony had been held. They were lost in one another's eyes as they mirrored each other's glowing smiles. "Um, Lori, I've been thinking about something," Connor clumsily said as he looked down on his large, shuffling feet. "Um, well, you know, we've been going together for quite a while now and, um, well, I've just been thinking that I love being a part of your family so much that, um, well, I was just kinda wondering if maybe I could ask you a question about, um..." Lori's heart was fluttering as her anticipatory mind was whirling with thoughts of flowers, wedding gowns, and vows. The awkward, tender moment was then interrupted. Rather rudely.

"Good game, Connor!" a cackling Maddy exclaimed as she

slapped his ass. "Good game, Lo…" her hand was caught in mid-air by a very frustrated Connor. "Don't do it." He ordered sternly. "Don't you *dare* slap my girlfriend's behind again, Maddy." "Hey! Let go! You're hurting me!" Maddy yelled out as nearby on-lookers began paying attention. "This is police brutality, and I won't stand for it! I'll call your boss! I'll call the mayor! I'll call the Governor! And don't think I won't! Whatevs. I'm outta here! Too much touchy-feely shit for me, anyway. I'm going home! Who's giving me a ride? Anybody? Anybody wanna give lil' ol' me a ride? I mean, it's like eight blocks to my house and I'm wearing heels so…"

The nearby people shook their heads in bewilderment, turned to one another, and continued their conversations. "Fine! I guess I'll just have sore feet for our trip to Berlin then! But until then, I'll call the Senate! I'll call the President! This indignity, sir, shall *not* go unpunished! Maddy out!"

Connor and Lori watched as their unlikely ally stormed off through the crowd of celebratory graduates and parents. They burst out laughing when they heard her yell out, "Oh just great! Now I've broken a heel! I was just put on this Earth to suffer, I guess!" "Wow," a dismayed Connor stated. "Well, you're going to have an interesting trip to Berlin with *her* in tow. Why is she going, anyway? Why not just leave her here? She's not a witch or a medium."

"I know," Lori answered. "But Queen Zenobia wants to keep her close. She's being groomed as her personal bodyguard. Not that the queen needs one. Even *without* her incredible spiritual prowess, she is still a physical phenomenon. I mean, just look at those muscles. She could take out twenty men without even blinking an eye. But she says that she has special plans for Morgan's creation, and she wants to tutor her. Help her to not be so, um, what's the word I'm looking for?"

Connor was more than happy to contribute to Lori's search for the perfect word. "Arrogant? Bratty? Snotty? Vicious? Self-serving? Pain in the ass? *Literally?* Violent? Gluttonous? Annoying?"

"That's the one!" Lori exclaimed through her laughter. "Annoying! Although the other words seem to fit as well. Yes, the queen wants to try to temper her annoying side and build upon her caring side. And, as much as I hate to admit this, she actually does have a caring side. She's mostly just bluster when she's bragging or whatever. And the pranks she pulls seem to never stop. But if anyone were to ever threaten us, especially Morgan, that young woman would pick up a knife, or bat, or axe, or, well, just pretty much anything that she can find, and protect us with everything that she has. Her protection of us and anyone who she perceives as downtrodden, is instinctual. But, oh my lord, is she annoying. This ass-slapping is just her latest trick. Remember a couple of months ago when she would say 'an idiot says what?' to absolutely everything that someone said to her? That finally ran its course, thankfully. Then came the whole good game, ass slapping thing. Hopefully, the queen can exorcize some of this out of her so that she isn't so…um… annoying. Plus, Taylor at the diner begged us not to leave him in charge of her. He simply can't keep her from spitting in people's food."

"What?" Connor shouted out. "She spits in people's *food*? I eat there every day! And she always insists on waiting on me! No matter where I sit, she's always my waitress. And always sweet. Like, *overly* sweet with a pasted on wicked little smile. Do you think she's been spitting in *my* food?" "Um, probably," Lori sheepishly replied. "And, um, from what I've heard, you may not want to order the iced tea."

"Why? What does she do to the iced tea?" a concerned Connor asked. "That's my go-to drink, Lori! You know that! What has she been doing to my iced tea?" "Um, never mind. Just don't order it anymore, okay?" Lori replied while trying to suppress her laughter. "Let's change the subject. What were you wanting to ask me before we were interrupted?"

Connor turned bright red as his eyes darted down to his nervous, shuffling feet. "Ah, nothin' important, Lori. I can talk to you about it when you get back from Berlin. Why is this big shindig happening in Berlin, anyway?"

"Queen Zenobia has planned all of this, and she wants it to be perfect. Nearly all of the mediums and witches of the Earth will be there. Hundreds of us will be together in one hall for the very first time. And for the very first time, mediums and witches will have an opportunity to break through their past differences and build a new coalition of unity. And the queen believes that Berlin is the perfect city for this to occur. There could be other appropriate locations, but the city of Berlin certainly understands the consequences of following a mad man. The horrible, bloody consequences. And they were a city that was divided, literally, by a wall. Freedom, opportunity, and democracy on one side and dark oppressiveness on the other. It was one city that represented both the promise of humanity and the cruelty of it simultaneously. But through years of valiant persistence, the wall came down and the people were unified. Just as the wall between mediums and witches will soon come down. So, you see, Berlin has been chosen as a symbol of hope, persistence, and unity."

"Plus, the night life is off the hook!" Queen Zenobia exclaimed as she wrapped her constrictor-like arms around Lori and Connor. "Yep, if you're looking for trouble, you can certainly find it in Berlin. But before we get to the celebration, we must do the hard work. We must bring our brigade together and end this centuries-long feud once and for all. But then, it's party time, bitches! Come on, Lori. Say good-bye to your squeeze here and let's get to Berlin!"

Queen Zenobia was encased in her customary armor and red-flowing robe as she led her court through the hallway and approached the mahogany door of the stage entrance of the grand ballroom in Berlin. She proudly looked into the eyes of each of her cherished collaborators. Eighteen hopeful yet apprehensive pairs of eyes looked back. Sophia, Lori, Morgan, Victoria, Naomi, Papa Doc, Agatha, Minnie, and Sruja stared at their leader with reverence. They each nodded at Zenobia and smiled.

"Hey! Are ya gonna open the door or what?" Maddy exclaimed from the back of the troop. "Chop, chop, sister! I was out late last night and need a nap! And how come I'm way in the back? This is bullshit. Excuse me. Coming through. Coming through. Move your ass, Victoria. Z-Bomb's bodyguard coming through. Don't look at me like that, Lori. Just move your skinny ass to the side. The more quickly we get this done, the sooner you can get back to your lover boy. Although, I wouldn't kiss him after he's eaten at the diner if I were you. He really likes his iced tea, if you know what I mean, and I think that you do, heh, heh, heh. Okay. Good. Here I am. By my queen's side. In the front. Like I'm supposed to be. Okay, Queenie, open the door and let's get this shit on the road."

The ten-foot-high door swung open, and Queen Zenobia braced herself for an onslaught of celebratory applause. Instead, she was greeted with absolute mayhem. Hundreds of exceptional women were literally at each other's throats. Witches were flying between elegant chandeliers and dive-bombing furious mediums. There was name-calling and hair pulling. The frantic voices of mediums could be heard reciting incantations from their respective books sending witches to plummet from their brooms or to crash into walls. The rich flora that decorated the room had been turned into weapons and screaming mediums were being squeezed by elongated branches, leaves, and petals. A gale force wind swirled around the cavernous chamber sending ornate curtains, paintings, and other priceless ornaments crashing to the floor. And there was spilled popcorn. Everywhere.

Queen Zenobia stood in shocked silence as she witnessed the unnecessary carnage unfold before her disappointed eyes. "Enough!" She commanded to no avail. The bitter women continued their frenzied battle against one another. "Not to worry, Zens," Minnie confidently stated. "I got this." Minnie closed her round eyes, lifted her arms and concentrated. From the heating ducts came bright yellow swarms of smiling emojis. They circulated around the room and attached themselves to the faces of each individual combatant. Within moments, anger turned to confusion as the women attempted to remove the smiling spheres from their heads.

"Are you done now?" Queen Zenobia forcefully asked. She was greeted by hundreds of nodding, smiling emojis. "Would you like to have those removed from your faces?" She was greeted once again by silent nodding. "Are you going to behave and listen?" The embarrassed congregation nodded a final time. "Fine. Minnie, let them have their faces back."

There were loud suction sounds heard as the smiling emojis removed themselves from the beleaguered faces of the witches and mediums. They momentarily floated in front of their respective woman, winked, and kissed them lightly on the cheek before dissipating into the air.

"Well, I must say, this is quite disappointing, ladies," Queen Zenobia admonished. "Yes, quite disappointing indeed. And we shall not begin our program until this mess is cleaned up. Do you know how much of a deposit I had to put down on this room? Now, you will clean up this disaster. And you shall do it...*together*."

Hundreds of brooms were sweeping the floor while ghostly silhouettes rehung curtains and paintings. One witch said to another, "Oh, this is just great. Now we're not going to get S'mores. Stupid mediums." "You're stupid," a medium countered triggering a back and forth of, "No, you're stupid." "No, you're the stupid one." "No, you are. I am rubber and you are glue. You want me to prove it, bitch?" Morgan and Naomi held hands and approached the front of the stage while glaring at the pair of arguing women. Naomi concentrated while Morgan recited an incantation. The entire crowd let out an astonished gasp as the bickering medium and witch were lifted into the air. The pair of combatants screamed as their limbs, torsos, and heads merged together like a demented swirled ice cream cone. Their hideous contorted frame hung over the bewildered crowd as Queen Zenobia stepped up to her lectern.

"Do you see, my friends?" a smirking Zenobia stated. "Do you see the power that we could have if we put aside our petty differences and join forces? And I mean, *truly* join forces. To join forces not for our personal enrichment or for our survival, but to join forces out of genuine love and caring for one another and all decent creatures upon this Earth. You have just witnessed the power of true love. These two friends, Morgan, a medium, and Naomi, a witch. They truly love one another. And it is out of this love that they are able to combine their powers and do this. And so much more. As can you.

Ladies, put down your books of incantations. Put away your brooms and crystals. Please, take your seats and listen. But, to begin to build our trust, we shall sit medium, witch, medium, witch. That's right. Break out of your little cliques, find someone of opposite abilities, introduce yourself, and take a seat. No, you two are both mediums. Find another seat. Yes, shake hands. Good. Everybody settled in now next to your new lecture buddies? Alright, then I shall begin."

The grotesque figure floating above the proceedings pleaded out of their combined mouths, "May we please be separated and take our seats as well? Our internal organs are rubbing against each other and it really hurts. We will sit next to one another and not argue. We promise." Morgan and Naomi smiled at one another, concentrated, and waved their arms. There was a loud ripping sound as the conjoined figures were torn from one another and the embarrassed women were gently placed upon their chairs. In the back of the hall. Behind a support beam with a restricted view.

"Ladies," Queen Zenobia began. "Today is the dawn of a new age. An age of kindness. Of fairness. Of equality. Of prosperity. It is the dawn of the age of people of all walks of life cooperating to achieve peaceful coexistence and understanding. It is an age of embracing our differences out of true love and caring. And this new age shall be led by you, my most wonderfully gifted friends. No longer shall you be enemies. The trivialities of the past are now gone. From this day forward, witches and mediums shall march in lockstep and build our Brigade of Persistence. We shall work together to enhance *all* women's natural abilities. We shall cleanse their souls and open their minds to their connection to nature or the spiritual realm. They shall march into battle with us against the Earth's *true* enemy. Men. Now, not *all* men. Most men, although generally meek, are decent people and we shall allow them to join our movement. In equality. Although *I* think they need to relinquish their control over the TV remote, but that is a fine detail that can be negotiated later. No, the decent men are not our enemy. But everyone in this room knows who is.

"Brutal men. Soulless men. Men who are men in name only. They may be homo-sapien, but they are not *human*. And they are not *human* because they lack any trace of *humanity*. They are heartless demons. And it is *these* men who have dominated the world order from the beginning of recorded time. They began by clubbing women over the heads and taking from us whatever they wanted. And they have continued that vile tradition until this very day. They have figuratively clubbed us over the head economically, politically, and religiously and taken everything that they wanted from us. They have raped our bodies, our psyches, and our souls without any regard for us. We have been stripped of our independence and of our dignity. They have dominated us and kept us at odds with one another. Why? Divide and conquer. They understand how powerful women can be if we were to ever join forces. They understand that the only way they can retain power is through brutal acts of division. They understand that the rise of a united female front, the rise of our Brigade of Persistence, shall be their painful downfall. Well, my friends, *today* is the beginning of their end. *Today* is the first day of their downfall. *Today*, we shall all unite and begin our task of uniting all women of the Earth! *Today* is the first day of the march of our Brigade of Persistence! Are you with me? Are you fired up yet? Are you ready to get to work? Each and every one of us, holding hands, and finally defeating the power of demonic male power? Are you with me?"

The entire chamber was filled with voluminous applause, cheers, and whistles. Former enemies embraced one another while tears of unbridled joy ran down their feminine faces. The giddy, smiling women could feel the yokes of centuries of oppression being lifted from their worn shoulders as their hearts exploded with the love of their sisters. Their spines straightened. Their resolve hardened. And they lifted their fists in unity. "Alrighty then!" Zenobia yelled out. "Tonight, we shall devour S'mores! And tomorrow, we shall devour the patriarchy!" The applause exploded again until Queen Zenobia hushed the crowd. "Alright everybody, alright. We'll get to the S'mores here in a second. It appears we may have a question in the front row. Yes, miss. What would you like to ask?"

"Uh, Hi, Gabby Gillespie from the Transylvania Times. Thanks for taking my questions. Um, first, what role, if any, do you see vampires and werewolves playing in this scenario? I see that you have a voodoo priest here, but no vampires or werewolves."

Queen Zenobia huddled for a moment with her spiritual advisors. Agatha whispered something into her ear and Zenobia returned to the lectern. "Thank you, Miss Gillespie, is it? Very good question. We have not yet made a decision as to whether to invite vampires or werewolves into our movement. There would be a number of factors to be considered before extending an invitation to either group. One factor, for example, would be personal hygiene. I don't think I need to tell any of *you* just how smelly those two groups are. Vampires refuse to bathe because they're paranoid that someone may have blessed the water and then they'll burst into flames. Understandable, but doesn't exactly make them date material. And werewolves certainly *try* to clean, but there are just some areas that they can't quite reach, and their hair gets all filthy and matted and gross. Then, there are the fleas to consider. So, to answer your question, we are not opposed to either group joining our movement, but it would be after some very complicated negotiations."

"Okay, great," the witch reporter stated. "And my second question is, once we have every woman on the Earth incorporated into our brigade, what is it exactly that we are going to do with the demonic men? Will they be banished someplace? Or just monitored? Or perhaps executed? I mean, there are going to be hundreds of millions of them. What are we going to do with them?"

Queen Zenobia once again huddled with her spiritual advisers. There was a great deal of whispering back and forth before she finally emerged once again in front of the lectern. "Again, very good question. And again, we're still working out a few of the finer details on this point. Like, how can we be certain that a man's soul is demonic? We certainly don't want to punish a decent man who has simply made some bad decisions. Hell, if *that* were the case, I'd be punished for all the bad decisions that I made last night! Am I right, girls?"

The entire hall burst into laughter before Zenobia calmed the crowd. "Okay, okay," she stated through her chuckles while wiping joyful tears from her eyes. "But all joking aside, back to your question. We need to make sure we're dealing with a demonic man, and we're in the process of developing a system for that. But your question was what we will do with a man once he has been determined to be demonic, correct? Okay, that one is simple. They will be allowed to live in society and contribute, but will be on parole, so to speak. They do some oppressive, violent shit? We're going to castrate them and put them into work camps. They do that shit again?" Zenobia's face turned dark as her lips curled into a devilish smile. "They screw with us again, and we'll torture and murder the assholes and use their bodies for goddamned fuel. That's *exactly* what we're going to do to these deplorable pricks."

Cheers, laughter, and applause once again erupted and echoed around the chamber. "Good game, Z-String!" Maddy exclaimed through her laughter as she firmly slapped Zenobia's ass. A smirking Sruja approached her annoyed queen and whispered into her ear. "Not to worry, my queen. I have done it. I have broken through. Her distraction shall be waiting for her upon her return to Plymouth."

"Wow, what a trip," a weary Morgan stated as she dragged her slumping body through the front door of her Plymouth home. "Yes, but how inspiring," Lori contributed. "All of those women. Hundreds of them finally joining together in unity for a common cause. It may have been the most emotional experience that I've ever had. I mean, except for, um, I need to call Connor and let him know we made it home."

"Oh, give it a break!" Sophia shouted out. "I mean, I've heard of guys being pussy-whipped but you two are ridiculous! You just called him from the airport! And when we got into town! And when we pulled onto our street! And thirty seconds ago, when we pulled into the drive! And..." She was suddenly silenced as she clicked on the overhead light and found the quivering bodies of Gabriel and Larry the Leopard cowering with one another.

"Larry! What's wrong!" Morgan exclaimed. "Oh, thank goodness you're finally home," a shaking Larry answered. "A strange man is upstairs and we're all alone!"

"A strange man, huh?" Maddy roared as she retrieved the axe that was hidden under the couch. "Well, *I'll* teach this sonofabitch to break into our home and scare my friends!" She flew up the stairs, opened Morgan's bedroom door, and shouted, "You'd better get your sorry ass out of here or I'm gonna hack you into little bits or my name's not Maddy Sommers! And that's my damned name, so you'd better get goin' prick!"

The man who was casually lying on the bed lowered the book that he was reading and revealed his face. He smiled at the ferocious, red-headed, green-eyed woman, stretched, and playfully said, "Waz-zup, Buttacup? You maybe wanna drop the axe and give your husband a kiss, or what?"

CHAPTER 11

LOOPHOLES

"Oh, this is just ridiculous," Sophia lamented as she once again turned the volume of her television up. "I can't even hear my stories, let alone concentrate on what is happening with all that racket going on upstairs."

"Yeah, they do seem to be enjoying themselves," Lori responded while the sounds of loud moans and creaking bed springs echoed from an upstairs bedroom. "But, Jesus, how long can they, um, keep this up?"

"Well," a red-faced Morgan stated. "I mean, I *did* write them as being inseparable soul mates and they haven't seen each other for a while. Not since Christmas when Sruja took Maddy out of my book and brought her here. Poor Erick was all alone in my book. His wife was there, but she was just frozen. He didn't understand what was happening. For several months all he could do was stare at his comatose wife and weep. And now, they're reunited. Here. So, I guess maybe they're making up for lost time or something."

"Well, I think it's really romantic," Naomi contributed. "Two lovers who had lost one another are now reunited. It's really cool. It's kinda like this one time when I lost one of my favorite socks. It was pink with little ladybugs on it. Do you remember those socks,

Morgan? You always said they were really cute. Anyway, I looked all over the place. The washer. The dryer. The hamper. The laundry basket. Under my bed. Under my dresser. I looked everywhere, but my poor sock was lost. I kept its mate on my dresser as a reminder to never stop looking for my lost sock. It just lay there on my dresser like it was depressed. It was so sad. And I kept looking, but I could never find it. Then, one day, my mom came into my room and said, 'Naomi, is this your sock? It got mixed in with your father's things'. And there it was! My lost sock! I was so happy, and I put them both on right away and my socks were just so happy to be back together and resting on my feet!"

"Yeah, this is *exactly* like that, Naomi," Sophia stated in a surly, sarcastic tone. "Except your socks don't screw at a billion decibels. Now, everybody be quiet. Look, they're about to search that guy's house. Oh, I bet he's the murderer." The dialogue was suddenly completely drowned out by an explosion of orgasmic moans from above them. "Oh, damn it! What did they just say? This was the most important part!"

"Sorry, Gramma," Morgan sheepishly said. "I think they're almost done." She was interrupted by a loud slapping sound and the voice of an enthusiastic Maddy yelling out, "Good game, Erick!"

"Ow!" Erick exclaimed. "Would you *please* stop slapping me in the ass? That really (expletive) hurt!" "Oh, you know you love it, you kinky ol' bastard," a chuckling Maddy replied as she draped her five-foot-four-inch frame in a bright pink robe. "Oh, and we're not supposed to use that word around here."

"What (expletive) word?" Erick shot back. "Well, that one. (Expletive). We're not supposed to use that word," Maddy answered. Erick burst into laughter as he put his jeans on. "(Expletive)? We can't say (expletive)? Why the (expletive) not? You're (expletive) joking, right? And, if so, being brought to real life really hasn't helped your humor. Because that joke (expletive) sucks."

"Well," Maddy began to explain while trying to retain her calm. "First off, my humor does *not* suck. It is not *my* fault that *some* people's minds are not *sophisticated* enough to get my great sense of humor. But, since you are recently brought to life, I am going to assume that your hurtful indiscretion is because of confusion from going through the universe and being brought here or some shit. So, you get a pass. This time. Secondly, no that was *not* one of my great jokes. The Ladies Cabot do not care for that word. Plus, the author of this thing is writing it for a slightly younger audience, and he is trying to tone down the language and violence. But he's a dumbass, so what does he know. Anyhoo, no we cannot say (expletive). Or (expletive). Or (expletive). Or (expletive). Or (expletive). Or, um, no I think that's it. Oh no! Wait! We also can't say (expletive)."

"Well, what the (expletive) *can* we say?" Erick roared back. "Um, I mean, we can cuss a little," Maddy answered. "But just the minor league cuss words. You know like 'shit' and 'damn' and 'hell' and shit like that."

"Well, what about (expletive)?" Erick inquired. "And also, what exactly do you mean by tone down the violence? You had better not mean what I think you mean." "Well," Maddy responded. "To your first question, no, I think that (expletive) would definitely be frowned upon in this household. And to your second question, um…" Maddy's voice trailed off as her emerald eyes looked down at her shuffling size-six feet.

"What?" Erick asked again. "What do you want to tell me?" "Um, well," Maddy began to clumsily respond. "I mean, I really don't want to disappoint you. How can I put this exactly? Um, you see, it's kinda like this, um, well, we kinda can't kill anybody."

"Noooooo!" Erick exclaimed as he flopped face first on the bed and began sobbing. "This can't be happening. Why were we brought to this hell hole? We can't say (expletive) or (expletive) or (expletive) and now, we can't even (expletive) kill anybody? What do they do with all of their traitors to democracy, and rapists, and wife-beaters? Just let them walk around and hope the so-called justice system takes care of them? This is totally (expletive) up, Maddy!"

"I know, I know," Maddy stated as she gave her husband sympathetic rubs on his back. "I know. This world is *totally* insane. These lunatics who tried to overthrow their democracy are still walking around free. And get this! They actually have a good shot at rising to power again! Yeah, no shit! Half of the people in this stupid fu…um, country are actually going to vote for this shit *again*! These assholes aren't patriots. And they sure as hell aren't Christians. They are stupid. They are bigots. They are misogynists. They are the uber-wealthy wanna-be oligarchs who want to rule this country and gobble up all the wealth. I mean, how many damned yachts, houses, toys, and mistresses do these pricks need, anyway? They are the worst that humankind has to offer. And they get away with it by wrapping themselves in the flag while clutching a Bible. It's sick and disgusting how many dumbasses there are that fall for their manipulative, con-artist shit. And why? So they can get cheaper eggs. So, I understand, baby. This world is totally (expletive) up."

A still sobbing but more hopeful Erick asked through his tears, "So, we can say prick?" "Yeah, baby," an understanding Maddy answered. "We can say prick. And that's not all! Sure, we can't kill anybody right *now*. But these bitches kill people all the time! Some of these women are mediums and some are witches. And there's this whole plan to take down all of the male assholes of the world! In fact, there are four vengeful spirits coming over late tonight for a big meeting. So, all we need to do is be patient. We'll be able to do some twisted shit to somebody. Don't you worry. We just have to wait for it to be approved by the spirits."

"But *I* want to kill somebody *now*!" Erick whined while pounding his fists on the helpless mattress. "How come *they* get to tell us who to kill and who not to? Who made *them* our boss? *We're* not mediums or witches. Why do we have to play by *their* rules? This isn't fair, Maddy! I mean, what if we're threatened? Are we supposed to just stand there and let some douchebag beat us over the head with a baseball bat? Oh, gee, I wish I could defend myself against this assault on my life and take this knife and slash this (expletive) into tiny pieces, but I have to get clearance from a bunch of old bitch spirits. So, if you would please just stop assaulting me for a moment, mister dickhead, I'll check to see if I can fight back. See how stupid that sounds?"

"Yeah, that actually does sound pretty stupid. I've missed you baby," Maddy replied. "And that gives me an idea. Nobody has told me that I can't act in *self-defense*. Sooooo, you maybe wanna go for a little walk with me?"

Erick's tears began drying on his pale cheeks as he looked up into his beloved wife's glistening green eyes. He reached up and pulled her to him before embracing her in a long, loving kiss.

"Oh, dear lord, not again!" Sophia yelled out as moans and creaking bedsprings once again drowned out the dialogue of the pivotal courtroom scene of her story. "I give up! I'm going to prepare some snacks for our guests! Who all is coming? Let's see here. Victoria, Queen Zenobia, Sruja, Grandmother Agatha, Minnie. Oh, and Papa Doc. I think he's coming to our little shindig too."

"And don't forget Maddy and Erick, Gramma!" Morgan contributed. Sophia forlornly looked up at the shaking ceiling and said, "No, how could we ever forget *them?*"

"Good game, Erick!" SLAP! Thundered down the steps as the fully dressed couple descended into the living room. Their faces glowed while they held hands and looked at the gathered annoyed faces. "Wazzup, bitches?" Maddy exclaimed. "Oh, good you are done making the loud sound," Larry the Leopard gleefully stated as his goo-goo-googly eyes rolled around in their sockets. "I sure wish I had a companion that *I* could pound!" "Larry!" a shocked Morgan yelled out. "What has come over you? You're not supposed to think like that!" "Sorry, Morgan, I'm sure this will pass," an embarrassed Larry answered. "It's just that sometimes I wish I had a little ass."

"Um, while we're on the, um, subject," the ever-diplomatic Lori chimed in. "Well, I mean, we all think that it's *really great* that you two are re-united. And it really is *nice* to see a couple of, um, well, a couple that is so much in love but um, well, we were just wondering if, um, well..."

Lori was cut off by her less tactful mother. "You maybe want to get a room the next time you want to bang? I mean, holy hell, you two! Do you know how many stories I've missed since he's come along? Eight! That's how many! And I love my stories! So, the next time you two are feeling frisky, go to a cheap motel or something!"

"Oh, yeah?" an irritated Maddy shot back. "Well, what about *you*, Sophia? How many nights have I had to listen to you and Vince go at it, huh? And what about you, Lori? Your squeals are so high-pitched they could nearly break glass! And I've had to listen to it all. I've had to listen to all of *you* enjoy the fruits of your lovely relationships. And all while I was without my love. My soul mate. My prince. Every time I had to listen to you all carrying on, it was a reminder of how much I missed my husband. But did anybody ever think of *that*? Nooooo. Nobody cares about *Maddy's* feelings. All we care about is our stupid stories on TV. Which, by the way, you do *not* have to watch live, Sophia! You can watch them on-demand at any time! I've tried to show you! You maybe wanna pull your wrinkled ass into this century? Whatevs. Screw you guys. Erick and I are going for a walk."

"Um, Maddy," Lori stated. "The others will be here soon for our big meeting. Please don't be late." "Yeah, yeah, yeah, we'll be here," Maddy responded. She and Erick looked at each other wearing wide grins and chuckled as they pulled their black hoods over their heads. Maddy slammed the door and Morgan said, "Huh. I wonder what they're up to. It's kinda warm for hoodies tonight. And I have a bad feeling about those chuckles. And I should know. I created both of them."

"Oh, what a pleasant evening," Erick stated as he and his wife slinked through dense bushes in order to peer into yet another house window. "Nope. No abuse going on here. Dammit. This town just *has* to have some douchebags." "Oh, we'll find one," Maddy replied. "We just gotta keep turning over some rocks. Eventually we'll find a snake, heh, heh, heh. Here. Let's try that house over there. Looks the part. Beat up car on blocks in the front yard. Stupid confederate flag. Truck nuts on the, um, Pinto. Man, there really are dumbass rednecks everywhere, aren't there? But we'd better check. Not *all* rednecks are drunk abusers, after all. But that stupid flag and Pinto nuts certainly are encouraging signs."

They wiped years of dirt and grime from the cracked living room window and stared at the horrific sight inside the dilapidated home. Two small children were cowering in fear in a corner of a ripped-up sofa while their father stood over them. The shirtless man stumbled over empty beer and whiskey bottles while gripping a well-worn thick leather belt. The children were pleading, "Please, daddy. We won't be bad again." The drunken abuser continued to lurch forward until he heard the sound of his front door being kicked in. "Hey! Get away from those kids!"

The vile abuser turned and looked into the beet red face of Erick Parker. The veins in Erick's neck were throbbing and he wore a twisted smile upon his demented face. "You better get outta here, mister!" the abuser shouted out. "This is nonaya goddam business! If you don't get outta here, I'm gonna kill you!"

Erick paused for a moment and looked down at his amused wife. "Huh," he said to her. "Well, *that* certainly sounded like a *threat* to me. How did it sound to *you*?" "Yup," Maddy replied. "Definitely sounded like a threat. "Well," Erick continued. "I do believe that my life might be in danger. What do *you* think?" "Oh, definitely," Maddy answered. "Your life is *definitely* in danger. I don't think that you have any *choice* but to act in self-defense. And baby, this one's all yours. Welcome home." Erick looked back at the confused abuser and his demented smile returned to his reddened face. He continued his unblinking stare as he pulled a large butcher knife from under his black hoodie.

The blood-soaked couple opened the front door of their newly adopted home. They were giggling like mischievous children as they entered the living room. They were greeted by the astonished faces of Naomi, Papa Doc, the Ladies Cabot, four bewildered spirits, and...Detective Connor O'Sullivan.

They stood frozen for a moment before saying in unison, "It wasn't our fault!" "Oh, dear god," Connor stated while rubbing his weathered face. "Just tell me who it is and where you put the body." "Um, well, detective," Erick began answering. "You'll need to be a bit more specific. Are you talking about the head? Or torso? Or arms? Or legs?" "Or his little dick!" Maddy enthusiastically contributed.

"Oh, yeah, we put his dick someplace else. Do you mean where is his dick, detective?"

"Oh, dear lord," was all that Connor could say. Queen Zenobia leaned over to Sruja and whispered, "Well, *this* little distraction didn't seem to work. In fact, now we have *two* of them to worry about. You maybe wanna give it another shot there, Ace?" Sruja nodded in understanding while her mind searched for a new solution to their vigilante serial killer problem.

"And hey, listen," Erick continued. "The kids are just fine." "There are *kids?*" Lori exclaimed. "Well, yeah," Erick answered while nonchalantly staring up at the ceiling. "I mean, it was all in self-defense. We were just walking along, minding our own business, and enjoying this beautiful evening when we heard the cries of children. We looked into the window and this man was threatening them with a belt. So, we went inside, and I politely asked him to stop. Well, then this guy turned around and threatened *me*. I know we aren't to be violent unless instructed, but I had to defend myself. And my wife. Just look at her. She's tiny and helpless." Maddy looked at him, shook her confused head, and mouthed "What?" Erick patted her auburn locks while wearing a conceited smile and continued. "And, of course, we had to protect those innocent children. So, Maddy hit him on the head with a club and knocked him out. While I was dragging him into some nearby woods, Maddy called the police and reported the children as being abandoned."

"Oh, so *that* was what that call was about," Connor muttered. "Yeah, we totally made sure the kids were alright before defending ourselves against this unconscious dick who was being dragged into the woods," Erick continued. "So, anyway, we could see the flashing lights on the squad cars while we were taking off that guy's arms. And legs. And head." "And his dick, baby," Maddy reminded. "Don't forget about his dick." "Oh yeah, and his dick. And I must say, it certainly is handy to live near the ocean. Why couldn't you have written us as having lived by the ocean, Morgan? It would have made body disposal much easier."

"You two are sooooo full of shit," an unconvinced Morgan stated.

"Innocently walking along enjoying the evening, my ass. You two went *looking* for trouble. I *knew* you were up to something when you left wearing those hoodies. I created you, remember? You can't pull shit around me."

"Well, of course not, morgan," Erick replied. "You are our creator. You understand us better than anyone. But that's beside the point. The point is, why couldn't you have written us to just dump bodies into the ocean? You've written me as being in my mid-forties. I'm no spring chicken, and that shit's hard on the back."

"Well, yeah, I guess you have a point," Morgan answered. "But you *were* in Brooklyn, which is *kinda* near the ocean. Plus, how interesting would it be to just have you throw body parts into the water after every kill? Kinda boring don'tcha think? Don't you want to be more creative than that?"

"You're right!" Maddy yelled out. "That would be totally boring! Good game, Morgan!"

CHAPTER 12

TODAY'S ASSIGNMENT

The brilliant stars that were shining outside of the home of the Ladies Cabot began to disappear behind dark foreboding clouds as Queen Zenobia cracked her knuckles and stared at her brigade. Her face was illuminated by the crashing lightning over Plymouth Harbor as she began to speak. "Okay, okay," Queen Zenobia stated as she tried to regain control of the meeting. "Okay, you two. What's done is done. No sense crying over spilled milk or dismembered limbs. And, it sounds like this guy had it coming. Plus, you were acting in self-defense, so there is no need to split hairs here. Just put something down on the couch so you don't get blood all over it, sit down, and let's get this meeting started."

At that moment, Connor's cellphone rang. "Yeah? O'Sullivan here. Uh, huh. Missing father? Kids taken to their aunt's house? Good, good. No sign of the father, huh? But blood found in the woods behind the house? A lot of it huh? And a penis? Well, that doesn't sound good. No sign of the rest of the body, huh? Well, you know the drill, Deputy Holloway. Seal it off. I'll be there in a few. And thanks." Connor stood up and glared at the blood-soaked couple sitting on the adjacent couch. He clenched his fists in frustration while the pair nonchalantly whistled, twiddled their bloody thumbs, and innocently gazed at the ceiling. "You know, you are *really* becoming a pain in my ass. And now there's two of you. Great. Just great. Thanks for this." He went to the front door and opened it before shouting, "And one other thing! Stop spitting in my food!" SLAM!

"What does he mean about spitting in his food?" Erick inquired of his smirking wife. "Oh, nothin'," Maddy replied. "It's just a little game I play with him. You see, I work as a waitress at Sophia's diner, and if somebody treats me less than respectfully, which *he* frequently does, then they get an extra topping on their burger. Or salad. Or soup. But, come to think of it, he didn't tell me to stop pissing in his iced tea, heh, heh, heh."

"Wait, wait, wait," an astonished and outraged Erick loudly responded. "This is just *disgusting* Maddy! This is *horrendous*! I can't *believe* what I'm hearing! Are you telling me that you are working as a *waitress*? This is *ludicrous*, and I won't stand for it! No wife of mine is going to work as a common waitress! Don't you people see the potential that you have sitting right in front of you? Why, she's the most gifted vigilante serial killer ever created! And you are using her as a common waitress? Well, this insanity ends right now!"

"Okay, okay," Queen Zenobia interjected. "I totally get why you're pissed, Erick. I really do. But rest assured that there is a plan for both your wife and you. Once the battle really gets engaged, you two will be my personal bodyguards and there will be plenty of opportunities for you both to use your unique skills. Please just trust me on this. Okay? Now, can we please get back to business? There's a show in Vegas that we want to see that starts in a couple of hours."

"Yeah, let's get this shit started!" Maddy yelled out. "Chop-chop sisters! And since I don't have to work tomorrow, it looks like I'll be jetting off to Vegas. Oh, baby! We could re-do our vows and shit. Wouldn't that be romantic? Do you want an Elvis or a Wayne Newton? I'm thinking Elvis. But a young Elvis. Not the weird, sequined jump suit, karate chopping Elvis."

"Maddy," Sophia firmly stated. "You will *not* be going to Vegas. You can't teleport like these four can. And you are mistaken about one other thing. You *will* be working at the diner tomorrow. We are expecting a large breakfast crowd and an even larger lunch crowd, and you will not abandon your position. So, let's get on with this meeting. You need to get to bed. To *sleep*. You need to be up bright and early tomorrow morning."

"Oh, no!" Erick roared back. "I just said that *my wife* will *not* be working as a waitress, and I meant it! I'm sorry, Sophia, but you're just going to have to find somebody else to sling your hash! And another thing!" He was suddenly silenced by a large leaf from a houseplant wrapping around his mouth.

"Hey!" Naomi exclaimed. "You're getting pretty good at that Morgan! Wow! My bestie is a Fabula. Both a medium *and* a witch. It's so cool. Especially how I can link *my* connection with nature to yours and turn you into a supercharged witch! Yep, all we gotta do is hold hands and you can feed off of my energy! It's really cool. Remember when we lifted that car with the wind? It was so effort-less! Or how we created that huge tidal wave in the ocean? So cool. Yep, nobody's gonna want to mess with Sister Shade! It reminds me of this one time at summer camp, when..."

Naomi was abruptly silenced by another leaf wrapping around her mouth. "Whew! Thank you, Victoria," Queen Zenobia said as another flash of lightning lit up the room. "Now, could you all please be quiet so we can get on with this? Alright. First off, let me just say what a privilege it is to have you all as the high council of the Brigade of Persistence. You are all incredibly gifted and I appreciate each and every one of you. Okay. Status report. Agatha and Sophia. You have been assigned to pair up witches and mediums throughout the world so that they can begin opening the minds of the women in their respective regions. How's that shit going?"

"Well," Sophia began. "I must say that it has been such a pleasure to be able to work with my grandmother. She is such a delight. Although, I think I know where my daughter got her stick-up-the-ass-itis. They're both a bit stuffy. But, regardless, it has been a plea-sure. Grandmother Agatha, would you like to present our report?"

"Uh, sure," Agatha replied. "Thanks for that. I guess. You know, you could learn something from Lori and myself. Rules and order are in place for a reason. Emotional constraint is an asset, not a liability. You always have been a delightful woman, Sophia, but this hippie-trippy lifestyle of yours, well, I suppose that isn't important right now. Let's get on with it. I'm really looking forward to that Sounds of the 40's tribute show tonight."

"Wait," Papa Doc interjected as his hunched over frame rested on a chair. "You're going all the way to Vegas, just for a cover act? With all the great shows that you could see, you're going to see some third-rate crooners do shitty Sinatra covers? Why not go to that cool punk club down on Fremont? Or see one of the big acts at the Sphere? Why waste time watching a bunch of old men belting out boring songs that you've heard a million times? How are you supposed to boogie to *that*? I'm really surprised at you, ladies. Sruja. Minnie. Z-String. I thought you were way more hip than that." An embarrassed Minnie replied, "Yeah, well, it was Agatha's turn to pick, soooo…"

"They kinda got a point, Grandmother," a chuckling Sophia stated. "That sounds like a D-R-A-G, drag." "I happen to think that it will be quite enjoyable," a slightly hurt Agatha responded. "I just happen to enjoy the old-time crooners. The 1940's was a time of much more decency and civility."

"Really?" an incredulous Sophia yelled. "The 1940's were a time of *decency* and *civility*? Are you *serious*? That's *exactly* the time that these neo fascist assholes want to take us *back to*. Yes, a *decent* and *civil* time when Black people were second class citizens, at best. If they weren't being beaten in the streets and lynched. A *decent* and *civil* time when women were expected to play the part of the good, obedient little housewife while the asshole man of the house played golf and chased his secretary around the desk. A *decent* and *civil* time when people like my granddaughter had to suppress who she truly was as a human being or face the discriminatory wrath of society. Oh, yes, the 1940's were just so *civil* and *decent*. You might want to tell *that* to all of Western Europe who watched the *civil* and *decent* Nazis marching down their streets and committing genocide! It is the *decent* and *civil* 1940's bigoted mindset and oppression that we are fighting against in 2024, grandmother!"

"Well," a hurt Agatha responded. "I suppose if you wish to be a nitpicker, then I admit that the 1940's contained a few societal flaws. But I still maintain that the music was just wonderful. Now, can we *please* stop the critique of my personal musical tastes and get back to our report? Thank you. As I was stating, I think that we've completed the task of partnering one medium with one witch. It wasn't easy. We tried to pair witches and mediums up by common interests. Which makes *my* being paired with my granddaughter seem a bit curious, but I won't go into that now. We have a complete list of names in each region of the world. They have been given the names of their partners and have been working together to practice combining their powers. So, yes, my queen. The partnerships have been established."

"Okay, good," Zenobia stated. "Well, *that* took a lot longer than I *thought* it would. Alright. Victoria and Lori. You were to identify women in each region who are the most evolved and ready for their enlightenment. So, wazzup with that?"

"Thank you, my queen," Lori began. "And let me just say that *I* also appreciate the music of the 1940's, Great Grandmother." "Why thank you, Lori. That was very nice of you to say," Agatha replied while wearing a haughty grin. Sophia glared at her daughter and mouthed "kiss-ass." Lori smiled and shrugged at her mother before continuing. "Victoria used her connection to nature to reach out for others around each region of the world who will be the easiest to, um, inspire." "Yeah," Victoria chimed in. "We wanted to start with the low hanging fruit first, so I found women whose souls were as closely evolved as ours. Then, Lori used an incantation to find a vengeful spirit who led us to these women. We were able to peer into their worlds and see what their lives were like. And we *definitely* found many women in each region who not only are the best candidates to be awakened but who are also in really bad situations with an abusive man. We have the list all compiled and ready to go."

"Excellent!" Zenobia exclaimed. "Now, *that's* what I call a concise report! Good job ladies! Maddy. Just sit down. I said good *job*, not good *game*. Don't go over and slap their asses, please. Okay, now let's put this shit together. Lori, Victoria, Agatha, and Sophia. Match our brigade partners up with the women that will be the first batch to evolve. Our mediums will summon one of our spirits who will guide the witch to the selected woman. Then, our witch shall whisper a spell into the ear of that woman that will open her heart, mind, body, and soul to her natural abilities. And Viola! We've just given birth to a new witch or medium! Over and over and over again throughout the world, women will be enlightened to their natural abilities. Then, our *newbies* will be paired up and they will be given *their* assignments of *more* women to evolve. And so on, and so on, until we have *billions* of witches and mediums recruited into our Brigade of Persistence in sisterhood. And this is only possible because witches and mediums now genuinely care for and love one another. And it is this heartfelt union that allows them to combine their powers to evolve other women. But before our newbies can get into the game, they must hone their skills. They must be trained. Which brings me to Morgan and Naomi. Are you two ready?"

Morgan wore a sly smile upon her teenage face as she put on her sunglasses and crossed her feet on the coffee table while her disapproving mother looked on. "Yup, we're ready Queen Z," Morgan arrogantly stated. "Just send us your new recruits and we'll get 'em trained up. I've already made contact with several spirits who will be able to link all of our students together through their souls. Naomi can then use their connections to nature to bring all of their minds together at the same time. So, their *souls* will be connected, and their *minds* will be connected. We'll be able to hold virtual classes to thousands at a time from all over the world. It'll be like witch Zoom or something. And we've already put together the curriculum. The history of witches and mediums. The spiritual and biological make-up of women. The history of brutality by the patriarchy. And finally, how to focus and connect their abilities with each other to evolve other women. It'll be about a three-week course with a multiple-choice mid-term and essay final. We figure every woman in the world will be evolved and trained up by Halloween 2025. So, yeah. We're ready. Right, Naomi?"

Naomi began answering through the leaf that continued to cover her mouth. "Mmmm. Mmm, mmmm, mmmm. Mmm, mm. Mmmmm, mmmm, mmmm, mmmmm." "Yep, she says she's ready," Morgan stated while wagging her black Vans on the coffee table.

"Oh, this is so very exciting!" Zenobia shouted out. "But, as we have discussed, having every woman in the world become evolved spiritual warriors in our brigade may not be enough. The bad men will fight back. And it is the bad men who will still control the levers of society. Economic levers. Religious levers. Control of the media. Control of their governments. And, most dangerous, control over their militaries. So, we shall construct another, rather unconventional, army that we can call upon. Just in case we need them. Sruja, how is your part coming?"

"I'm piecing together incantations that medium authors have used throughout time so that I can bring their characters into the real world," Sruja answered. "I'm still working on it. Just like with Erick, I have to find these remnants of incantations that are floating around, piece them together, then apply it to that author's creations. And we need to be careful with that. We don't want to repeat our mista...um...we want to make sure we have the right characters for our army. So far, I just have a cartoon piece of toast and a fictional bar maid. But it's coming together. I'll have them all here by Halloween 2025. Not to worry."

"Good," Zenobia replied. "And don't forget about working on another distraction for you know who. Alright, Minnie, how is *your* project going?"

"Supa! Just Supa!" Minnie squeaked. "I'm getting' really good at using Lori's incantation on more and more emojis! I'm buildin' up quite the army of little images that I can conjure up and control! Why, just look outside in the back yard! That's right ladies! We're gonna be travelin' to Vegas in style tonight! That's a life-size airplane emoji that we can fly there! All that teleportin' kinda makes me queasy. So, all of Sruja's brought to life characters are gonna have *my* emojis that they can use as weapons!"

"Oh, Minnie, you are a delight," a thrilled Zenobia stated. "And to think that this all started out with a simple idea about 'Liking' some bastard up the ass. And now, here we are. Using them to topple the patriarchy. I am so proud of you, my friend. And that black flapper dress does *wonders* for your figure. Now finally, Papa Doc. Thank you so much for joining our movement. You truly are one of the good ones. And, by that, I mean men in general. Not voodoo priests. What have you got for us?"

"Oh, I think you'll be quite pleased," Papa Doc answered as he adjusted his black leather biker cap on his 104-year-old, wrinkled, bald head. "I have obtained and combined all of the necessary ingredients for my potion. I know just which recitation to use. It is just a matter of going from grave to grave, sprinkling a bit of my potion upon the ground, and saying a few words. Then, my queen, we shall have an army of zombies at our disposal. But there is one problem. I can certainly raise them from the dead, but I have no place to put them all. There's only so much room in my basement, and we're going to have thousands of these things."

"Hmmmm, that *is* a quandary," Zenobia replied while stroking her broad chin. "What to do with an army of zombies? Let's see here. It needs to be in a centralized location in this country so that they can be quickly deployed. Yes, someplace with a lot of trains so we can put them in box cars and whisk them off to anywhere they may be needed. Oh! I've got it! A storage place near a bunch of trains! There's a cool old, abandoned mall in Galesburg, Illinois! We could house thousands of them there!"

"Oh, how perfect!" Papa Doc stated. "Yes, I could create them here, put them on a train to Galesburg, then our midwestern witches could place a compliance spell on them and march them, um, like zombies, into the mall for safe keeping. It's perfect! It will be a zombie mall! Figuratively *and* literally! And better yet! With all that space, we could hold a killer zombie dance and really boogie! Oh, that would be perfect for an 80's night. I must start going through my records. But that is not all, my queen. Once we have used our zombies, we will need to oversee them, and I am quite happy to say that I have initiated talks with the ambassadors of the Vampire Syndicate and The International Assembly of Werewolves to assist us in that endeavor. Now, no promises, but I do believe that we may be able to get them to cooperate with one another to watch over the zombies once they have completed their mission."

"Well, that *is* good news!" Zenobia yelled out. "We're gonna smell like garlic for a while, though. And we'll probably need to wear flea collars. But a small price to pay for a responsible and efficient zombie babysitting service." Zenobia proudly beamed as she looked upon all of the members of her Brigade of Persistence. Her eyes then fell upon the sullen faces of Maddy and Erick. "What's wrong with *you* two? Aren't you happy? Look at how our plan to eradicate this world's patriarchy is coming along. Why do you look upset? Morgan, remove Erick's leaf gag, won't you please, dear?"

Maddy looked up at Zenobia. Her once-brilliant green eyes began filling with tears as she inquired in a disappointed, child-like voice, "Gee, I don't suppose you have any cool assignment for *us*, do you? I mean, we kinda feel left out."

"Oh, my darlings, no," a sympathetic Zenobia replied. "No, we would *never* leave you out. In fact, I have an assignment for the two of you which is just perfect. As you have just heard, we are going to have a mall full of zombies, right?" "Yeah, I suppose," Maddy meekly replied while twiddling her thumbs. "And zombies have to *eat*, right?" Zenobia asked. "Uh, huh," Maddy answered in a pathetic tone. "Well don't you see?" Zenobia excitedly continued. "*You* two are going to feed the zombies! You are going to find deplorable men who deserve a gruesome death, and you are going to take them to Galesburg, throw them in the mall, and feed the zombies! Now, don't *kill* these men before you get to Galesburg. Zombies like their brains active when they're eating them. Just knock them out, tie them up, toss them in the zombie mall, and watch natural selection at work!"

Maddy and Erick jumped off the couch and began jumping in a

circle while clapping. "Oh, Erick! This is just like Christmas! Except, instead of ripping open presents, we get to rip open a bunch of dickheads!" Maddy excitedly shouted. "I know!" an equally excited Erick replied. "This might be one of the greatest days of my life! Fictional *or* real! It's kind of a bummer that we can't kill them ourselves, but it's going to be *so much fun* watching these douchebags get eaten alive by zombies! Come on! Let's get to bed so we can get up early and start looking for meat!" He then glared at Sophia and tersely said, "Yes, we will go to bed now so that we can get up early. But *not* so my wife can go waitress at *your* slop shop. My wife has much more important work to do, so the days of her being your slave labor are over. Come on, dear. Let's go to bed. But we may want to screw on your side. I think we popped a spring on mine. Good night, ladies and Papa Doc. Good night, Sophia. I sincerely wish you the best of luck in your pursuit of a new waitress."

"Orders up!" The short order cook at the diner yelled out. "Good game, Erick!" Maddy exclaimed as she harshly slapped her husband's ass. "Goddam it, Maddy!" Erick shouted out. "Would you *please* quit slapping my ass? Now I've dropped another burger on the floor!" "Eh, it's okay," Maddy replied. "It goes to table twelve. And table twelve just happens to be a dick. Which reminds me. He'll need some special sauce on his bun. And he ordered iced tea. Better slam some lemonade before his order's ready. Gotta get my bladder nice and full for *this* douchebag, heh, heh, heh. I wonder if the zombies would enjoy *him*? Hey baby, didja bring the baseball bat and zip ties?"

CHAPTER 13

ORIGINS

"This is going to be awesome!" Carmen exclaimed as she and her new witch partner, Angelica, entered their hotel room in Jefferson City, Missouri. "Yeah, this is going to really be something," Angelica replied as she tossed her overnight bag on a pastel sofa and flopped her ebony body onto one of the queen beds. "It has been so cool meeting you, Carmen. I can't believe there was a time when mediums and witches hated each other. And *why?* Because we were different? So damned stupid. You would think that we evolved women would have known better. But we are also human, I suppose, and susceptible to the same petty bigotry as anyone else. But not anymore. Queen Zenobia has brought us all together. And I've not only found my spiritual partner, but I've also found a best friend. I can't wait for your daughter's Quinceañera next week. It's been so cool watching our families come together too. Our husbands and kids hanging out while you and I were training with Morgan and Naomi to prepare us for this moment. All the hard work that Morgan and Naomi have been putting us through is about to pay off. Tonight, will be the first woman that we shall evolve. Right here in southern Missouri. I'm gonna turn up the air. Man, it's crazy hot even for early July."

"Yeah, well, better get used to it," Carmen replied as she unpacked her bag. She smiled slightly as she retrieved an ancient, glowing family heirloom and placed it on her bed. "The dumbasses are running the world, and the Earth is just going to keep getting warmer and warmer. Stronger hurricanes. Droughts. Floods. And, in this section of the world, more frequent and stronger tornadoes. Yes, man is about to pay dearly for his ignorance and greed."

"Yes, men will," Angelica agreed. "Old, rich evil men who only care about their bottom line. They could give a shit less about the plight of billions of people around the world. The only billions they care about are in their stock portfolios. Well, *that* shit's going to disappear too. But that isn't enough. They need to suffer *more*. They need to suffer for their oppression of the masses. Especially women. The way evil men have brainwashed us. Divided us. Kept us from connecting with our true potential. Well, the beginning of the end to *that* shit is tonight. It begins with us, and other partnerships throughout the world. Oh! I wonder if we will give birth to a medium or witch tonight?"

"Does it matter?" Carmen inquired. "Naw, we'll love her no matter who she is," a giggling Angelica answered. "You maybe want a drink before we get started? We need to wait until she's asleep, so we have a little time to kill."

The pair of newfound friends lounged by the pool while sipping on their margaritas as the brilliant, setting orange sun was reflected in their sunglasses. The sky was awash with vibrant pinks and purples as Earth's star said goodnight to its satellite. "So, when did you first discover you were evolved?" Angelica asked. "Oh, man, that was such a wild night," Carmen answered.

"I was sixteen and I had just come home from a date. Well, more like a mauling session. I swear, I always hated watching pro wrestling with my father, but those moves certainly came in handy *that* night. I was so into that boy. And he did everything that he could to get into *me*. I finally had to claw his stupid, smirking face and knee him in the balls to get him off of me. I ran home, in tears. I tried to sneak upstairs, but my parents saw me. And they saw my tears. And they knew. They just knew. My father, bless his departed soul, got up from his recliner, went over to our bookshelf, and handed my mother an old book that had been there since I could remember. He nodded at my mother, kissed me on top of my head, and silently went upstairs. My mother said nothing to me.

"She opened the book while holding my hand. There were all these things written in Latin in what looked to be dried blood. We just silently sat there together and flipped from page to page until we came across a passage that began glowing. It was like the book and I were connected somehow and it knew what I was searching for. My mother placed my hand over the glowing passage and smiled. I felt utterly intoxicated as my mind opened. I repeated the passage three times. Each time I said it, I floated a bit higher into the air. I can control that now, but the first time you connect with the spirits, it's a total trip, let me tell you. Anyway, I finished reciting the incantation and floated back down on the sofa. My mother smiled at me and kissed me on the forehead and told me to go to bed. My worries were now over. I wasn't sure what had just happened, but man, did I sleep like a log that night.

"I went to school the next day, and all the kids were chattering about the boy who I had dated the previous night. I *knew* that I had caused what they were saying happened to him. I *knew* that I had caused his dick to somehow get caught in the blender that he was using to make some energy drink or something. And I *knew*, that because of *me*, that boy would never, *ever* try to force himself on another woman again. My mom explained what had happened and explained how the women in our family were more evolved than most other women. She trained me and mentored me. Hell, she still does. And from that moment on, I've never taken shit from anybody. Ever. It's so funny, there are all these white redneck assholes who tell me to go back where I'm from. It's gotten worse the last ten years or so as racist bigots feel more and more empowered. Anyway, I have a vengeful spirit who kinda follows me around, so when one of these assholes says that to me, all I have to say is, 'I'm from *here*. I was *born* here. Why don't you go back to where *you're* from?' This asshole gets all pissed off, puffs out his chest, then starts looking around all confused as his body starts sprouting hair, and his forehead slopes, and his back arches until his knuckles are literally dragging on the ground. They have no idea what to do with these guys, so they've been sent to some research facility in Montana. There have been about, um, let me see here..."

Carmen's sentence was interrupted by a thrilled Angelica. "Twenty-three! There have been twenty-three unexplained cases of men around here suddenly devolving. Oh my God! That was *you*? I've been following those cases trying to figure it out. I kinda *thought* that maybe it was a local medium, but we used to have that moratorium on fraternizing together, so I was afraid to look too hard. Holy shit, girl! You're my hero! Cheers!"

The pair giggled together while a leering, pudgy white man stared at their bikini-clad bodies. The women noticed him and Angelica began lifting her middle finger while muttering a spell. There was a sudden gust of wind on the far side of the pool, and the man's swim trunks blew down his legs and fluttered into the chlorinated water. The blushing man shrieked and covered himself with a small towel. The women laughed and pointed as they listened to the patter of his pasty feet head toward his room.

"Ah, shit, that was fun," a chuckling Carmen stated. "Talk about heroics. That was cool as shit, Angelica. So, how about you? When were you first awakened to your evolution? When did you first discover that you were a witch?"

"Well," Angelica replied through her continued laughter. "Nothing quite as exciting as *that*, I'm afraid. I was ten years old. My dad was in the army and had been killed in Afghanistan. My mom was devastated, and she did everything that she could to provide for us. She had to hold down two or three jobs to make ends meet, y'know? And she was a witch, but one who did not like to use her powers. She felt that it was unnatural, so she buried them. Anyway, she was almost always working, and me and my two older brothers were responsible for the housekeeping and making dinner and everything. We would come home from school and have this whole list of chores to do.

"Now, I'm not exactly proud of this, but I was kind of a bratty little bitch when I was a kid. Not unlike *my* eleven-year-old. I love her, but my lord is that girl trying. Hopefully she'll be more mature than I was when she is awakened. Anyway, I was ten and I came home to this long list of stuff that we had to do. My brothers were sitting on the couch watching TV and eating the last of the chips and dip, which really pissed me off. I told them to get started with helping me with the chores and they just laughed, threw chips at me, and told me that *that* was women's work and to let them know when I had supper ready.

"So now, I'm *really* pissed and all of a sudden, my mind kind of opened up and these words started flashing in my brain. I focused and started repeating the words and suddenly, the broom came flying in from the kitchen, went between my legs and lifted me up. I started laughing and dive-bombed my brothers until they got their asses off the couch. When my mom came home from job number two, she found me sitting on the couch watching TV while my brothers were being whisked around the house with the broom, mop, and dust rags. I had conjured the wind to lift them up and carry them around until they had finished the chores. My mom comes in and said, "Oh, shit." But she couldn't help but smile. She knew what I had done and why I had done it, and it made her smile. My heart melted at that moment because I hadn't seen my mother smile for so long. Well, after that, let's just say my brothers didn't screw with me anymore. Or any *other* female for that matter. They turned out to be nice guys. And my mom explained that she had chosen to abstain from using her powers, but it was my choice if I wanted to use them or not. I, of course, *totally* wanted to use them, so she hooked me up with a nearby witch to mentor me and here we are."

"Very, very cool," Carmen stated before sucking the final remnants of her margarita down. "And speaking of origin stories, how about we go create one? It's dark. One of my spirit guides is telling me that she's going to bed. Time to have some fun. Well, for us. And her. Her dipshit husband? Well, maybe not so much."

The women went back to their room and poured themselves into their pajamas. They sat next to one another on one of the beds. Carmen held Angelica's trembling hand as she opened her family's ancient book. "I don't know why, but I'm kinda nervous," Angelica stated. "Yeah, me too," Carmen agreed. "Just focus on my energy. I'm going to summon a spirit who will guide the both of us to our target. Then, you can cast your spell upon her true nature and open her mind to her abilities. And to her compassion. This shouldn't take long. She isn't far away. And I think it's pretty cool that a Black woman and Hispanic woman are going to convert a lily-white, blonde woman who has been brainwashed into this deplorable insanity. Up to this point in her life, she has been a bigot. She has been indoctrinated into believing that women are less than and to hate anyone who doesn't believe exactly what the men in her life have told her to believe. There are so many of these unfortunate souls in these rural areas. She will be our first triumph. Our first addition to Queen Zenobia's Brigade of Persistence. But certainly not our last. Now focus with me. We'll be there soon."

The room turned to a deep red as Carmen stared at the glowing incantation that had been placed in every medium's book throughout the world. She smiled as the words began rolling off her tongue. "Unitas nostra formata est. Missio nostra adest. Duc nos ad sororem nostram. Permitte nos excitare eam ut ab glorioso motu nostro amplectatur (Our unity has been forged. Our mission is at hand. Guide us to our sister. Allow us to awaken her so that she may be embraced by our glorious movement).

Angelica's eyes rolled into the back of her head, and she gasped as her soul was being carried by that of Carmen and an ethereal female spiritual form. Her eyes adjusted to the dim lighting, and she focused on the scene that she had been transported to. Laying beneath her was a slumbering young blonde woman. She could hear a drunken man shouting and breaking glass from the other room. Angelica smiled at the young woman and moved close to her ear.

"Hello, my young friend," her soul whispered to the sleeping female. "It is now your time. It is now your time to evolve into your natural being and embrace the wonders of your womanhood. It is now your time to break from your shackles of patriarchal oppression. Just listen to my voice. I shall guide you. Just listen to my voice and open your mind to the wonders that I shall now show you."

An explosion of colors bombarded the young woman's sleeping mind. Her brain began conjuring images of words that began organizing themselves into phrases. The words changed into brilliant, blooming flowers, then dark, billowing clouds. Her eyes darted under her shut eyelids as life-like images of erupting volcanoes, massive tornadoes, powerful hurricanes, and crushing tidal waves washed over her. All the forces of nature with their associated spells penetrated her peaceful psyche. Her mind ripped open, and the words attached themselves to her soul. She awoke with a start and looked around the room.

"My God, what have I done?" She said softly to herself while looking at the cracked plaster walls which were covered by hate-filled propaganda, racist flags, and banners celebrating undeserving idolatry. She began weeping as her soul was flooded by guilt. "What have I done? What have I become? My God, the hatred of others for no reason. The cruelty that I have rejoiced in. The laughter as I watched children crying as they were ripped from the arms of their parents. The screaming at strangers because they loved differently from me. The enjoyment of watching my husband beat on others for no reason. The excitement I felt as I watched the blood flying from the mouths of innocents. The rejoicing at the arrival of what we thought was Christ's chosen one. And now, I see. I don't know how, but I see the inhumanity that this man and this movement inflicts upon the innocent. I now see that this is not good, but pure evil. I now see that this is not Christ-like. Oh, dear Lord, please forgive me. How could I have been so stupid? So blind? So damned ignorant? How could I have ever rejoiced in the coming of the Anti-Christ?"

"But no longer," she said with determination as she dangled her feet over the bed for a moment before planting her sweat-soaked body onto the floor. "My mind has been awakened. I can now feel my power. My connection to nature. My connection to humanity. And I now see how it was that I harbored such abhorrent beliefs. Men. *Evil* men. My father. My Uncles. Every boyfriend I ever had. And now, my disgusting husband. *They* are the cause of my fall from grace. *They* are the ones who have indoctrinated me into their perverse, hate-filled beliefs. *They* are the ones who have kept me from my true nature. Kindness. Understanding. Empathy. Civility. *They* are the ones who stripped it *all* away from me. Day by day. Week by week. Month by month. Year by year. Until I was nothing more than their spineless, pathetic, subservient parrot. Well, my darling husband, that shit ends tonight."

"What the hell are you doin' up bitch?" the drunken husband yelled out as his sweaty wife emerged from the bedroom. "You gotta git up early tomorrow! What? You gonna lose this job? How we gonna put food on the table if ya lose yer job? How am I gonna play my horses at the track, huh? Think of that, you stupid bitch? Now git yer ass back ta bed. But before ya do, clean this shithole up. I'm tired'a livin' in a goddamned dumpster."

The young woman could feel her anger rising with every word that slurred out of her husband's serpentine lips. Her body temperature began to increase, and she began glowing red as he spoke his last words upon this Earth. "Can'tcha hear me, bitch? I said, get this shithole cleaned up and…wha…wha…what the fu…"

The man began screaming and flailing his arms as his entire body burst into flames. The woman silently stood while wearing a sly smile as she watched her enflamed husband fly from wall to wall. The newspapers that covered their windows began to blaze. As did the banners depicting his Anti-Christian golden calf. And posters. And pamphlets. And hats. And shirts. And shoes. The television which was spewing his source of inhumane propaganda and conspiracy theories began to melt. The plastic oozed over his charred, bare feet just before the entire dilapidated trailer exploded in a magnificent display of emancipation.

An unscathed blonde woman emerged from the raging inferno.

She got into her run-down car and started the engine. The beaten machine sputtered for a moment before roaring to life. The woman took one last look at her past life of repression, smiled, and flipped it the bird. She placed the car into 'Drive' and began her journey to her new life in the Brigade of Persistence.

"It's a witch!" Angelica and Carmen proudly shouted out. "And now," Carmen said. "Our spirit will guide her to one of our sanctuaries where she will meet others like her, get partnered up with a new medium, and begin taking Morgan and Naomi's classes. Then, she and her partner will evolve *more* women. And so on. And so on. Until every woman in the world has been evolved! This calls for a celebration. Let's break out the whiskey and cigars!" "You got it!" Angelica yelled out. "Ah shit. I forgot my lighter. Ah well. Let me just warm up a bit and I'll light that for you. Huh. I wonder how the *other* partners around the world are getting along. Any news?"

"Um, let me check," Carmen answered as she pulled out her phone. "Just a second. Let me log into our secure network. We wouldn't want to do something stupid and broadcast our battle plans on some hackable app now, would we? Um, hey. Here's something. Looks like Papa Doc has started raising the dead for his army of zombies, and is loading them on a train to Galesburg, so that's cool. Some gossip about Lori and Connor. And *more* gossip about Sophia and Vince. Oh, cool. We're invited to dinner with Agatha, Sruja, and Minnie next week. Oh, but it's a dinner theater that Agatha picked out. I suggest we maybe tell them we have other plans. Her shit is so boring. Let's see here. A lot of 'good games' from Maddy. Well at least she can't virtually slap anybody on the ass. Here's an interesting truffle mac and cheese recipe that the queen has posted. Maybe I should make that for my, um, white friends who are coming to my daughter's Quinceañera. A lot of them don't like spicy food. Oh! Here's one! From Saudi Arabia. Well, do we have a new witch or medium? And the survey says...."

CHAPTER 14

IT'S A SMALL WORLD AFTER ALL

The fourteen-year-old Saudi Arabian girl suddenly stopped her sobbing. Her eyes were wide open as her final tears rolled down her unblemished olive cheeks. Her mind was whirling with new insights and perspectives on the world. A world that had seemed like an unforgiving cage of disempowerment, humiliation, and servitude that was guarded by her own father. A cage that would soon inflict the ultimate grotesque mutilation of her womanhood. She looked around her room as she heard her father's approaching footsteps. There was a second pair of footsteps that she assumed belonged to the physician who was to perform this most brutal indignation upon her.

Then, something unexpected happened. The girl smiled. She smiled from ear to ear for perhaps the first time in her life. As her eyes continued to scan her bleak room, she no longer saw bars. She saw the promise of freedom. And empowerment. And self-fulfillment. And dignity. She looked down at her hands and saw the glorious key that would release her from her brutal confinement. She did not know where this ancient book had come from. She heard whispering in her psyche as she slumbered. When she had awoke with a start, her mind and soul had been opened to a world of new possibilities. And resting in her hands was this book. She somehow knew that the words written in this book represented her freedom. And power. She knew that there were spirits watching over her. All she needed to do was call for them. And she was prepared to do just that. As she flipped through the pages of the book searching for the perfect incantation to reveal itself, she wondered why this book did not have a cover. It was simply ancient paper bound tightly together with twine. The answer to that mystery would also soon be revealed.

Her father and the physician threw open the door. The father tried to explain to her the reasons for this upcoming violent desecration of her tender body. He was confused by his daughter's stoic silence. He was more confused by the smile upon her innocent face. And his confusion turned to anger as he heard her daughter say these blasphemous words, "Minae sunt mihi. Mulieri meae. Ut vitae ipsum mi. Fac ut dolorem et cruciatum sentiant in me et omnes similes mihi infligantes. vindictam meam portabo mecum in aeternum (They are a threat me. To my womanhood. To my very existence. Make them feel the pain and torment that they would inflict upon me and all like me. I shall carry my vengeance with me forever)."

Lightning crashed inside the room and the father and physician were encased by dark, billowing clouds. The door slammed and would not open for the hysterical men. The father looked up and found his laughing daughter floating above him. "A...a witch!" He screamed out. "You are a heretic! A witch! And you must be destroyed!" His daughter continued to laugh at the trembling men and replied, "No, father. I am not a heretic. Nor am I witch. I am a medium. And I am a woman. And you, my dearest father, are about to no longer be a man."

The father screamed as an invisible force came through the black clouds, tore his pants off, and sliced his scrotum open. The physician frantically tried to open the door while his own scalpel was used to repeatedly slash his throat. The father continued his high-pitched wails as he watched the physician bleed out on the floor. His cries increased as the menacing scalpel floated near his tearful face. His flesh was suddenly sliced from the skull in one perfect sheet. There was the cackling of an invisible entity as the bloody mask floated around the room, then flew to the book and attached itself around the treasured pages. The girl floated down through the dissipating clouds and picked up the book that was now covered by her father's bloody, anguished face. "Huh," she said through her chuckles. "Well, this is *one* book that you can *definitely* judge by its cover, heh, heh, heh. And now, time to pack and find my sisters. I can feel them calling for me. Oh, and Daddy. You don't mind if I borrow the car, do you?" The lifeless, bloody skull responded with dead silence. "Yeah? I *can* take the car? Thanks Daddy. You're the best. Oh, and I *really* hope you get to watch what I do in the *back seat* of your car one day. When I'm ready for that. And do you know what, Daddy? I'm going to enjoy it. Rot in Jahannam, Daddy!"

The twenty-year old woman from the Democratic Republic of the Congo looked around at her two dozen shackled sisters and wept. Tears rolled down her ebony face as she contemplated the horrific future that was in store for them. There would be no higher education. No wedding vows. No children to raise. Just beatings. And back-breaking work. And rapes. There would no longer be joy or laughter or pride for any of these women. Those celebrated human expressions would be replaced by continuous inhumane degradation, humility, and pain. Until finally, the women would no longer be of use to their owners and would mercifully be put to their death.

Her mind flashed to the night when she was abducted off the city streets. She had been grabbed by four men, knocked over the head, and thrown into a rickety van. She was bound and her gag prevented her from screaming out as each man brutally forced themselves into her. The excruciating physical pain that she was experiencing was numbed by waves of horrific torment in her psyche. She was exhausted. Her mind, body, and soul had no strength remaining. She resigned herself to her tortured plight, laid her filthy head down on the dirt floor, and drifted into a tenuous slumber.

She was awoken by a man lifting her to her feet. He laughed as he brutally slapped her across her face. All the other women were being rousted in the same manner. Two dozen evil, sadistic worms were once again beating two dozen helpless women. Tears rolled down her face once again as she absorbed yet another blow to her ribs. She was ordered to get on her knees and open her mouth. She gladly complied as tears of torture were transformed into tears of determination, joy, and dignity. She opened her mouth as ordered and said something in a foreign language while staring up at her marauder with piercing black eyes. He began to unzip his pants. It was the last act that he would perform on this Earth.

All of the women but one screamed in confusion as they were encapsulated within impenetrable spheres of condensed air. Their shrieks of panic became exclamations of wonder as they watched from within their protective cocoons the cruel men being lifted by multiple violent vortices and thrown about the wooden shack. Man after man was mercilessly crashed against the wooden walls. Blood and teeth swirled within the howling winds and the sound of cracking bones were heard as the men's bodies were repeatedly bashed against the walls, floor, and each other. The vortices dissipated as quickly as they had arrived, and two dozen broken and twisted male bodies could be seen through the bloody mist lying still on the dirt floor. Cheers of joy erupted as the women began kicking at the lifeless, contorted frames of their former captors.

The young woman smiled at her sisters, waved her hands, and released them from their chains. Heavy clinking sounds echoed off the battered and blood-stained walls as each woman's shackles snapped open. The woman opened the door of their hellish shack with a huge gust of wind. She saw a large transport truck and ushered the women into it. She promised to take the women someplace safe. Someplace where they would be welcomed and embraced. Someplace where their true natural power would be achieved. She promised to take them someplace where they would never feel pain or humiliation or indignity again. She was asked if she was riding along in the transport truck. She smiled, shook her head, and pointed to a nearby broom.

———

The elderly Texan woman sighed deeply as she looked upon the piles of medical bills on her dining room table. "Why is it that I worked so hard for my entire life? What did I get out of it?" She wondered aloud as she picked up her basket of prescription medications and contemplated which ones she could possibly live without. Waves of dull pain swept over her recently replaced hip as she continued her ruminations. "Years and years of hard work. Factories by day. Waitressing or bartending by night. Always on time and never missed a day. Even when I, or one of my children, were ill. For decades. I dutifully paid my taxes. I watched as my money went to the government. Money that I could have used to put food in my children's mouths. Social Security, my ass. It was supposed to be my savings for when my weary body could no longer stand for hours. I was promised financial comfort and health care in my golden years. And what did all of those years of toiling get me?

"A child so disillusioned by the working class being exploited by the wealthy that he joined a gang of drug runners. I barely had enough to pay for his modest funeral, let alone a headstone. A daughter who was so desperate to escape this dystopian hellhole of a town that she married a horrible little man. Yes, she has a bit of financial security. But at what price? Her freedom? Her soul? It breaks me apart thinking that my children have been forsaken by this so-called 'Land of Opportunity.' That my children have been sacrificed at the altar of corporate greed. And that I will soon be their next victim. Even with Medicare, my medical bills are insurmountable. My hip surgery exhausted my savings. I have only my pittance of Social Security to live on. And now, if that madman and his corporate henchmen get elected, I fear they will take that from me as well.

"I know what they are doing. They want subservience. They wish to exploit the able-bodied at their yokes of industry until they are no longer productive. Until they are no longer a benefit to their bottom line. And what is to become of those that they do not find to be of benefit to them? The elderly or the disabled? Why, they simply want us to die. They want to kill us off. They may not succeed in building murder camps in this country as they had in Nazi Germany, but they sure as hell will try. And if they fail in that, then they will kill us off in other ways. They think they are clever, but they are not. I've lived long enough to understand their diabolical plan. They will poison us. In our air and water and food. They will create another pandemic to kill off the weak. Or they will simply starve us to death by cutting off our only financial means of support. We are nothing but cogs in the machine to them. And we broken cogs must be disposed of. They are inhumane and cruel. They disgust me. So many people do not see who they truly are. So many people are blind to the truly evil people in this world.

"Just like this banker. Ah yes, my balloon payment is due. I have paid my mortgage on this home for twenty-five years and now I must come up with another twenty-thousand-dollars. Or I get kicked out. He smiled at me the last time we met. He had a big ol' smile on his pudgy, evil face as he assured me that as long as I kept up with my mortgage payments, everything would be fine. Why, they would *never* kick a little old lady to the curb. Hogwash. I signed the extension on my loan so that I could have cheaper monthly payments. This balloon payment in the fine, legalese print was never explained to me. No, this letter was quite the surprise.

"I literally begged them to allow me to go back to my previous terms. I would somehow pay the increased mortgage. But there was no way I could come up with this lump sum. He just smiled at me and said that there was nothing that he could do. Suggested maybe moving in with my daughter. Yes, that would be a nice ending to my life. Watching my daughter and grandchildren being beaten by that brute that she married. I'll be a bag lady before I let that happen. Or perhaps these pills might be my exit strategy. Just pop a handful and drift off to sleep. It isn't that he *can't* help me. He doesn't *want* to. He wants my land so that infernal on-line supermarket can build yet another one of their distribution centers. Yes, this town is perfect for them. Cheap land and plenty of ignorant cogs to do their bidding. I'm too old and too tired for this. I simply can't fight them anymore. Yes, perhaps I will just take a nap. I do believe it is time for my medications. All of them."

She awoke to the sensation of violent retching. Vomit covered her wrinkled lips and the front of her faded floral nightgown. She began chuckling. "Wow, I can't even do *that* right. I truly am a worthless old bitch, aren't I? But it seems as though I am stuck here because I can't even kill myself. And what are these words pounding in my brain? The book. The book. Get the book. What book? What are you talking abo…"

She cut off her sentence as she looked over at a pile of books that was stabilizing her decrepit end table. She got up from the dining room table, steadied herself on her cane, limped over to the end table, and tipped it over. Cheap porcelain figurines and a green glass candy dish shattered on the stained hard-wood floor. Her rocking chair creaked as she plopped down upon it. She slowly bent over and lifted a glowing, flesh bound book from the top of the pile. Her mesmerized eyes were fixated on the bloody passages that she found within as a tender woman's voice whispered to her through her drugged haze. She turned to another page and an inscription began glowing. The dark green illumination reflected off of her bifocals as she read the passage to herself. She then smiled as the whispers succeeded in penetrating her soul and her understanding of her true nature and power encompassed her consciousness. She had evolved. She now understood the meaning behind the whispers. She understood the meaning behind this book. And she understood the awesome power that she now wielded.

She let out an evil little chuckle as she read the glowing incantation aloud. "Qui in pauperes insidiantur, suam interitum obviam se habebunt. Avarici iis quae optaverunt poenam ferent (Those who prey upon the less fortunate shall meet their demise. The greedy shall regret that which they wished for). "Well, now, that was fun," she said to herself as she carefully placed the book next to her pile of bills. "I feel like a bit of tea."

Her frail body had just re-entered her home the following day. "Okay, you can do this," she said to herself while gasping for air and clutching her pounding heart. "Just take this one last box to the car and we can get on the road. One more little workout for my new hip. Now, who could that be?" she asked as her phone began ringing. "Yes, hello. Oh, hello, how are you dear? No, I haven't heard the news about the bank president. You don't say. He was on his way home after purchasing one of those hideous swasticars when it just blew up? Right in the middle of the highway? Well, perhaps they should have performed a few more safety inspections on those ticking time bombs on wheels before they let them on the road. Oh well, there will be a new bank president who will also want to steal my house from me. Well, you know what? They can have it. I'm going on a little trip. I've found a new group of friends. I'm on my way to Dallas right now. To pick up my daughter and grandchildren."

———

"It's haaaaaapeniiiing laaaaadiiiiiees!" an exuberant Queen Zenobia sang down the staircase of the Ladies Cabot. She was followed down the stairs by the giddy spiritual trifecta of Agatha, Sruja, and Minnie Marples. "We've been looking through our portal and shit is really starting to happen! All around the world, our medium and witch partners are evolving our first batch of newbies. They are giving birth to new mediums and witches in every country! Morgan and Naomi, are you ladies ready for your first class of pupils?"

"We sure are!" Naomi exclaimed. "We have everything ready to go. All the power points are put together and we've established a way for us to connect with their souls so that we can hold our classes to everybody all at once. But do you think we should print up some binders? I know that *I* like to have a binder where all my class materials are organized and stuff. But what color should they be? Red is kinda evil, and even though we're not evil, we're going to do evil things to evil men. Or, how about green? That would match the color of the glowing incantations. But do you think the witches will feel left out? And we're going to need lots and lots of paper. We'll need billions of binders. Oh, who can we get to put the binders together? Let's see here. Victoria, do you think you could help us put billions of binders together and…"

Her mouth was then covered by an extended leaf from a house-plant. "Nope, not gonna do it," Victoria tersely answered. "And we don't need binders. They'll have access to the power point in their souls. Plus, save a tree why don'tcha!"

"Yeah, we don't really need binders, Naomi," Morgan agreed. "All we need are our kick-ass abilities, our natural charisma, and some cool shades. We're going to be the coolest teachers on the planet. But tough. We're not going to put up with any gum chewing or passing notes while we're lecturing. And no letting somebody slide a little just because we like them. No, we're going to be cool but tough. And fair."

"Yeah, okay, whatever," Zenobia stated. "Just get 'em trained up. Like I said, this shit's really starting to cook. Oh! And speaking of cooking, I tried that truffle mac and cheese recipe. It's in the oven. Anybody want some?"

"Um, none for me thanks," Lori replied. "Why not?" Morgan inquired. "I've never seen you turn down *any* type of mac and cheese, Mom! What gives?"

"Um, well," Lori awkwardly tried to answer. "You see, I'm kinda avoiding carbs at the moment because, um…" Her voice trailed off as she looked up at a beaming Connor. "Well, you see, we weren't planning on announcing this just yet because of everything that's going on but, um, well, I kinda need to fit into a wedding dress that I've ordered because Connor and I are engaged."

"Engaged?" the entire group yelled out as they began embracing Lori and shaking Connor's hand. "*Chika-Chika-Wow-Wow,*" Maddy said as she sauntered through the crowded scene on her way to the refrigerator.

"Chika-Chika-what?" Connor asked. "It's kind of her new thing," Morgan answered. "Just ignore her. Gramma, isn't this awesome? Connor's going to be *your* son-in-law, and *my* stepfather. And Naomi's going to be my stepcousin or something! Gee, it sure would be nice to have a *grandfather* to round out the ol' family unit. Hint, hint. Catch my drift, Gramma? A *grandfather*? Hint, hint?"

Sophia sat silently while twiddling her thumbs and staring up at the ceiling. A blushing Vince cautiously approached his girlfriend and got down on one knee in front of her. "Oh, Vince. Get up. You're being foolish," Sophia scolded while trying to hide her smile behind her hand. "Aw, come on Sophia," Vince awkwardly said while fishing in his pocket. "We've been friends for forever. We've been lovers for quite a while now. I'm really kinda already a part of your family. I just adore Lori and Morgan. And your extended family of witches and spirits and shit are, um, really nice too."

"Aaaaaand?" a curious Maddy asked as she poked her head from out of the refrigerator. "And what?" Vince shot back. "And aren't you forgetting about someone that is in this family and that you care about?" Maddy replied in a sing-song voice. "Nope," Vince bluntly answered. "As I was saying Sophia, we're a good fit. I know it, and you know it. You have nothing to hide from me. I know everything about you. And then some. Listen. I've been carrying this ring around with me for weeks just waiting for the right time. And, dammit woman, this is it! Come on Sophia. Won'tcha stop this little cat and mouse game and just marry me?"

There was dead silence in the room as the observers leaned forward in anticipation of Sophia's response. Sophia blushed, said something quietly, and turned her face from the on-lookers. "What did you say Gramma?" Morgan asked. "We couldn't hear you." Sophia let out a deep sigh and once again whispered a response. "Mom! Could you please speak up?" Lori ordered. "I've never known you to be so quiet."

"Oh fine!" Sophia roared. "Yes! I said yes! Are you all happy now?

I already told you that we were thinking about this silliness anyway, so why are you all so surprised? So, yes. I say yes to this foolishness that I am far too old to be a part of. But since we're going through with this, Lori, I believe that we should go dress shopping together. And yes, I'm wearing white! Or maybe a cool tie-dye. Oh, and we need to find a florist, and a photographer. Oh! And a DJ or maybe a really great seventies cover band and..." She was cut off by her amused daughter.

"Mom, I have an idea," Lori stated while clasping Connor's sweaty hand. "I would love to do all that with you. In fact, I would love it if we got married together and had a double ceremony. Two generations of the Ladies Cabot finding happiness with great guys. Right after we, um, you know, kill off a bunch of bad guys. What do you say, Mom?" Sophia burst out in uncharacteristic tears and tightly embraced her daughter while saying through her sobs of happiness, "It would be my honor to share this day with you. To share our good fortune together will be a dream come true. This will be one of the happiest days of our lives."

"Oh, my dear, this is the greatest news!" Larry the Leopard shouted out. "There will be so many guests, I hope there will be enough pews!"

"Shut up, Larry!" the crowd yelled out before Maddy made her way back through the room carrying chips and dip and ice cream and cheese. *Chika-Chika-Wow-Wow*, she said as she sauntered up the staircase.

"Okay, seriously, what in the hell *is* that?" Vince asked. "Like I said," Morgan explained. "It's just her new thing. She does that anytime anybody talks about sex or about anything related to sex. She sees somebody kissing? Chika-Chika-Wow-Wow. Holding hands? Sharing dessert? A couple wearing matching outfits? Yep. Chika-Chika-Wow-Wow. It's already wearing pretty thin. And that's why she does it. She enjoys annoying people. She's really not very mature sometimes."

"No shit, huh? Well at least she's not slapping everybody on the ass anymore," Vince stated. At that moment, Maddy could be heard from upstairs yelling out, "Oh! I almost forgot!" She came bounding down the stairs and shouted, "Good game, Connor!" SLAP! "Good game, Vince!" SLAP! "Congrats on your upcoming nuptials. I bet it'll be a helluva honeymoon for both of ya. *Chika-Chika-Wow-Wow*. Oh, and I wouldn't mind trying some of that mac and cheese, there Queen Z. Then Erick and I gotta get our duffle bags packed. There are some hungry zombies heading for Galesburg and we need to get them some snacks. Hey, Connor. What do you know about the manager of the jewelry place at the mall? I was there the other day, and I felt he was a bit rude to me. You think he might make a good zombie snack, *hmmmmmm?*"

CHAPTER 15

MALL RATS

The Sandburg Mall in Galesburg, Illinois was bustling with more activity than it had seen in nearly a decade. Hordes of shuffling feet were making their way from store to store over the cracked, checkered tiling looking for the most perfect treat. They let out high-pitched wails of disappointment from their decaying mouths as their search of the vacant, dilapidated shops proved to be fruitless time and again. Their frustration was palpable and could be felt by a group of on-lookers from behind the locked security gate of a former jewelry store.

"Well, this is just sad," the black leather-clad Papa Doc stated to Victoria, Lori, and Sophia. "I feel so guilty. I am the one who resurrected these poor corpses from their eternal slumber, put them in box cars, and placed them into this abandoned mall. Just look at them. How pathetic. Wandering from store to store looking for live human flesh. And brains. Zombies certainly do love eating brains. They are trapped and starving. Thank you, Victoria, Sophia, and Lori, for assisting me in this. I may be a very powerful voodoo priest, but controlling over one thousand of these creatures is a bit much, even for me. A hundred? Sure, sure. I can control that number. But I needed your combined powers to keep this many in check. A spirit summoned by Sophia who is whispering to them combined by a brisk wind summoned by Victoria to keep them moving along. But they have been here now for days, and I wonder how long it will be before they take notice of us." He then lifted his bent frame and gulped hard as he saw hundreds of dead eyes staring at him from behind the security gate. "Well, I guess that answers my question. They have finally noticed us, and they are ignoring the spirit's suggestions and the wind. They have live humans right in front of them and they are hungry."

"And pissed off," Sophia contributed. "If we don't find another distraction for them it won't take them long to break down this security gate. I may be old, but I'm not ready to die yet. Plus, there's an old bridal shop at the other end of the mall that I want to check out. Maybe they left some stock in there."

"Oh, that would be perfect!" an excited Lori exclaimed. "We haven't had a chance to do hardly any planning for our weddings, Mom. We've all been so busy the past couple of months. Our ranks are swelling so rapidly that we hardly have time to run the diner, let alone do any wedding planning. All over the world, more and more women are becoming evolved. And more and more abusive men are waking up to a former lover who is now a powerful witch or medium. And these women are pissed and not shy about using their power. From every corner of the Earth there are strange accounts of men spontaneously bursting into flames, or having their limbs ripped off of them by unseen forces or being suffocated after their windpipes have been crushed. The women take care of their former abusers, then follow their instructions and go to their assigned headquarters.

"Queen Zenobia and her spirits have done such a wonderful job refurbishing abandoned buildings in every country in the world to serve as these women's new homes and training complexes. The new witch or medium gets paired up with her new buddy, gets settled into their new apartment, and take Morgan and Naomi's three-week training course. Then, they are ready to be unleashed upon the world and begin to evolve yet more women. This is spreading like a highly infectious plague. Yes, our Brigade of Persistence is growing and spreading and yes, we are a plague. At least to all of the abusive men of the world. But they are still too blind to see it. They don't yet know what is happening. All they know is that seemingly random men are dying in unexplained ways and women are disappearing. They haven't connected the dots yet. But they will. Which is why we need our little zombie distraction. We need to keep them occupied with the living dead to buy us time to complete our Brigade. It is all working as Queen Zenobia has planned. Although I don't remember anything in the plans about *our* becoming a zombie buffet."

"We aren't going to die, and we aren't going to get eaten alive," a frustrated Victoria stated as she rolled her eyes. "Lori, just use your book and call up Minnie Marples. I'm sure she'll be able to come up with a fresh distraction for us until we can get them fed."

"Alright, good idea," Lori agreed as she took her family's ancient book of incantations from her bag. "I think we'll just go with a classic. No need to be fancy about this," she said as she opened the glowing pages and looked for the proper incantation.

"You might want to hurry this shit up," Sophia said as the zombies began violently shaking the metal security gate. The force of hundreds of zombies began bending the gate while outstretched, decomposing arms reached for their prey. "Um, just a second," Lori replied as she furiously scanned the incantations. "Don't rush me. No, we don't want to turn them into snakes, although that would be interesting. No, not this one either. No need for their limbs to fall off. They're already doing that anyway." The thunderous sound of shaking metal echoed around the zombie mall, attracting the attention of more and more of the starving undead. The metal gate creaked as it strained against the weight of the zombie army. "Here it is!" Lori exclaimed as her relieved face was illuminated by a glowing green incantation. "Oh shit, I hope this works. Here we go. O magne protector. Mitte eos qui mihi nocere volunt longe a me (Oh great protector. Send those that wish me harm away from me).

A giggling, high-pitched voice came over the mall's PA system.

"You got it toots!" Minnie Marples stated. "Check this shit out!" A swarm of smiling, bright pink brain emojis suddenly appeared and flew around the mall within Victoria's conjured winds. The gullible zombies began following and reaching for the bite-sized sustenance. They cried out in frustration as they attempted to grasp what appeared to be floating treats, only to be denied that which they craved.

"Well, shit," Papa Doc stated. "This seems even more cruel. At least they aren't trying to break in here. Just look at this gate. They nearly bent it in two. A few more seconds and I'm afraid we would have been a main course. We need to be behind another store's security gate. This one won't hold out much longer and those imitation brains aren't going to hold their interest for very long either. Where in the hell are their meals on wheels, anyway?"

At that moment, a large overhead door opened from the loading dock revealing the back end of a semi-trailer. The door of the trailer rolled open, and a woman's voice yelled out "Wazzup bitches!" The smiling pair of Maddy and Erick stood triumphantly inside the trailer with their fists planted on their hips. "Sorry we're late, but *somebody who shall remain nameless* had to keep stopping to take a piss!"

"Hey!" Erick roared back. "I can't help it! I have prostate issues!" "Yeah, yeah, yeah," Maddy dismissively replied. "Prostate issues. Did I, or did I *not*, tell you to watch your fluid intake? Why, yes. I believe that I did. And did you listen to me? Gee, the answer to *that* little question would be no!"

"Oh, yeah?" Erick countered. "Well did I, or did I *not*, tell *you* that we didn't have to shop for souvenirs at every damned truck stop we passed? Seriously, Maddy, how many shot glasses, post cards, ashtrays, and magnets do we need? Where are you going to put all that shit?"

"Well, excuse *me*, mister tightwad!" Maddy yelled. "Excuse *me* for wanting a few trinkets to memorialize our adventures together! I am putting together a collection of memories and I'm going to get a cool cabinet to put them in! Right in Sophia's living room! Which reminds me, Sophia, you're going to have to move your bookshelf. I need to put my cool cabinet there. Anyhoo, that isn't the point! The point is that while you were relieving your aging bladder for the bajillionth time, I was collecting memories. Plus, how many bonus 'Chads' did we find at those truckstops? Of the sixty-three dumbasses we have in the back of this truck, I'll bet twenty of them came from truckstops! Like this asshole!"

Maddy grabbed a naked, bound and gagged man by his thinning hair and dragged him over to her husband. "Remember *this* dickwad? Remember how he couldn't keep his eyes off of my tits? Remember how when I went back to his semi with him, he tried to club me over the head? Remember how I used my really cool judo moves on him, threw him to the ground, and knocked him out? Remember how we found a bunch of kidnapped women in the back of his semi? Poor women who we saved from a life of human trafficking? Remember that?"

"Oh, I remember all right!" Erick screamed back while the trembling, naked man looked on through tearful eyes. "I remember that we had to stop at *that* particular truck stop because I had to take a piss. So, you can thank my so-called aging bladder for that! And I remember following you two back to his truck and when he took out a club, I yelled 'duck'! Which you did, and he fell over. There *were* no really cool judo moves because you don't know judo! You just ducked and he fell over when he took a swing at you! Then I bashed him over the head with a bat! We released the women, stripped him down, tied him up, and threw him in the back of our rig with these other douchebags!"

"Well sure, that's *one* interpretation of events!" Maddy yelled back. "But did you see the cool ashtray that I bought in that giftshop that I didn't drop when I ducked because of my cool judo moves?"

"But why do we need an ashtray?" a defiant Erick responded. "Neither of us smoke!" "Well, maybe I'm gonna start!" Maddy exclaimed. "Why in the hell would you start smoking?" Erick countered. "Because it looks cool!" Maddy retorted. Their senseless bickering was finally silenced by the agitated voice of a bewildered Papa Doc.

"Maddy, Erick, please. We have more pressing matters here. Or can you not see what is surrounding your truck?" The pair looked down and saw hundreds of drooling, snarling zombies anxiously awaiting their meal. "Oh, yeah, the zombies," Erick nonchalantly stated. "Alright zombies, alright. We have some snacks for ya. But you're going to have to share. Here, start with this guy." Erick lifted the man and threw him into the awaiting crowd of the undead. The man screamed out as decomposing hands ripped his chest open and began tearing out his internal organs. His squeals intensified as his skull was cracked open and rotted teeth began chewing on his brain. His bound body finally stopped shaking as his heart was pulled out and rapidly consumed by a zombie.

"Wow," Maddy stated. "They're not much into table manners, are they? Well, better get the rest of them fed. Bring me that dickhead over there. See what happens? See what happens when you evict innocent families from their homes that don't deserve it? Yup, that's right. If you evict innocent people from their homes who don't deserve it, then you get fed to zombies. It's called natural selection or some shit. Byeee!" The man screamed as he was pushed out of the truck and into the pungent jaws of the awaiting crowd.

One by one, the abusive, naked men were thrown out of the back of the truck. "Hey now, no shoving," Erick admonished the zombies. "There's plenty for everybody. Here you go dear, have a nice, thick pedophile. And here *you* are. A nice flabby redneck insurrectionist. Mmmm. I bet that's really good isn't it? Nothing like southern cooking. Yes, yes, share with your friends. And what would *you* like miss? How about a nice, juicy wife beater? Yeah, I knew you'd like him. Hey Maddy! Check this shit out! She went right for his eyes! Just popped them out and down the gullet in one bite!"

"Ooooh, that's so cool," an awestruck Maddy replied. "And check these three out. They're taking turns slamming that asshole's head into the ground. They really want his brains. And crack! There they are!" Maddy jumped down from the truck and made her way over to the three feasting figures. "Good game, zombies!" SLAP! One of the zombies looked up at her with brains drooling out of his mouth and began standing. "Oh shit! Back in the truck for lil' ol' me!" she exclaimed as she hopped back into the trailer and stood next to her exasperated husband.

"Well," Sophia observed. "They truly are enthusiastic about their work. I have to give them that. Wait. I think I recognize that one. Isn't that the guy who works at the hardware store?" "Huh, yeah I think it is," Lori replied. "Shit. That's going to piss Connor off. He explicitly told them *not* to hunt for zombie snacks in Plymouth."

"I can heeeaar you!" Maddy cried out. "And he's not from Plymouth! He may *work* in Plymouth, but he *lives* in Kingston, so you can tell your stick-up-the-ass detective boyfriend of yours to kiss my ass! Who's next? Oh baby. Hand me that one over there. No, not that one. The one with the big thighs that we found in Kentucky. Yeah, that one. Time to crowd surf asshole!"

"Okay, ladies," Papa Doc stated. "I think that while the zombies are preoccupied, we should find another safe haven. Plus, I need to get my stereo equipment in here. This is gonna be a dance party to raise the dead!"

While Papa Doc was setting up his DJ equipment behind the security gate of a former novelty store, Lori and Sophia were glee-fully exploring the other end of the mall. The giddy pair had to yell at each other in order to be heard over the tortured shrieks of men being eaten alive.

"Well, not much to choose from, Mom, but this one has poten-tial!" Lori stated. "Yeah, that's not bad! Maybe with a few alterations and add some of the lace from this little number and it might work!" Sophia loudly replied. "And how about this! I mean, it's utterly hideous, but I kinda like this light blue fabric! Plus, Victoria will be really pissed if I make her wear it! We're family and have buried the hatchet, but there's no harm in getting a harmless jab in on her once in a while! Besides, she agreed to be my maid of honor! She's got youth, better hair, and a better figure! I'll be damned if she's gonna get a better dress too!"

"Agreed!" Lori answered. "Just tell her that the blue will bring out her eyes! How about something like this for Morgan? There's a lot of material here and I think we can convert it into a really nice pants suit! Oh! And look at *this* hideous piece of shit! Why did anyone ever manufacture something so *ugly*? But wait a minute. I think we might be able to use this one. And we won't have to change a thing! You know who would fit perfectly into this monstrosity?"

The pair began giggling as they looked down the long corridor at the red-headed sprite that was enthusiastically flinging yet another plagued man into his grisly demise. "Hey! Sophia! Lori!" Maddy yelled out. "Try to find me something to wear to your weddings! I wanna look good! Oh, gross! Come look at this! I think those two zombies are making out! *Chicka-Chicka-Wow-Wow!*"

"Oh, don't worry dear," Lori yelled back. "I think we've found the *perfect* dress for you!" Sophia squinted her eyes so that she could see the face of the latest shrieking morsel that was about to be thrown into the zombie pit. "Aw shit," she stated remorsefully. "What is it, Mom?" a concerned Lori inquired. "Well, it looks like I'm going to have to find a new auto mechanic. Look at who's about to be dessert. Yeah, there goes his hands. His car repair days are done. I had always heard he was an asshole, but he sure was pretty to look at. Not anymore. There goes his face. Ah well. Well, lookee here at what I've found in *this* box! Anybody need a veil? And a garter? Chicka-Chicka-Wow-Wow. Oh shit. Now *I'm* doing it. She really is a bad influence."

CHAPTER 16

——————

LET'S MEET OUR VILLAINS, SHALL WE?

"Preposterous," Elder Dante sneered from under his pitch-black hood. His frail, seventy-nine-year-old body was draped in a black robe with an ornate gold medallion hanging across his chest indicating his regal stature within the secretive Nationalist Society. He leaned back in his crimson throne and looked upon the grand portraits of his illustrious predecessors that encircled the room.

For centuries, these White, supposedly Christian men had dominated the Earth. And they had done so by wielding ruthless control over those that they found to be beneath them. People of different religious beliefs. People from non-European or non-American cultures. People of darker skin-tones than translucent white. But they asserted most of their control over women. They understood the power that the female of the species was capable of wielding. Women were a threat to them. A threat to their global dominance. And their very existence scared the living hell out of them.

For centuries, this group of men, and other similar groups in other regions of the world, came to realize that women were naturally more evolved than men. That women possessed souls that were capable of expanding their spiritual connections to the universe or to the natural world. Yes, these men were quite aware of women known as 'mediums' who could connect to the spiritual realm and summon the great power from beyond. And they were quite familiar with those women who were 'witches' and could tap into and control the forces of nature. And it was believed by them that should women ever evolve in great numbers, that they would use their awesome power to usurp men from their thrones. This was a correct assumption and not a risk that these men were ever willing to take. They knew how they had treated women, and they trembled at the prospect of the tables being turned upon them.

So, for centuries, many men assumed the dominant role of master to the woman's slave. They believed that the only way to keep women from evolving and ascending to the world's thrones was unbridled superiority over them. The vile men treated them as property. As cattle. As sex slaves. When a young woman was believed to be gifted, her natural aptitude would be berated out of her. Beaten out of her. Raped out of her. Until she was nothing more than a shell of her natural self and was completely subservient to the cruel men in her life. Of course, less gifted women were treated in the same manner. These men did, after all, believe in treating women with equality. Equality in the torture that they would be forced to endure simply because of their gender.

But as the centuries wore on, the ranks of the evil men began to diminish as other men began to evolve in their own right. They weren't evolving into the acquisition of supernatural abilities. Their humanity was evolving to see women, and *all* human beings, as equals to themselves. They did not understand the senseless brutality against others. They did not understand racism and xeno-phobia and antisemitism. They did not understand homophobia or transphobia. And they most certainly could not comprehend how so many men could be so cruel to women. It was beyond their mental capacity. It could not be understood by their souls. So, many of these privileged men joined the various causes for equality for all. They marched for LGBTQ rights. They voted for women. They supported the different cultures that enhanced their communities. And their combined efforts bore fruit.

As yet another decade slipped into history, another set of barriers would be torn down through men and women tirelessly marching and advocating in lockstep. Slavery was ended. Women obtained the right to vote. People could love and marry whomever they desired. Work conditions were negotiated between the uber wealthy and their throngs of employees. By 2024, the advanced societies of the world certainly weren't perfect. There was still so much more to do. But society was *better*. It was more *diverse*. It was more *equal*. It was more *inclusive*. And it offered every person the opportunity to compete within society on an even footing. These people would not be given stature or lofty positions or greater pay because of who they were. They simply would not be *excluded from consideration* because of who they were. And this was accomplished because of men and women of all walks of life banding together. Supporting one another. Respecting one another.

The members of this Anglo version of the Nationalist Society had seen this coming. They had thought that they had been able to squelch this unholy uprising with the rise of Hitler. It was thought that he would usher in a wave of brutal dictatorship throughout the world that would secure White, male dominance for eternity. But people of other races were too persistent in their yearning for equal opportunity. LGBTQ persons were too persistent in their desire to be recognized and respected for who they truly were. Women were too persistent in their fight against the dominant patriarchy. And enlightened men assisted them all in taking steps toward their rightful recognition and respect until the world-wide fascist movement was soundly defeated.

"We shall bide our time," a thirty-year-old Elder Dante said in 1975 during his coronation address. "Yes, they may have defeated us now, but we shall have the ultimate triumph. We have accumulated too much wealth. Too much political power. Too much influence over business and religious institutions. And we *most certainly* have accumulated far too much military might for these piss-ants to be of any real threat. Let them have their minor victories. Let them have a woman elected to a political position now and again. Let them have mixed races in the schools and in the workplace. Let them share restrooms and water fountains. Let the deviants love whomever they desire. Let them all believe that the arc of history is bending towards justice for them. Let these movements continue. Let them have these minor victories. Let them be lulled into a false sense of security. Let them be lulled into apathy. Let them believe that the world is a safe and just place for them. No, my friends, they shall not succeed. They shall not succeed because they shall defeat *themselves*. They shall eventually act against their *own* self-interests. We shall bide our time and wait. We shall wait for another puppet that we can use to launch a new, glorious populist movement. A movement that will be successful. And why? Because the lemmings will be sound asleep in their cocoons of apathy. They will have lost their hunger for the fight. They will have lost their drive for equality. They will have lost their persistence. We shall roll over them quite easily. Another thirty or forty years perhaps and the fruit shall be ripe to be plucked. And pluck it we shall, my friends. And we shall gorge ourselves upon it.

"The only thing that could possibly thwart us is if the evolved women were to somehow join forces. Should the mediums and the witches combine their might, we could be defeated. But there is very little risk of that now, is there gentlemen? Not only have we spent centuries dominating women and keeping most of them from evolving, but we have also spent centuries indoctrinating women to be distrustful of one another. And, when it comes to the mediums and witches, why we have turned that distrust into absolute hatred. Those two groups would just as soon die a grisly death than to break bread with one of their enemies. Heh, heh, heh. No, let those two groups of blasphemous women live their lives as well. Let them hate one another. Let them war against one another. And then, when the time is right, they shall be vanquished from this Earth. As will any of their sympathizers. Now pass me that goblet filled with the blood of a newly born infant. I am ready to take my oath and take my rightful place as leader of the Nationalist Society. Mmmm, yes. It is quite good. And the religious fanatics think that we are against abortion because we believe in the sanctity of life. Stupid fools. We simply do not want to be denied our simple pleasures, right gentlemen?"

Elder Dante's sly smile could be seen under his hood as he recalled his speech from decades before. He believed those words then and he believed them even more now. He had been prophetic. All of the civil rights victories over the last seventy years had indeed lulled his adversaries into a sheep-like trance. Especially in the world's most powerful country, millions of people believed that their rights were truly unalienable and could never be violated or taken away. Persistent battling for equality and freedom had been largely replaced by their constant, greedy search for immediate gratification. Salty or sugary treats. Sex. Money. Leisure. These were now the priorities of the American population. They wanted it all and they wanted it now. And it would be through this self-absorption of the masses combined with the bigotry that remained prominent that the Nationalist Society's ultimate victory would be attained. And it would be attained through the actions of their latest dullard puppet. So, when Elder Dante heard concern coming from his ranks, his only response was a light chuckle followed by his sneering, "preposterous."

"This is truly quite preposterous gentlemen. Men disappearing all over the world? So what? Their wives or girlfriends disappearing as well? What does *that* prove? Perhaps there is a bit of an uptick in domestic violence. Good. Thin the herd a bit. What does this have to do with mediums and witches calling a truce? You say that there have been no reports of medium against witch hate crimes in months? Couldn't it be that they are simply avoiding one another? Or perhaps our budget cuts to our intelligence department are having an impact on our ability to obtain accurate statistics. You all know as well as I do that mediums and witches have hated one another for centuries. And that hatred persists to this very day.

"So do not come to me and waste my time with this unwarranted handwringing. Not now. Not when we are so close. Our puppet is once again in position to claim the reins of the most powerful nation on Earth. He will do our bidding. He will tear down the democratic pillars of this society. He will destroy any and all legal boundaries. He will make the masses dumber and sicker and poorer, which will make them even *more* dependent upon us and the crumbs we are willing to give them. He will divide this nation from the other democratic nations of the world and align it with the autocrats. He will burn it all down so that we may rebuild it in our vision. The (derogatory term omitted) will once again be our slaves. The (derogatory term omitted) will be forced to hide once again in their closets with their pretty little sequined gowns and Marilyn wigs. The working-class whites shall toil at the yoke of our industry until they die of black lung disease or some other preventable malady. And the women? They will finally and completely be put in their place. They will be stripped of their rights. Of their dignity. Of their freedom. Of their humanity. They will be nothing more than living, breathing baby factories. They will pump out our labor force. Of course, a few of those screaming brats shall become our little treats, yes? We are nearly there, gentlemen. There is no need to alter our course and certainly no need to panic. We have bided our time, and the fruits of our indoctrination efforts are about to be consumed by us. Just a few more months, my friends. We are guaranteed a victory. We now have enough of our own on local election boards and in the judiciary. Especially the Supeme Court. Plus, do you *really* think that the citizens of this country will vote for a woman? Our constant messages of misogyny will not allow it. I've said it before, and I shall say it again. Preposterous. Now, get me my goblet. I yearn for an infant's blood. Then perhaps a round or two of golf."

"You are mistaken," the forty-seven-year-old Elder Himler replied. "You are mistaken about this just as you have been mistaken about biding our time. Yes, we have succeeded in making the majority of the people in this country apathetic. This is true and was quite wise of you. And you have succeeded in selecting the perfect puppet to lead our uprising. He is as evil as we, but dimwitted and easy to manipulate. Once again, an excellent choice.

"But you were mistaken to not simultaneously hunt down and kill the witches and mediums. We should have been burning those bitches at the stake for decades. And you are wrong now. We know that the mediums and witches have formed an alliance. We know that they are swiftly evolving more and more women into more and more mediums and witches. Their ranks are swelling at an incomprehensible pace. They will be a threat to us. And very soon."

Himler's voice deepened as he strode behind Elder Dante's throne while continuing. "Yes, they are a threat, and they are a threat right now. You have been a great leader, but the masses are not the *only* ones who have become apathetic and lazy. With all due respect, it is time for you to retire." Himler retrieved a dagger from under his flowing black robe and thrust it into the throat of the astonished Elder Dante. Himler twisted the knife around in the struggling man's bloody throat until he gurgled his last breath and planted his deceased face on his altar. Himler lifted the gold medallion from Dante's neck with his sticky red hands and placed it around his own. He beamed with maniacal pride as he placed the medallion over his head and said, "Yes, they are a threat, and it is now time for new leadership. Leadership that will not be afraid to take the necessary action. We must extinguish this female uprising now! We must crush this Brigade of Persistence before they can crush us! And it will be quite easy. They may have called a truce, but their mistrust of one another runs quite deep. We know where this all started. It started by a teenage medium and a teenage witch unwittingly befriending one another. All we have to do is kill one of them and frame the other for the murder. Then, the mistrust and hatred will once again rise to the surface, and the two groups shall battle each other to the death. And then, no more mediums and witches. And no more threat. Quite simple. Now, which one to kill? Hmmmm. Yes, I know. I do hate Black people anyway. Kill the witch. Kill that little bitch named Naomi. And fetch me that goblet. I yearn for an infant's blood."

The bright yellow 'listening' emoji that had been hiding in the corner of the room immediately dissipated as Naomi yelled out, "*Kill* me? They're going to *kill* me? But why? Because I'm a witch? Because I'm Black? OMG Morgan! They're going to kill me and frame you for my murder and then there will be a war between the witches and mediums and that evil man is going to be elected and the whole world is going to suffer and people will lose their jobs and go hungry and be bombed and die and I won't be able to help because they're going to kill me and..."

"Now just calm down," Morgan interjected. "Naomi. Just breathe. Nice big breaths. There. Good. Nobody is going to kill you. And I'm not going to be framed. And there will be no war between us. We have recorded this little conversation, and we will broadcast it to our entire brigade, so they will know what's happening. Okay? Am I right Queen Zenobia?"

"Oh yeah, kid, you're right," Queen Zenobia replied after swallowing her latest mouthful of frothy ale. "And nice job with the eavesdropping emoji, Minnie. You're getting really good at this. But yes, Naomi, you have nothing to worry about. The two of you have done such an incredible job of training the new recruits and getting them paired up. Scores of women are evolving every day and joining our ranks, and I need you two to begin the next phase. It is time to begin building the camps. Naomi, you and a whole shitload of witches will use the forces of nature. You know, the trees and wind and shit to build the camps while Morgan and *another* shit-ton of mediums will shroud the camps from detection. Got it?

"Now, Papa Doc. It seems as though these assholes are on to us. I think it's almost time for our little distraction. Are the zombies ready?"

"Oh, yes!" Papa Doc's hunched over frame exclaimed. "My zombies are ready to boogie! I have already selected several small midwestern towns that we shall transport them to on the trains. And, I have perfected my zombie repellant and have already had Lori, Sophia, and Victoria plant it in their local water supply. Just one sip and it will be absorbed into the skin of any woman or enlightened man which will make them repellant to the zombies. They will emit the exact same pheromones that zombies emit, and the zombies will think that they are one of their own and leave them alone. Took quite a bit of hemlock and just the right amount of onion, but it is perfect. Yes, my queen, just a few months to ensure my little potion gets absorbed by the local community then we will be ready for our groovy zombie dance."

"Good!" Queen Zenobia yelled out. "Everything is going just as planned. But Naomi, why do you still look so worried?"

"Um, I'm sorry my queen, but, um, I'm still just worried about being targeted for murder. How will they do it? Are they going to poison me? Or run me off the road? Well, that's not a problem I guess, since my parents still won't let me drive. But what if they shoot me with an arrow? Or a gun? Do they have snipers? Oh, I bet they have lots of snipers. Really good ones. Really good ones that are gonna snipe my brains out of my head! I'm too young to die! I want to grow up and go to college and fall in love and get married and have kids, um, someday. Probably not right away because I think that me and my husband should focus on our financial security before we have kids. Plus, I'd like to travel and that's really hard when you have kids. OMG, I'd just die from embarrassment if I was on a plane and my baby was crying. Could you imagine? What if I can't keep them quiet? So, how am I going to travel if I have kids? No, it would be best to wait. But not too long. Maybe when I'm twenty-five or something. Oh, Morgan! Would you be the godmother to my children? I just know you'd be great with them, and we're besties so I'll be godmother to your children as well! You know. If you want to have kids. And if you want me to. I don't want to butt in where I'm not wanted. But my point is, how are you going to keep me from being murdered?"

Queen Zenobia looked over at a pair of dark silhouettes that were lingering in the doorway. "You got this?" she asked.

The male stepped forward into the light and said, "Yeah, we got this. We'll take out *anybody* that tries to harm Naomi. And we'll do it with a goddamned smile on our face, right buttacup?"

"Oh, hells yes, baby," the short female said as her green eyes glimmered. "Erick is right. Nobody but *nobody* is gonna mess with our Naomi. We'll take them out. And we'll be creative about it too, heh, heh, heh. Yep, that's what's going to happen, or else my name's not

Madeline Ruth Sommers and that's my fu-uh-damned name, so that's how it's going to be!"

Morgan and a relieved Naomi smiled at one another, snapped their fingers, slapped their hands together, and put on their respective sunglasses. "Come on, Naomi," Morgan confidently stated. "Let's go round up some troops. We have some camps to build. It's time for Sister Shade to get into action."

CHAPTER 17

SCENE FROM AN ITALIAN RESTAURANT

"Oh, I just love the layout of this place, don't you dear?" Sophia asked her daughter as the pair looked over a brochure from a potential venue to hold their weddings. "Oh, yeah. I think it would be perfect, Mom," Lori answered. "What do *you* think, Connor?" "What? Oh, yeah, sure looks swell to me Lori. What do you think Vince? Vince?" Connor replied.

"Yeah, yeah, yeah," Vince abruptly answered without taking his eyes off of the television screen. "Yeah, whatever you ladies want. Oh, dear lord. Just look at this. The stinkin' Pats are down by fourteen and it's only the second quarter. Yeah, what a way to start the season. It's only week one and we may as well start planning for the draft next April."

"And speaking of April," Sophia replied. "I believe that Morgan and Naomi will have most of the encampments built by then. And then, heh, heh, heh, well, *then* there will be quite a number of surprised, evil men who will find their lives to be a bit, um, *lacking*."

"Yeah, great," Connor stated as he rolled his eyes. "Millions of newly evolved witches and mediums are gonna round up millions of men, put them into camps, and *then* what? What are you going to *do* with them? Just keep them caged up? And what happens if you mistakenly imprison an *innocent* man? Like me or Vince? How are you going to know who deserves to be there and who doesn't? Seems like a cockamamie idea to me ladies."

"Well, yeah," Lori admitted. "That last part is something we need to work out. Queen Zenobia is working on a triage process to better identify which men should be targeted. Many will be obvious, of course. Public figures who abuse their power to exploit the innocent, for example. But just run of the mill humdrum men will be more difficult to identify. Queen Zenobia has said that she is working on a fool proof process. She said that Sruja is working on bringing somebody into our fold who will be uniquely qualified to help us with that. She is a fifteen-year-old young lady who is said to be a genius. And a great archer, for some reason. But she also has a great intuition. She has a connection to living things, especially animals. She just loves animals and they, in turn, love and trust *her*. Sruja believes that this young lady may be very helpful in determining which men deserve imprisonment and which ones may be invited to be our allies. Please, Connor darling, don't worry about it. Queen Zenobia is brutal to her enemies, but she has no intention of harming any innocent person. Okay? Now, let's take this brochure to the restaurant and discuss our wedding plans there. I'm starving."

"Wazzup bitches!" Maddy exclaimed as the front door was flung open and she and her husband strode in. "Did I hear something about dinner? *Hmmmm?* And am I and Erick invited, *hmmmm?* I need some sustenance so I can be at full strength for later tonight. Know what I mean? Nudge, nudge. You know. *Chicka-Chicka-Wow-Wow.* Right baby?"

"Yeah, we're invited, right?" Erick inquired. "We haven't eaten since, um, let's see here. We had breakfast at six before we opened the diner. Then our mid-morning snack at nine. Then our pre-lunch snack at eleven. Then we *finally* had time for lunch at two. Wow. That was a long stretch. Then our pre-dinner snack at five and it's now... Jesus! It's almost eight o'clock! We haven't eaten for nearly three hours! Oh, my lord. I'm feeling weak, baby. Weak from the hunger. I don't know if I can even make it to a restaurant. Just hold me. I want to look into your beautiful green *eyes* one last time before I fade away. Y'know. From the hunger."

"Hey, hey," Maddy implored. "Just look at me, okay? Just look at me and breathe. It will be okay, baby. We'll get you some food. I'm sure they won't let you starve to death. Right guys? Please. Just *look* at him. He's about to fade away from us. We need to get him to a restaurant fast or else he won't survive." The room was filled with silence except for light wheezing coming from the overacting Erick. Finally, Sophia spoke up.

"Oh, my lord, what a pathetic display! Yes! Yes, you two are invited! Happy now? But we're discussing wedding plans, and we don't need any input from you two, got it?"

A giggling Maddy slapped her husband's ass and yelled out, "Good game, Erick! So, where are we going for eats?"

"We're having Chinese tonight," Lori answered. Erick and Maddy looked at each other with scrunched up noses and began making gagging sounds. "Well, we don't really want *that*," Erick stated. "Nope," Maddy agreed. "We'd rather have Italian. So, how's about we go to the Italian joint instead, *hmmmm?*"

"You know what?" Sophia roared. "If you two are so *starving*, then you'll be happy with Chinese! It's either Chinese or you can dig around in the fridge for whatever crumbs you two may have left in there. My lord, I've never seen anybody eat as much as you two! So, it's Chinese or nothing! Got it? And don't forget to feed your zombies before we go!"

"GAAAAWD! Feed the zombies! Feed the zombies! Cook the burgers! Clean the diner! Protect Naomi and Morgan! Eat crappy Chinese! Then feed the zombies again! This shit's getting old!" Erick exclaimed as he and Maddy rolled their eyes at one another and stomped out the back kitchen door toward the garage to retrieve the zombies' meal.

"Wait! What?" a shocked Connor yelled out. "There are zombies in the *basement*? And those two have been *feeding* them here? Dammit, Lori! I love you but I've gotta put my foot down on this. I've *told* you that I don't want anybody from my jurisdiction to be used as zombie feed! I mean, I have to think of a way to cover up the missing persons reports so that nobody knows it's you doing this, then I have to deal with the distraught families. And just think of all the paperwork that I'll have to do! Hours and hours of paperwork while I'm leading a sham investigation! No, Lori, I just can't have this."

"Now just calm down, Connor," Lori replied. "There's nothing for you to worry about. Yes, there are zombies in the basement, but just five of them. Maddy and Erick wanted a few as back-up in case the Nationalist Society sends more assassins than they can handle. And there's no threat to *us*, because we have all drank Papa Doc's potion, so the zombies think that we're one of their own. They just hang out in the basement and play with Larry the Leopard and Gabriel. They're really no trouble. And the zombie feed is not locally sourced. Maddy and Erick have gone out of state to abduct men and bring them here. Well, I mean, just to Rhode Island, but it's still out of state and out of your jurisdiction. And these *latest* meals have come to *them*. They are assassins that the Nationalist Society have sent to murder Naomi. Isn't that right you two?"

"Right as rain, Lori!" Maddy grunted out as she and Erick were struggling to carry a frantic, naked, bound man toward the basement stairs. They dropped him on the kitchen floor and the man wailed from the impact on his ribs. "Yep, these douchebags have come to *us*. It's almost like ordering a pizza or sumthin'. A pizza for zombies. Plus, it's a really efficient way to get rid of the bodies. Those zombies eat everything! Well, except the bones, but we've been carving those into weapons for Queen Zenobia. We've made her knives and spears and swords and all sorts of stuff out of their bones. Even a back scratcher. You know how itchy Queen Z gets when she wears her armor? Well, no more uncomfortable itches when you have the official Maddy and Erick backscratcher 3000! It'll get to the hardest to reach places! And, it's made from all organic materials, so no waste to worry about! Available at all fine retail stores! Pick yours up today!"

"Yeah, these assassins really suck," a laughing Erick added. "All we have to do is lurk around outside in the trees and wait to see their little red dots from their stupid little guns. Then, BANG! POW! SNAP! We knock 'em out! They fall from the tree, we strip them down, tie them up, and wait for feeding time!"

"That's so right, baby," a chuckling Maddy replied. "But I have to take issue with one part of your explanation, if you don't mind."
"Okay," a curious Erick answered. "What exactly did I get wrong?"
"Well, it's not so much *wrong* as it is *incomplete*," Maddy chortled. "You see you said that once we see them it's BANG! POW! SNAP! Which is accurate. But sometimes it's ZING! BASH! SLASH! And then there was that one time that it was SMASH! SLICE! BOP! Remember that one?"

"Oooooh yeah," a reminiscing Erick replied. "You're right, Buttacup. I stand corrected. Oh man, just listen to those zombies whining. They must be *really* hungry. Kinda ridiculous to whine like a baby though. You'll never catch *me* acting that way. Alright one, two, three, lift!"

Erick and Maddy lifted the squealing man and tossed his naked frame down the basement stairs. "Here ya go zombies! Don't forget to wash your hands first!" Maddy yelled out as the thuds of the tumbling man echoed throughout the house.

"Oh my god, this is just getting worse and worse," Vince lamented as the tortured screams of the man being eaten alive bellowed from the basement. He hung his head in his hands while the sounds of the chomping, biting, and chewing zombies continued.

"I'm so sorry, Vince," Sophia tenderly stated as she sat next to him and thoughtfully wrapped her pale arm around his shoulders. "I know this is hard for you. It's a travesty really. Twenty-seven to three at half-time. But it's just the first game of the season. They might get better."

"Nope, doubt it," a disgusted Vince stated as he got up from his seat. "I just can't stand to watch any more of this atrocity. I'm gonna go upstairs and get ready for dinner. Those zombies are making me hungry. Man, I'm really looking forward to my sweet and sour chicken."

"I think I'll have the chicken parmesan," a delighted Erick told the waiter while Sophia, Vince, Lori, and Connor glared at him. "Mmmmm, that sounds good, baby," Maddy replied as her stomach made churning sounds. "Hey, you maybe wanna share? Like, could I have some of yours and you can have some of my broccoli alfredo?" "But of course," Erick answered before placing a light kiss on Maddy's forehead while the other diners shook their heads in disgust.

Throughout the evening, other patrons at the restaurant requested to be moved to a table far, far away from the Cabot's. "I'm so sorry, ma'am," Connor said regretfully. "She just gets a little excited at dinner. Maddy! Would you *please* stop taking food off of other people's plates? It's rude!"

"Rude?" an incredulous Maddy roared back. "Rude? I'll tell ya what's *rude*. This bitch has barely even *touched* her spaghetti, and she expects me to just sit here and stare at it. And what's up with the garlic bread? Are you gonna eat that shit or what? And if not, can *I* have it, *hmmmm*? What's with the look bitch?"

"Yeah, what's with the look?" Erick jumped in. "Is it too much for my wife to ask for a bite if you're not going to eat it? And are you gonna finish your appetizers or what?" "Oh yeah, good point, baby," Maddy agreed. "Yeah, are you gonna finish your appetizers or what?"

"Oh, dear lord," Lori whispered to her mother. "We really thought that bringing her husband out of Morgan's book would be a good influence on her. But now, there's *two* of them. I'm so embarrassed. I'm never going to dinner with them again." "I know it's hard. *Believe me*, I *know* it's hard," Sophia replied. "But just be patient. I believe Sruja is close to our new distraction. And I think *this* one may very well be the moderating influence we've been hoping for."

Several minutes later, a fuming Erick and Maddy were leaving the restaurant followed by the slumped bodies of the embarrassed Lori, Connor, Sophia, and Vince. "I can't believe this injustice! We should have gotten Chinese!" Maddy bellowed as the party made their way toward the dimly lit parking lot. "I can't believe you're kicking us out! Just for asking to sample another patron's food! You should be *thanking* us for appreciating your cuisine! This is ridiculous! This injustice, sir, shall not stand! I'll call the mayor! I'll call the governor! I'll call my congressperson! You have not heard the last of this…"

Maddy was cut off by her husband yelling out, "Down!" Sophia, Vince, Lori, and Connor ducked behind a large black SUV while they watched a pair of blurs instinctively zigzag in the direction of a thin red laser beam that was aimed at them. Maddy and Erick dodged several bullets before leaping at a person who was crouched behind a rusty dumpster. Erick headbutted the assailant before they both began pummeling him with their fists. The four on-lookers gasped as they watched streams of blood erupting from behind the banging dumpster. The struggle suddenly ended, and they heard Maddy yell out, "Hey! Good news! We got zombie dessert! You wanna bring the car around? This asshole looks heavy! Oh, goddamit. Look baby. I broke a nail." "Well, maybe I was wrong," Lori observed. "Maybe they *aren't* such bad dinner guests after all."

"Next time, let's just get take-out," Vince grumbled as the group re-entered the home of the Ladies Cabot. And "guests". "And just look at this score. Forty-four to ten. Yeah, good game, guys. Good game." "Ooooh shit, why did you have to say that," Sophia mumbled before her backside was blindsided by a firm slap. "Good game, Sophia!" Maddy squealed. "Thanks for letting us get Italian. It was really good. Plus, we got another snack for the zombies. Yep, all in all I'd say this was a successful evening. Well, except for that bitch at the next table. I'm gonna have to talk to Z-String about her. I don't think she should be welcome in our brigade. Nope. Not unless she's gonna share her garlic bread."

At that moment, Larry the Leopard's bright yellow furry frame came bounding up the stairs. "Oh Maddy! Oh Erick! Please come and see! Come see the wonderful surprise that is waiting for thee!"

"What the hell is going *on* down there?" Connor asked as the group approached the basement door. "Are those zombies…laughing?" They cautiously descended the creaking wooden stairs and gasped at a most improbable sight. The five zombies were indeed laughing. And dancing. And putting their whole self in. Then their whole self out. There was a small record player that was playing *The Hokey Pokey*. And in the middle of this improbable display was a barefoot, teenage girl. Her copper, curly locks hung around her cute, freckled face while her flowered yellow dress swayed to the rhythm of the song.

Erick's eyes filled with tears as he yelled out, Oh…my…God! Josie!" "Hi Dad! Hi Mom!" the teenage girl squealed through her laughter. "Surprised to see me? This really nice spirit named Sruja brought me out of Morgan's book and here I am!"

Josephine Patricia Sommers Parker, otherwise known as Josie, was written by Morgan to be the beloved daughter of Maddy and Erick. She was, indeed, a genius and a master archer. And she adored all forms of life, especially those with fur. Throughout her childhood, Josie was written to believe in the best of people. She believed that all people had good in them that could be brought out if only they were met with kindness. With understanding. With compassion. By the age of fifteen, Josie's view of the world had changed considerably. Through tragic personal loss, she came to realize that there were some human beings who were inherently evil and that no amount of nurturing would dispel them from their malicious actions. She understood how they were obsessed by greed and lust and power and that they would do anything in their pursuit of personal enrichment. She understood the senseless, brutal atrocities that these demonic men were capable of. She understood that they were soulless and weren't truly human because they did not possess one shred of humanity. And from the age of fifteen, Josie was in a constant internal struggle between caring for all of humanity and seeking revenge for the downtrodden. Yes, by the age of fifteen there was no doubt from whose loins Josie had sprung.

Maddy and Josie stared at each other in silence with their identical glimmering green eyes. Their five-foot-four-inch frames faced each other while their copper hair swayed to the movement of the still-dancing zombies. "Hello, mother," Josie quietly said. Tears welled up in Maddy's effervescent eyes as she embraced her daughter and yelled out, "Oh my lord, my daughter is alive!"

Erick joined the sobbing pair, and the family tightly embraced for the first time since they had been written by Morgan. Lori, Sophia, Connor, and Vince fought back their own tears as they looked at this tender reunion. Larry the Leopard was sprinkling water around the basement as his tearful goo-goo-googly eyes rolled around in his bright white sockets.

Josie chuckled slightly and wiped her eyes while stepping back from her parents. "Yep, here I am. Sruja said it took a while to put Morgan's incantation back together and bring me here and I'm so glad she did. I was so alone in those books without you. I mean, you were both still there, but you were frozen. Your souls were gone. I knew what had happened. I knew that somehow you had been brought out of Morgan's pages and into the real world and I was happy for you. But I missed you both so much. I'm just so happy to be alive and with you both.

"Sruja told me all about the Brigade of Persistence and said that I have a special assignment. Three actually. The first one is to look into men's character and determine whether they were worthy of joining our brigade or whether they needed to be incarcerated or put down. So, *that* sounds super fun. My second task is to help you both protect some girl named Naomi. That should be easy enough. I brought my bow and arrows. And my *third* assignment, um, well..." Josie's voice trailed off as her advanced mind struggled to find the right words.

"Yeah, what is it, sweetie?" Erick asked. "Yeah, out with it sister!" Maddy demanded. "What's your third assignment? Helping us feed the zombies? Hell, you'll enjoy that! You're *always* feeding goddamned strays!"

"No, that isn't quite it," Josie meekly replied while shuffling her bare size-six feet. "Well, what the hell is it then?" a frustrated Maddy asked. "Come on! Out with it! What's with all the hubbub-bub? We got shit to do!"

"Fine!" Josie roared at her mother. "You want to know what my third assignment is? Well, I'll tell you! It's you! And Dad! I'm supposed to keep an eye on the two of you and make sure you don't go off all half-cocked and murder a bunch of people that you're not supposed to! And I'm supposed to always go out to eat with you! It's ridiculous! A fifteen-year-old girl having to chaperone her own mother to go out to eat! But otherwise, you'll steal food from the other diners then get kicked out! Right? Right! Plus, you need to watch your language and…"

She was cut off by an infuriated Maddy. "You were brought here to babysit *us*? Oh, hells no! *I'm* not taking orders from my teenage daughter! And I'm sure as hell not taking you to dinner with us! You'll totally embarrass me when you order a hot dog and put ketchup on it! Who in the hell does that? It's barbaric! I've said it before, and I'll say it again! Ketchup on hot dogs is doing it wrong!"

Maddy then felt herself spun around by her husband. He looked into her eyes and smiled. "Hey. Listen. Don't you see? Our daughter is here. She's alive. She's with us. We're a family again. This is the happiest day of our new lives. This isn't a time for bickering, although you're right about the whole ketchup on hot dogs thing. This is a time for celebration. This is a time to appreciate what we have."

"Yeah, I guess you're right," a backpedaling Maddy conceded. "But I don't see why Sruja couldn't have brought back sweet *eight*-year-old Josie and not smartass *fifteen*-year-old Josie." "Because," Erick whispered into his beloved wife's ear. "For what we are doing, we *need* fifteen-year-old Josie. We need her intelligence and tenacity. And we may as well admit it. It really wouldn't hurt us to have a chaperone when we go out to dinner. Or on late night walks. Or when we go to the grocery store. Or pretty much any place where there are, um, y'know. People." The pair broke into hysterical laughter before their daughter joined them once again.

"Besides," a laughing Josie playfully stated. "You may not want to mess with me mother. Or have you not met my new zombie friends?"

"Oh yeah, the zombies," Sophia said. "I wonder if Papa Doc, Victoria, and her Plymouth coven have launched their attack yet? Come on everybody. Let's see if we can get ahold of Queen Zenobia and see what's going on. Plus, I wanted to speak with Grandmother Agatha and get her cupcake recipe. I was thinking cupcakes might be more fun than a big intrusive wedding cake. Oh, um, and by the way you three, congratulations on your reunion. We're all really happy that you're together. Or something. But young lady, let me just say, that you *really* have your work cut out for you. And I'm not talking about tasks one and two."

"Don't I know it," Josie muttered under her breath as she followed the others up the rickety basement stairs while the exuberant zombies continued to dance.

CHAPTER 18

NOW THIS IS AN INVASION

"And make sure you don't overcook the pot roast…again!" the husband was ordering his wife over breakfast. "Yes, dear. I won't," the seemingly submissive woman replied. "And would it kill you to clean this place up a bit? Look at all the crumbs laying around the toaster!" he bellowed. "Alright dear," the wife dutifully agreed. "And I'm almost outta beer. Get me a case today. Or two. The guys are coming over tonight to watch the game. And maybe you should try to cover yourself up this time. That dress you wore last week made you look like a cheap whore! And put some makeup on your black eye! They don't need to see that shit!" "Of course, dear. I'm sorry for embarrassing you," the wife meekly replied.

"And one more thing!" he shouted before being cut off. Literally. Just as he was about to issue his final command a zombie broke through the back kitchen door, grabbed his head, and ripped it from its shoulders. Blood gushed out of his neck like a geyser before cascading into the couple's eight-year-old boy's cereal bowl. The shocked tike was frozen in fear as his innocent face was splattered by bloody cornflakes and pieces of his father's brain which was being ravenously consumed by the tenacious zombie.

"Oh my, they do make a mess, don't they?" the wife stated

through light chuckles. "Oh well. No use cleaning it up. We'll be leaving here today," she added while the zombie was pulling the husband's intestines out of his cavity like morbid magician's scarfs. "It's time for me to join my sisters. Now, junior, do you see what happens? Do you see what will happen to you if you grow up to be an asshole like your father? That's right. You will be eaten by zombies. Or worse. So do *not* turn out to be an alcoholic, abusing lout like him. You will be a caring, loving, and understanding man. Or you will be eaten by zombies. And there's not a damned thing that I'll be able to do about it. Now, just run upstairs to your room and color or play with your action figures. I'm pretty sure school will be cancelled today. Y'know. Because of the zombies. Just run upstairs and play and don't worry about what is happening. The zombies won't bother you. We've both drank a potion that was placed in the water supply, and they think we're one of them. Oh, and don't worry about cleaning your room. This place is going to be condemned anyway."

She went to the front door, opened it, and smiled widely as she witnessed the brutal carnage that had descended upon her Midwestern town of nearly 2,000 people. "Yes, this entire damned town is going to be condemned, heh, heh, heh," she muttered as she heard the boy's footsteps frantically thumping up the staircase. She began laughing hysterically as most of the town's men were being swarmed by zombies. They were shrieking and praying to their lord as their faces were being torn off of their skulls. Their lord did not answer these men's prayers. Their lord had forsaken them. Their lord had forsaken *them* just as *they* had forsaken their lord. While it was true that these men dutifully attended their local churches and prayed and sang reverential hymns, their practice was not true to their supposed faith. Their practice was to directly or indirectly hate and oppress and terrorize people different from themselves. Their practice was brutal bigotry. No longer did they worship their lord or pay respect to their lord's teachings. They now worshipped a corrupt, immoral golden calf that was the antithesis of everything their lord represented. They now worshipped an Anti-Christ. And their punishment would be to be eaten by zombies, be banished from Enlightenment, and be sent into the fiery pits of hell where a smiling Satan would open his welcoming arms before thrusting a blazing poker up their ass. For eternity. The chaotic scene made the wife smile and laugh.

She looked at the simple home across the street just beyond an exploding car and waved. "Good morning, Gladys! Nice morning, isn't it?" "Oh, just beautiful dear, just beautiful," the sixty-eight-year-old Gladys replied. "What a wonderful day. It is a day of cleansing. A day of freedom. A day of reckoning for these asshole men. And a wonderful day to do some gardening. But I really must speak with Morgan and Naomi. Although we learned of this zombie invasion during our orientation into the Brigade of Persistence, I did not realize just how *horrible* it would be. They did not prepare us for such carnage. Why, just look at my marigold garden. Those zombies have absolutely trampled them. Oh, I know it's the end of the season, but I *was* hoping to get a couple more weeks of enjoyment out of them and…oh no. Now listen, you. My yard is *not* a shortcut to the Peterson's house. I know he's cowering in his garage but use the sidewalk. Yes, right over there. Use the sidewalk. Good zombie. Enjoy your breakfast. And if you're still hungry after that, I think that there's some leftovers of my husband in the bathroom. He's been pretty picked over, but there may still be a few bites left, and you are welcome to them. Alright, dear? Yes, you're welcome. Now go get your breakfast. Oh, zombies. They are so good natured, but I swear, they have the manners of a toddler."

"Yes, they do make a mess, don't they?" the wife replied through her laughter. "You should see my kitchen! But no matter. We'll be going to our camp soon and preparing for the arrival of surviving men. And I spoke to Victoria last night after our zombie invasion preparation meeting and she said that all of the camps will have plenty of space to plant gardens around our houses. I just can't wait to see our new homes. Thousands of cute little brightly painted houses encircling a large concrete barracks big enough to house 100,000 men. Morgan and Naomi have been so busy training us, then building thousands of these camps throughout the world. And the dumbass Nationalist Society has no idea what is happening. The mediums have summoned spirits to cloak the camps. And the caravans of zombies. They are completely undetectable. The towns have no idea that the zombies are coming. Until they attack. Then they can be seen. Then we can *all* be seen. Which is exactly what we wanted. Especially *them*."

The pair of friends and hundreds of other women from the town looked to their west and saw four figures ascending a grassy hill to oversee their handywork. The townswomen began applauding as they looked upon the proud faces of Papa Doc, Victoria, Morgan, and Naomi. The quartet waved to the townspeople while screaming, half-eaten men were being chased by throngs of zombies. Trails of blood weaved through the warm asphalt streets as the hysterical men squealed and looked for refuge.

"And where do you think *you're* going?" the wife stated to a histrionic man who was running past her. "Not on *my* watch, Earl. Remember when you forced your hand up my skirt that night at the bar? Well, here. Have a taste of your own medicine." She closed her eyes and focused. A large tree limb extended up the man's pant leg and grabbed him by the genitals. The limb lifted the flailing man into the air, carried him several yards, and dropped him right in the middle of a circle of zombies. "No! No! Please! Lord help me! Noooooo!" were the final sounds the man made before his throat was torn out by an appreciative group of the living dead.

"Wow!" Naomi squealed with delight. "She really has come a long way since the first day of class! Just look at how easily she summoned that tree limb! Perfect control. Yep, she's almost as good at controlling her powers as I am now. And that's all thanks to you, Morgan. You helped me unclutter my mind and concentrate and now I can do all sorts of stuff with nature! Almost as good as you. But not quite, since you're a Fabula and have the powers of both witches and mediums. Yep, I've come a long way. But not with flying my broom. I don't know what it is. I'm really good in first and second gear, but once I put it into third, everything goes all wonky!

Just like when I had my Miata. Oh, I miss my little car. It was so cute and..."

Naomi was cut off by the gleeful voice of Papa Doc. "Oooooh hear we go ladies. Our latest zombies have arrived. Just watch that cargo van down there. Watch and listen." Papa Doc reached down and pushed play on a 90's era CD boombox. He turned up the volume and "Jive Talkin'" by The Bee Gees thundered out of the speakers.

Two members of the Plymouth Coven opened the back doors of the cargo van, and eight newly arrived zombies came gyrating onto the street. The four female zombies were all wearing bright red chiffon dresses that flowed down to their knees. The male zombies were adorned in an all-white polyester suit and white platform shoes. They looked up from where the music was coming from, smiled, and began grooving to the rhythm.

"Now, it's a party!" Papa Doc yelled out. "That's right zombies! Let's boogie!" The zombies grabbed disoriented, hapless men and began spinning them around the bloody street. Each time a zombie pulled one of its dance partners close to them, they would ferociously bite off a chunk of flesh. A shoulder here. A lip there. Then a nose. Another shoulder. Ears. Eyes. Blood spurted into the air as the hysterically wailing men were being eaten alive one bite and one dance step at a time. By the time "How Deep Is Your Love" was playing, the deceased men were lying on the blood-soaked pavement while the zombies gorged themselves in order to build up their strength for their next dance.

There was a thunderous boom in the middle of the street as an explosion rocked the town. "Well, here we go," Morgan calmly stated while placing her sunglasses over her hazel eyes. "Took them long enough. Here comes the cavalry. Come on Naomi. It's Sister Shade time." The pair of best friends snapped their fingers and looked at the oncoming artillery. "Need some help?" Victoria asked. "Nope. This is gonna be a piece of cake," Morgan confidently answered before reciting a memorized incantation.

"You got it, toots!" the disembodied squeaky voice of Minnie

Marples was heard before thousands of small airplane emojis circled the five incoming F-16 fighter jets. The confused pilots swerved to avoid the small, smiling cartoon aircraft. Two of the planes collided in mid-air and erupted in a huge ball of fire. The shrapnel from the fallen planes struck the three remaining jets, causing them to crash into a nearby field. Two surviving pilots crawled out of their demolished cockpits and looked up into the dead eyes of zombies who were licking their decomposing lips.

Naomi focused on the tips of her toes. She began vibrating them and pointing the energy at the oncoming tanks. The vibrations traveled under the town until it reached its destination. They then exploded in a powerful earthquake. The ground opened up from the violent shaking and the tanks plunged into the Earth. Naomi focused once again, and the ground closed around the tanks like the mouth of a snake around its unsuspecting prey.

"What the hell is going on? They said the women were powerful, but who knew they were *this* powerful? Oh, screw this! Retreat! Retreat!" the commander yelled out. As the troops began to fall back, Morgan held hands with Naomi. They both concentrated and hurricane force winds blasted the marauders in their fearful faces, forcing them to halt. The soldiers were being violently pelted by dirt and rocks that were being launched by the horrific gales. They were then pelted by something much more deadly.

Morgan called upon Minnie Marples once again and thousands of dagger emojis emerged from the dust storm. The defenseless men screamed and fell to the ground as their bodies were shredded by hundreds of tiny razor sharp emojis. The screams of the final man were extinguished, and Morgan and Naomi opened their eyes while smiling at one another. "That's how this shit is done," Morgan arrogantly stated as the winds died down revealing hundreds of dusty, bloodied, deceased troops. "Jesus, you two are powerful," Victoria stated with awe. "And it's just the two of you that did that. Took out an entire battalion or something. And we now have millions upon millions of mediums and witches in our brigade. Oh, dear Enlightenment. We might actually pull this shit off."

The Brigade of Persistence had made its statement on behalf of every downtrodden person throughout the world. And that statement was 'We tried nice. Time to get naughty.' It was a statement that was clearly heard by the members of Nationalist Societies throughout the world. And the realization that the women of the Earth were now more powerful than they caused them to literally piss in their pants.

"Well, that was fun!" Papa Doc exclaimed. "Okay, ladies. Let's round up the zombies. On to the next town," a chuckling Minnie Marples could be heard saying as thousands of brain emojis began leading the zombies back into their semi-trailers. The moment the last zombie was safely locked away, the trailers disappeared as though they had never been there.

"Alrighty then," Morgan exclaimed. "That really *was* fun. Papa Doc and Victoria, have fun in the next town. Naomi and I are going to round up the few survivors and take them to our first camp. We want to cut the ribbon of our first officially opened camp and we want to personally see the reaction on our sisters' faces when they see their new homes. Then we'll turn the camp over to them to run, and we'll move on to the next one. Then the next one. Until every surviving evil man is incarcerated. Then the *real* fun will begin, heh, heh, heh."

"Don't remind me of that," Naomi stated. "It makes me hungry. I know it's gross, but it reminds me of hot dogs. I just *love* hot dogs on a nice warm, fresh bun. And lots and lots of ketchup! I just love it when I take a bite of my hot dog, and the ketchup runs down my chin and…"

Naomi was cut off by the stern voice of Morgan. "Ketchup on hot dogs is doing it wrong." "Well, now you just sound like Maddy," Naomi replied. "I *am* Maddy," Morgan bluntly stated. "Now come on. Let's have our sisters round up all the remaining men. There are bound to be some evil ones mixed in with the good and we need to figure out how to sort them. We'll keep the evil ones and let the good ones join our brigade and go home." At that moment, Morgan heard a woman's voice say, "I've been watching, and I am so proud of you all." Morgan then felt the firm slap of an invisible hand on her backside. "Good game, Morgan!" The congratulatory slapping continued down the line. "Good game, Naomi!" "Good game, Victoria!" Good Game, Papa Doc!" Oh shit, I'm sorry! Don't fall over Papa Doc!"

"Aw shit," Victoria lamented. "Now Queen Zenobia is doing it. You know, that Maddy really is a bad influence. Alright girls. See you at home. Good luck on opening your camp. And double-check to make sure the vengeful spirits are keeping it cloaked twenty-four-seven. Just one slip up, and the Nationalist Society could attack us. On the other hand, who cares? Just look at what we did today, so screw them. Maybe the more quickly they attack, the more quickly we can get this over with and get back to our normal lives. I haven't been out clubbing with my sisters for months and this figure is too cute to waste. So, let's just get this shit over with."

"P-please," the bound, pleading man sobbed in his small, concrete cell while staring at a pair of smirking eighteen-year-olds. "I swear, I'm one of the *good* ones. Look. The zombies didn't attack me. The potion that you put in the water had the same effect on *me* as it did the women. And all my female friends told me what was going to happen and that I'd be alright. Please? Please won't you go ask any of the women from that town. I've never been disrespectful or harmful. I'm not a bigot. I believe in equal rights and civility and humanity. Please. I just want to go home."

"What do you think?" a suspicious Naomi asked her friend while stroking her ebony chin." "I dunno," an equally suspicious Morgan answered. "I mean, he has a point. He wasn't eaten by zombies. But maybe that's because he was just a good hider. Yeah, that's it. Maybe he's really good at hiding. Like, hiding his true nature and duping women into thinking he's a nice guy when in fact he's just another abusive perv."

"Yeah, you're probably right, Morgan," Naomi agreed. "He's probably hiding that he's an abusive perv from his female friends. So, what do you have to say about *that* Mister Hiding That You're an Abusive Perv? How are ya gonna talk your way out of *that* one? If you *are* hiding that you're an abusive perv, then having a woman friend to vouch for you won't help much, now, will it?"

"Please, I swear," the desperate man pled. "I'm not an abusive perv." "Yeah, well, that's just what an abusive perv *would* say," Naomi countered. "Well, then what can I do to convince you?" the trembling man inquired. "It seems as though I'm damned if I do and I'm damned if I don't. Please, just let my female friends vouch for me. Please? My best friend was a lady in her sixties named Gladys. I used to enjoy helping her garden. Please speak with her."

"Alright, we'll give it a shot," Morgan stated. "Come on Naomi. Let's find his friend." Sister Shade walked down the cold, bleak concrete corridors of the encampment and came to a heavy iron door. The door let out a loud creak as they opened it and the pair was greeted by bright sunshine. And laughter. All around the foreboding fortress were rows of adorable, brightly painted two-bedroom houses. There was a bustle of activity as giddy mediums and witches were moving their belongings and children into their new homes. Morgan put on her sunglasses to dim the glare of the beaming sun reflecting off of the neon pink, yellow, blue, purple, and green homes.

"Wow," an awestruck Naomi commented. "It really is the dawn of a new day. Just look at this rainbow of houses that are being filled with all of these powerful women. Women who no longer have to cower in fear but can live their lives however they want. Raise their kids however they want. This isn't a torture camp. This is a camp that is filled with new beginnings and love."

"Yeah, well," Morgan replied as she hid her joyful tears behind her sunglasses. "There's still gonna be some torture. The same torture that these men have put these women through. For decades. Centuries, even. Their oppression and torture were endless. And the only way to finish this once and for all and to make this right is for the tables to be turned. The victimizers must now become the victims. Retribution must be made for us to finally be free. Inhumane crimes have been committed, and a price must be paid for humanity to be restored. But retribution against only the bad ones.

Speaking of which, hey! Anyone here named Gladys? Gladys? We're lookin' for a Gladys! Anyone here know…oh, hello."

"Hello girls, I'm Gladys. How may I help you? Oh, and I must say how impressed I was at how you handled those troops. I only hope to be such a strong medium someday. Now, how may I help you?"

"P-please, Gladys," the quivering man pled. "Please tell them that I'm one of the good ones."

"Yes, yes, he is," Gladys immediately confirmed. "He was always so kind to me and I have never heard him say a cross word toward anyone. He is, in my opinion, a fine gentleman." The man let out a sigh of relief and smiled at his friend. The smile was short-lived.

"Uh,huh," Naomi stated while rubbing her chin once again. "But isn't it *possible* that he was just putting on an act and that deep down inside he's an abusive perv?"

"Well, I suppose it's *possible*," Gladys conceded. "But he's always seemed so nice." "Yeah, well," Naomi countered. "That's what they say about pretty much *every* serial killer *ever*. And I should know. I know a couple of them. Although *they* aren't really nice. Kinda more annoying than anything. They do make good bodyguards though."

"Well, this just sucks," a pacing Morgan grumbled. "We can't torture an innocent man, and we have no way of knowing if he's truly innocent. I mean, I know Sruja has brought another of my characters to life who has unique intuition about these things. But Josie just got here and there's going to be millions of men to go through. We don't have time for that. Plus, she's going to have her hands full playing caretaker to her parents. Hopefully she can get Erick to stop eating so much and Maddy to stop slapping every-body's asses. And, you know, keep them from indiscriminately killing people. I mean, their victims are always assholes, but Connor just hates all the paperwork he has to do after they've murdered a local. No, Josie isn't the answer. At least not yet. I think we need to contact Queen Zenobia before we proceed. I'm really on the fence with this guy."

"Perhaps *we* could be of assistance," a British male voice came from a dark corner of the small cell. Gladys, Naomi, and Morgan looked in the direction of the voice and gasped as a couple appeared out of nowhere. The slender man was tall, had slicked back silver hair, a thin mustache, and wore a perfectly fitting grey, pinstriped suit. The woman looked considerable younger and had blonde hair and wore a styled business suit. And they were both holding worn brown leather medical bags.

"We are so sorry to have startled you," the man politely stated. "Please, allow us to introduce ourselves. My name is Alexander. Alexander Picklesbee. And *this* ravishing young woman is my wife, Melissa Bartlesworth. We became aware of your activities and thought we could be of service to you. You see, we are quite adept at looking into men's souls. Just one look into their eyes and we know everything about them. And then, we give the dark souls what they deserve and send them to our lord, Satan. It really is a very efficient process. So, we are here to offer our services to your brigade. On one condition. You need to take *those* four off of our hands. Deal?"

The women looked to the opposite corner and saw four cheer-leaders nonchalantly filing their sharp fingernails and snapping their gum. "Um, maybe," Morgan cautiously answered. "But who are you again? And, how in the hell did you hear about us? And where in the hell are you from?"

"In hell," a chuckling Alexander replied while clutching his medical bag as his black eyes glimmered. "What an appropriate use of words. Well, my new friends, let me just tell you where we're from. You see, my beautiful wife and I have indeed come to you... from *hell*."

CHAPTER 19

A Helluva Story

Alexander Picklesbee was an interesting sort. On the surface, he appeared to be a typical, mild-mannered British gentleman. But just a slight scratch beneath the surface would reveal a much more complicated and nefarious character. He was born in 1838 to a rigid and somewhat belittling pair of parents. As a young man, he showed a propensity for medical practice. Especially surgery. It was while at university that he met his one true love, Virginia Smith. He had grown completely infatuated with her and his happiness was dependent upon her love for him.

But that love was not to last. Virgina moved from London to New York with her family at the height of the American Civil War to start a clothier business and produce uniforms for the Union Army. It was a financial boon for the family. It proved to be a devastating loss for Alexander. As time passed, the lovers grew apart and Virginia inevitably fell for another. Thomas Bartlesworth had wormed his way into Virginia's father's business and into her heart. Following the mysterious death of Virginia's father, it was taken over by Virginia and her husband and Bartlesworth's Clothier Company was born.

Alexander would write to his love every day, sharing the most miniscule details of his life. She would, in turn, write him back. For a time. Her letters became less frequent until they ceased altogether following her announcement of her engagement to the vile Thomas Bartlesworth.

For several years Alexander attempted to win back the heart of his lost love. With each passing letter of pathetic pleas, he descended further into a madness born of frustration, jealousy, anger, and heartbreak. The weight of his loss became too great, and he crawled into many bottles of gin to medicate himself. The promising young surgical student was kicked out of school, and Alexander was forced into a meager living as a traveling salesman. The pain and humiliation finally reached an insufferable plateau and Alexander's demented mind decided to lash out against those who he felt were responsible for his despondent plight.

First, it was his parents. Then, more innocent victims. He thrilled at the sight of the blood and organs that he ripped from the bodies of working girls in White Chapel. He delighted at watching the constables scurry around aimlessly as they attempted to catch this monstrous killer. He would laugh hysterically as his letters to the authorities provided more confusion and fear than clues. And he absolutely adored the new name that he had given himself. He basked in the inhumane glory of Jack the Ripper.

He traveled to New York to claim his ultimate retribution. On Christmas Day, 1888, he had planned to murder his lost love's entire family while Virgina was forced to watch. And then, it would be Virginia's turn to…suffer. But he was denied his final victory by a misstep on an icy wooden staircase leading to his modest boarding house two days earlier. Alexander slipped and cracked his head open. And then, his living hell truly began.

He was greeted in Hell as a celebrity of sorts. After all, the great, sinful Jack the Ripper was now in their presence. And because of his notoriety, his eternal punishment wasn't so bad. Comparably speaking. For eternity, Alexander was to tend to a convenience store in Hell. Outside of scorching his hands on the white-hot security gate each morning, it was more tedium than torture.

Then, in 2024, Alexander thought of a way to break free from his eternal torment and return to Earth. He struck a deal with Satan to send damned souls to Hell by posing as a shopkeeper and selling soulless patrons that which they deserved. Repeatedly, Alexander would sell unsuspecting customers a seemingly harmless item, only to have that item be their downfall. And fall they did. Right into the lap of a delighted Satan. The deal that had been struck was an absolute success. Until Alexander saw *her*.

One day, Alexander saw a beautiful blonde woman who looked identical to his lost love, Virginia. His heart swooned and raged simultaneously. Her name was Melissa. Melissa *Bartlesworth*. A descendent of his Virgina. Alexander's mixed feelings for this vibrant young woman sent his mind into a whirlwind of confusion. And then, dead prostitutes began showing up once again. This did not sit well with Satan. Alexander was only to provide for the demise of the soulless, not the innocent. As Alexander and Melissa engaged in their rather complicated relationship, Satan conducted his own investigation into these unnecessary murders. And he was shocked at what he found. (AUTHOR'S NOTE: For more details, read *Satan's Shopkeeper*. I'm not gonna give *everything* away!)

Despite the complicated nature of their relationship, Alexander and Melissa's love flourished and they were married in a ceremony in Hell. The newlyweds were granted the opportunity to return to Earth and continue to provide the souls of evildoers to Satan. On two conditions. One was that they were not to murder anyone that was innocent. Satan was very clear on that. The second condition was a bit more challenging. The wedded couple had to tend to four young women. Well, four teenage mean-girl cheerleaders to be exact. For decades, Missy, Buffy, Sparkles, and Trish had tormented Satan, and he was tired of putting up with their attitudes, blasphemous graffiti, juvenile gossip, and relentless gum-snapping. They would now be the problem of Alexander and Melissa. And Satan would get the relief from those despicable girls that he so desperately needed.

"Which leads us to the events of just a few days ago," Alexander stated to the gape-mouthed Naomi and Morgan. "You see, a few days ago…"

"Alexander! Alexander would you please come up here?" Melissa screamed out from the second floor of their shared estate. "Yes, my love, what is it?" an out of breath Alexander inquired as he reached the top of the stairs.

"Would you please talk to them? I just don't have the strength today. I have to go to the bank and extend our line of credit, then try to negotiate lower prices with our Canadian and Mexican suppliers. Then, there's that pedophile over on West Fourth Street that I have to slice up and send to hell. Which reminds me. You haven't sent a damned soul to our lord in nearly a week. Do ya think it might be a good idea to get off of your British ass and contribute a little? I've done eight already this month!"

"Well, about that, my love," Alexander sheepishly replied. "There is actually something that I wish to speak to you about. I have an idea."

"Well, just save it until I get out of the shower. If it isn't all clogged up again with their hair!" Melissa stormed down the hallway and slammed the bathroom door. Alexander let out a frustrated sigh when he heard her yell out, "Yep! Clogged again! Just look at all this hair! Where's the damned plunger!"

He shook his head solemnly as he looked upon the various blouses, stockings, discarded bottles of make-up, and pom-poms that were strewn about the hallway. He walked several feet down the cold marble and lightly knocked on a bedroom door. "Ladies?" he cautiously asked. "May I please come in? I wish to speak with you."

"Yeah sure, why not," a female voice replied. Alexander grabbed the doorknob, then wiped his hand that was covered in chewing gum. He sighed once again and entered the room to find four teenage girls sitting in a heap of pizza boxes, soda bottles, soiled clothing, and teen magazines. "Yeah, what's up? You got our breakfast ready yet?" one of the young women asked without looking up from painting her toenails.

"No, I do not. I need to speak with you. All four of you. We have now been here for five weeks and not once have any of you lifted a finger to assist around our home. In fact, you four are creating quite the mess and I am here to tell you that your selfishness and laziness ends now. Your actions are placing a strain on our marriage and that, ladies, I simply won't tolerate. Now, you will get up, get dressed, and clean this home from top to bottom. I want to be able to see my reflection in the shining floors by the time I get home. Do you all understand?"

All four girls began laughing before one of them replied, "Oh yeah? What are you going to do about it? You can't send us back to Hell, 'cause, like, that'll piss off Satan. So, just go make us our breakfast and leave us alone old man. We're busy."

Alexander took a deep breath and exhaled heavily. His face darkened and his eyes turned black before he said, "Missy, Buffy, Sparkles, and Trish. Listen to me very carefully. You are correct. I am unable to send you to Hell. But, believe me ladies, I am more than capable of making your lives hell on Earth. Every moment. Every breath. Everything that you do will be met with excruciating pain. I can perform operations on each of you that will never heal and will provide you with an eternity of suffering."

The four young women rolled their eyes and went back to their primping. "Yeah, like we didn't experience pain in Hell. How original. Whatevs. Now go make us our breakfast." Alexander clenched his fists and began again. "Or I can ground you. No more dates with the local high school boys. No more cheeseburgers. No more pizza and soda and potato chips. No more chewing gum. And no more of your internets. Now, as I said, you will get up, get dressed, and clean this home from top to bottom. I want to be able to see my reflection in the shining floors by the time I get home. Or do you really want to try *Jack the Ripper*?"

Missy, Buffy, Sparkles, and Trish stared at one another with widened eyes then looked at the determined face of Alexander. "Fiii-iiine!" they bellowed out. "We're getting up! Gaaaaawd! This is soooo unfair!"

Melissa emerged from her bedroom wearing a form-fitting, dark blue business suit. She smiled as she passed four sweaty young women who were placing clothing into laundry baskets, sweeping, mopping, and dusting. She entered the study to find her demonic husband sipping tea and reading the paper. "Nice job with the girls," she said as she poured herself a cup. "Thank you," Alexander replied. "I can be a bit persuasive when I put my mind to it. Which brings me to the topic that I wish to discuss. I know you are quite aware of what this nazi regime is implementing in this country. All the pain and suffering and death that they are destined to create throughout the entire world. So many souls who have been converted from the pious to the damned. Millions of them. And, of course, their corrupted leaders. They are all paving their road to Hell. So, my dear, I have just one question for you. Would you like to assist me in helping a few of them along on their journey? Would you enjoy sending some sadistic fascists to Hell?

Melissa took a sip of her tea, placed the porcelain cup on its saucer, and smiled. "I sure as hell would, my love. And I know just where to start. Just look at this," she said as she excitedly retrieved a scrapbook album from her attaché case. "Look at all of these men who have disappeared. Or died in unexplained circumstances. And women are disappearing too. Their abusive husbands or boyfriends get whacked, then the women disappear for a couple weeks, then they return home. Oh, and suddenly their gardens are fabulous. And here's another weird report. Look at this article. I know this is a conspiracy-theory tabloid, but I think this may be real. There are reports of zombies being held in a mall in Galesburg. I've been monitoring this ever since our wedding, and I think I know what's going on. No, I *know* what's going on. Maybe it's my natural female intuition combined with my new hellish abilities to see into men's souls, but I'm just sure of this. This is the work of witches and mediums. Somehow, they are banding together and taking on the world-wide patriarchy. I'm just sure of it."

Alexander chuckled and said in a dismissive tone, "Oh, tut, tut, my dear. I do believe that your feminine mind might still be a bit cluttered from your experience in Hell. Witches and mediums?

Together? Perish the thought. Everybody knows that those two groups loathe one another. No, I do not believe that there is any merit to this. Now, getting back to *my* idea…" Alexander looked into the fuming blue eyes of his beloved wife and gulped. He suddenly realized how condescending his response had been. And Melissa was not someone that he wished to upset. For multiple reasons. "Um, I mean, well," he began stammering. "Perhaps it *might* be worth at least looking into. There certainly have been stranger things that have occurred than witches and mediums banding together. So, yes. Yes, my love. Let us look into this."

"I already have," a still annoyed Melissa bluntly replied. "It seems to have begun in Plymouth. A teenage witch and a teenage medium became friends. Really close friends. That was the first domino to fall. Since then, I believe that the mediums and witches have been successful in bringing vengeful spirits from Eden to Earth to lead a war against the dominant patriarchy. I think we need to find them. And join them. And help them send dark souls to our lord, Satan."

"Two teenage girls, you say?" Alexander mused. "Yes, if you are correct then our services may very well be of service to them." He then looked at the sweaty, bustling bodies of Missy, Buffy, Sparkles, and Trish and smiled. "Yes, perhaps we could offer our services to them. Well, for a *price*, heh, heh, heh."

"And find you we did," Alexander stated to the awestruck pair of friends. "We located the two of you here and, well, you see, we are able to transport ourselves to wherever evil men are, and so here we are. At your service. But, as I mentioned, for a price."

"Okaaaay," Naomi stated while stroking her chin. "So, if you can see into men's souls, prove it. Start with this guy. Is he good or is he bad? Because if he's good, we need to let him go and invite him to join us. Of course, he doesn't have to join us. He could just go back home and go back to work or whatever. But he could join us if he wanted. But if he's bad, then we have to torture him and keep him locked up and stuff like that. We've been thinking of all sorts of cool ways to torture evil men, haven't we Morgan?"

"We sure as hell have," Morgan replied. "Okay, you two. Show us what you've got."

Melissa smiled, retrieved a glistening scalpel from her medical bag, and stared at the bound man's crotch. Alexander took one look into the man's eyes and said with regret in his voice, "I'm so sorry, my love. I know how you were looking forward to castrating this one, but it is not to be. Just look into his eyes." Melissa looked into the hopeful eyes of the man, shook her head in disappointment, and said, "Yeah, dammit. He's a good person. You can let him go. Shit. Who else you got locked up in this joint?"

"Huh. That was kinda fun," Melissa gleefully stated as she fed a fifth severed phallus to a snarling German Shepherd. "So, we got a deal or what? We'll help you weed the good from the bad and all *you* need to do is take these four snotty bit…um…*girls* off our hands. Deal?"

Morgan and Naomi went to a dark corner of the room and began whispering to one another. Alexander and Melissa looked up at the ceiling and whistled as they waited. "Um, any day now girls!" an impatient Melissa shouted. "We got a deal, or what?"

"Well," Morgan began. "I'm not sure this is our call to make. I mean, your audition went great. You totally identified the bad souls. And Melissa, you are an artist with that scalpel, but, um, you see…"

"Well, what seems to be the problem, young ladies?" Alexander inquired. "Do you need more proof of our abilities?"

"No, it's not so much *that*," Naomi answered. "It's just that our Brigade of Persistence has been put together to, y'know, take out evil men and overthrow the world-wide male patriarchy. I mean, it just seems a bit, um, counterintuitive to include Jack the Ripper, y'know? I mean, you, like, murdered innocent women and stuff. And maybe you're nice *now*, but still, you have a reputation. It might cause a little bit of dissent in our ranks, if you know what I mean. I'm just not sure we're the ones to make this decision. I think we need Queen Zenobia for this."

"Oh!" an infuriated Melissa shouted. "So, just because he's a serial killer we can't get in? This is ridiculous! This is discrimination! *He* isn't a murderer! *I* am not a murderer! We're just, um, what's the phrase I'm looking for, baby?" "Emotional aggressiveness impaired," Alexander contributed. "Yeah! That's it!" Melissa continued. "We're emotional aggressiveness impaired and you are discriminating against us because of our impairment! This isn't fair!"

"Melissa, darling, please calm down," Alexander interjected. "I'm sorry ladies. We understand the difficult position that this puts you in. I knew that one day my being Jack the Ripper might place a damper on my vocational pursuits. We are merely here to offer our assistance. If you think that speaking with your Queen Zenobia would help in this matter, then we would be delighted to do so."

"Well, hey there Poindexter! What in the hell are *you* doing here? Well, since you're here, how 'bout whipping me up a gin and tonic, *hmmmm?* The stuff's in the kitchen. Chop, chop mister! Lil' ol' me needs to get her buzz on!"

"Hello again, Maddy," Alexander stated as he, his wife, and four disgruntled cheerleaders entered the home of the ladies Cabot. "I thought that we might meet again."

"Who in the hell is *this* joker?" Vince grumbled. "And what is this meeting about? I've got a game coming on in less than an hour, so let's get this over with."

"What do you mean, 'who is this joker'?" Maddy asked. "You should know. He was bartending at your place the night that I picked up my first victim here. Yeah, that was a fun night. Picked up a corrupt insurance executive, lured him to a construction site, then BASH! POW! CHOP! And one fewer dickhead insurance execs to worry about."

"Oh man, that sounds fun," Erick replied. "I wish I coulda been there." "Yeah, me too," Maddy answered while Josie rolled her eyes at her demented parents. Vince looked at Alexander once again and said gruffly, "Never seen him before in my life. And he sure as hell has never worked for me."

"What are you talking about?" Maddy retorted before Alexander placed his hand upon her shoulder and whispered, "Do not worry about it. It is a lengthy story and one that you can read about in a delightful book about me called *Satan's Shopkeeper*. It really is a good read. I think you'll enjoy it."

"Whatevs. I heard that author is a dick," Maddy stated as Lori, Sophia, Morgan, and Naomi entered the living room. "Okay, it's nearly eleven. Where is Queen Zenobia?" Lori inquired. "Oh, she and the others in her primary council will be here soon, dear," Sophia answered. "And I do hope Grandmother Agatha will bring her cobbler. It really is to die for."

At that moment, a giant plume of dark red fog erupted in the middle of the room. Through the haze, four female figures began to take shape. "Who *dares* to summon Queen Zenobia and her council?" a woman's voice boomed causing porcelain nicknacks to tremble and Larry the Leopard to cower behind the couch. "Oh Goddammit, Queen Z!" Connor stated. "Could we not go through all the theatrics every time and just get this over with?"

"Yeah, okay, sorry," Queen Zenobia stated as Agatha, Sruja, and Minnie Marples giggled behind her. "Alright, let's get this shindig on the road. Agatha, would you like to get us started?" "Why yes, my queen," Agatha dutifully replied. "We are here to determine whether Alexander Picklesbee and Melissa Bartlesworth are worthy to join our Brigade of Persistence. Does anyone have any objections to continuing? Hearing none, we may proceed, my queen."

"Cool. You really are a stickler for rules, aren'tcha, Agatha," Zenobia stated as she settled into her comfy chair near the television. "Okay, I've read the briefs, and I think I understand the gist of this whole thing. Basically, are we doing our movement a disservice by allowing Jack the Ripper into our little gang. Is that it? Alright you two. Make your case. And...what is that incredible *smell*?"

"I'm sorry for the distraction, my queen," Agatha answered. "I'm just warming up my cobbler in the oven. Please proceed." "Yeah, let's get this over with and have some cobbler!" a joyful Sophia yelled out.

Following a detailed explanation of his and his wife's exploits, Alexander concluded with, "So you see, my queen, we most certainly have made some mistakes in our lives. And after-lives. But we have learned from those, um, errors in judgement. And, as I mentioned, we are now prohibited from killing anyone who might be remotely considered a candidate to go to Heaven. That would make Satan very cross with us, and we would be permanently banished from the Earth and spend a torturous eternity in Hell. And we certainly do not wish that upon anybody. Well, perhaps on the dark souls, but that goes without saying. So, I will once again state that it would be our honor to assist you in identifying those dark souls and sending them to our lord, Satan. I, um, rest my case. Or something."

"So, you're now a servant of Satan, huh?" Queen Zenobia asked while looking at her dingy gladiator helmet. "Yeah, okay. If Satan is vouching for you two and allowing you to roam the Earth unattended, I guess it's good enough for me. You know, Satan really gets a bad rap. I mean, he has this reputation for being all evil and shit, but he's actually a really nice guy. Unless you're a brutal, bigoted asshole. He's a big dick to *them*. Literally. But to everybody else, he's pretty cool. But man, does that sonofabitch cheat at cards! So let that be a lesson to you all! Do not, under any circumstances, start playing cards with Satan. He'll cheat and win the tunic right off your back! I've learned that the hard way. That was a humiliating night, let me tell ya. The drunken orgy was kinda fun though. Anyway, yeah, alright. You're in. You two can team up with Josie. She can keep an eye on you."

"Wait, what?" An astonished Josie complained. "So, I have to bodyguard Naomi, help weed out good souls, keep my impulsive parents from killing people, and *now* I have to watch *these* two? I'm just a fifteen-year-old girl! This is too much pressure!"

"And what about our four teenage, um, *friends*, my queen?" Melissa awkwardly inquired. "Are you willing to take *them* off our hands?"

Queen Zenobia looked into the kitchen at the four self-absorbed, tittering cheerleaders, rolled her eyes, and said, "Sure. Why the hell not. I think I have an idea of how we can use them. We'll have Josie look after them too."

"Oh my God! You people are infuriating!" Josie screamed as she stomped up the stairs. "Oh, my," Zenobia stated while trying to spit-shine her helmet with her crimson cloak. "Teenagers. Am I right?"

Alexander and Melissa were smiling and shaking the hands of their new colleagues when Alexander was suddenly slapped on his backside. "Good game, Poindexter!" Maddy declared. "Welcome to the family! Now where are we at with that whole gin and tonic situation, *hmmmm?*

CHAPTER 20

HUH. WELL, THAT WAS EASY

Elder Himler was solemnly changing his piss-stained pants once again. The Nationalist Societies throughout the world had long understood the danger that a united front of evolved women posed to the dominance of their male patriarchies. But they had also long believed that by keeping many women submissive and sowing hatred between the few existing witches and mediums that their reign would be eternal. And even if they *were* to unite and somehow evolve millions more women, the political, economic, and militaristic dominance that the patriarchy wielded would be far too much for them to overcome. They would be silenced and crushed into brutal submission should they ever attempt a true uprising.

But now, as Elder Himler heard reports of a sixth small town being overrun by zombies, he realized that they had been wrong on all counts. The reports of hordes of zombies invading small communities without being detected and eating many of the local men were horrendous. The remaining men, women, and children who survived the onslaught of the undead simply disappeared. They had no idea to where. The men's military could not detect their whereabouts. Nor were they of any use against the zombies. No matter how large of a force that was sent into battle, their advanced killing machines and highly trained soldiers were immediately taken out by unseen forces and strange weather events. And deadly, flying emojis for some unexplained reason. Smoldering remnants of their military might lay strewn in the serene fields outside of the devastated towns and were now as useless as a petulant child's discarded toys.

But at least conditions in this country and Europe seemed manageable compared to reports from other regions of the world. Throughout Asia, the Middle East, South America, and Africa the entirety of the female populations were rounding men up. They were rounding them up from small villages and major cities. They were rounding them up from their boardrooms and their farms and their halls of government. Millions upon millions of women were rounding up millions upon millions of men. Only to then disappear into dense forests or swamps or into the middle of the desert. While zombies were distracting this nation's Nationalist Society on the home front, their contemporaries in other lands were being soundly defeated. And it all happened in the blink of an eye. The attacks came without warning as millions of men were subdued and disappeared into parts unknown. The women disappeared also, leaving ghost towns throughout many regions of the world. But their disappearance had been brief. It now appeared that many of these women and half of the men had suddenly returned once again from nowhere and were now assuming the levers of power and control in their societies. Women were now in control over their regions' infrastructure. Their electrical grids and water systems and health care systems were now in the caring hands of evolved women. They had assumed control over their economic institutions. And of their governments. And of the militaries which were now being dismantled.

"Stupid bitches," the bald, slithery Himler muttered to himself as he looked in his closet for a clean pair of slacks. "Why are you dismantling your military? Of course, the military capabilities of all those other nations combined pale in comparison to *our* might. But it is your only means of defense. It will now be so easy for us to take over the world. Once we have crushed this silly little rebellion here, of course. Yes, take out the subhumans for us, won't you? It only empowers us. It only empowers the world's Anglos to achieve our ultimate goal of world domination, heh, heh, heh."

Himler shook his head in disgust at his bare closet and at the heaping laundry hamper that was overflowing with his piss-stained trousers. "Why has my laundry not been done!" he bellowed. A dutiful, shaking White man came running into Himler's bedroom. "I-I-I'm so sorry, my lord," the wormy Elder Lee stammered. "Our entire housekeeping department has been deported upon your orders last month. Remember? And we cannot find any Anglos who are willing to labor for long hours for the pittance that we pay. I understand that we believe those sorts to be rapists, and murderers, and less than human, but they turned out to be essential, hard-working people who wanted nothing more than to earn a living and build a safe and fruitful life for their children."

Himler slapped Lee in the face and screamed, "That is not true! They are vile! Anybody who is not a White male is vile! They are not to be depended upon! They are not to be trusted! They are not worthy of living in this country! I have known that ever since eighth grade when that little bitch Ana Rodriguez turned me down for the dance! I knew then that none of them were worthy to be on my arm! None of them were worthy to breathe the same air as I! None of them were worthy to share in the prosperity of our great nation! None of them! Ana was just the first.

"Ooooh, I can see her now in her pretty little dress pointing and laughing at me with her dark-skinned friends. Yes, they all mocked my long face and premature baldness while standing by the punch-bowl having a grand old time. Well, how grand of a time are they having *now* as they watch their loved ones be kidnapped by masked men and sent off to torture prisons. It has taken me all these long years, but I am finally getting my revenge against her and her tight-fitting sweaters and little, short skirts and pouty lips. Reject *me*, will you? Well, *I* shall reject *you*, Ana! And all others *like* you! You will be rounded up and tortured and murdered! Now go find me some pants! And a clean shirt! And convene the rest of the elders! I now know exactly what needs to be done! I know how to put the fear of God into the hearts of these bitches while taking over the rest of the world!"

The 'Listening' Emoji transmitted Himler's demented diatribe back to the home of the ladies Cabot where Zenobia, Minnie Marples, Sruja, and Agatha were literally rolling on the floor in a fit of laughter. "Are you kidding me?" Zenobia roared. "All of this hatred and violence towards people just because he got turned down by a girl in the eighth grade? Wow. I mean, I know he looks like he could shed his skin at any moment but still, thin-skinned much?"

"Oh, I know," Agatha replied. "How utterly pathetic. I knew that man was disturbed more than most, but this is quite ridiculous." "No, it isn't," Sruja interjected in her native Hindi. "This is a microcosm of what is wrong with *all* men like him. The dark souled men strut around and act all powerful. They build armies and march them around. They harass and bully and suppress anyone who is different from themselves. And why? Because it is all a projection. They must project power to conceal the fact that they know they are worthless, untalented boils on the face of the Earth. Any time a man shows off his big, long, hard gun, it is a projection of his inner weakness. Any time a man harasses a woman, it is a projection of his unworthiness for true companionship. And any time a man throws a military parade in his own honor, it is a projection of, well, um."

"That's a projection of a *lotta* things, toots!" Minnie Marples squealed. "Let's see here. It's a projection of a small, well, you know. And a projection that his daddy didn't love him enough. And a projection that he knows that no cares about him. And a projection that he is unworthy of true love and companionship. And a projection of his self-absorbed greedy nature. And a projection of his lack of intelligence. And a projection of..."

"Yeah, yeah, yeah," Zenobia chimed in. "Yeah, it's a projection of *all* that stuff. A shrink would have a field day with a man like that. But who cares? As far as *I'm* concerned, it's a projection of him being an asshole. Just like this Himler. Just a bunch of pathetic little insignificant assholes who cause significant damage to innocent people. Come on, let's listen in. Minnie, send your 'Listening' Emoji into their board room. This really should be entertaining. Oh, and Agatha, is there any of that cobbler left?"

Elder Himler stood behind his lectern in the front of the board room wearing bright blue polyester shorts and a yellow T-Shirt that read 'I'm with stupid'. "All right, gentlemen," he said through his snake-like lips. "I warned you all, and now it is happening. Women have successfully evolved into witches and mediums, and they are overthrowing the patriarchies throughout the world. But it would appear that they are not yet powerful enough to launch a significant attack in this nation or in Europe. Otherwise, they would be doing much more here than these silly zombie attacks. This is all fine. The Anglo nations have always been destined to clean up the refuge that resides in other regions. They have done our work for us. And now, it is time to show them the true power that we wield. Once they see how powerful we truly are, they will bow to us. We shall capture them. Use them for breeding and our gratification. Harness their abilities for our own means. And also, to do our laundry. They think that they have succeeded in overthrowing the patriarchies. They are too stupid to see that these apparent victories shall actually serve as their downfall. All we need to do is demonstrate our might. And now, we shall do that. Contact our puppets in the government. Tell them to launch."

"Um, launch what?" Elder Lee meekly inquired. "What do you think, you idiot?" Himler sneered back. "Launch the nukes. We are going to nuke every country that these uptight bitches in their tight little sweaters have taken over. Africa. The Middle East. Asia. South and Central America. Nuke all of them. I want every woman, man, and child to disintegrate. I want every plant and animal dissolved in a fury of hellfire! I want to destroy everything so that we may rebuild it in our own glorious image!"

"Um," Elder Lee interjected. "But, if we do *that*, especially on a global scale, won't that cause radioactive fallout to impact us and Europe? Won't we be subjected to the blotting out of the sun and a nuclear winter? Won't *our* plant and animal life die as well leaving us with nothing to eat? And won't the radiation be carried here on the trade winds causing us to contract cancer?"

"Pffft," Himler replied through a sly grin. "Where in the hell did you hear *that* bullshit?"

"Well, sire," Lee answered while avoiding eye contact. "Um, it's, um, y'know. Like, science or something."

"Science," Himler scoffed. "You truly are an idiot, Lee. I can't believe that you actually buy into that leftist science bullshit. It has all been a lie, Lee! A lie perpetrated upon the masses to keep us White men from the prosperity that we are entitled to! There *is* no climate change! Windmills DO cause cancer! Vaccines DO cause autism! And there sure as hell is no nuclear winter! And even if there were, God shall protect us. You should pray more, Lee. You really should. Starting now."

Himler nodded to a nearby guard who nodded back, stepped behind Elder Lee, and plunged a dagger through his ears. Lee's dying body convulsed for several seconds before slumping onto the grey marbled floor. "And *that's* what you get for not having faith, gentlemen," Himler dully remarked. "Now, call our puppets. Launch the nukes. We'll watch all the witches and mediums in those regions be reduced to ashes in moments. And we'll watch all the mediums and witches in *this* country and Europe wet their pretty little panties at the sight, heh, heh, heh. I do wonder what color panties *Ana* will be wearing when she witnesses my might! Yes, I must find her. I am looking forward to her being on her knees in front of me, heh, heh, heh."

"Well, *that* took a turn!" Zenobia exclaimed. "Shit. Maybe we should have waited to take out the other regions until this country was at full strength. Ah, well. Hindsight is 20/20 as they say. Screw it. Morgan and Naomi. Do we have enough evolved women here? Do we have enough witches and mediums trained up to disable their military?"

Naomi and Morgan pulled out a red binder and began looking through their data as they whispered to one another. They snapped their fingers, put on their sunglasses, and Morgan said through her adolescent giggles, "Yup, we're ready to go. We haven't got *all* the women in this country evolved yet, but we have enough. We know where all of their military installations are everywhere in the world, and we have members of our brigade ready to take them out. All we need is a green light from you, Queen Z."

"Well, you girls have got it!" Zenobia cheerfully replied. "Your project is green lit! Let's get this shit done! And where are those mouthy cheerleaders? Missy, Buffy, Sparkles, and Trish! Get your little asses down here! I've got an assignment for you and…oh! Don't you *dare* give me that look girls! I'll knock that look right off of your face and into the next century! And don't you roll your eyes at me either! Just listen to me and do what you are told. Josie is going to be in charge of your mission."

"Ah, shit," Josie muttered under her breath as she sat on the couch with Gabriel and Larry the Leopard. "And I don't need any lip from you either, little missy!" Zenobia roared at the teenage genius. "Just get this shit done, alright? I've got to get to more *important* business. Sruja, have you found me a selection of outfits for me to try on for the wedding? I can't decide if I want a nice flowing gown, or a tight little number to show off my figure or…" She stopped to chuckle as she heard *Chicka-Chicka-Wow-Wow* come from a red head that was buried in the refrigerator. "Yeah, you're right, Maddy. I don't want anything too sexy. I wouldn't want to show up the brides on their special day and…Trish! Get your ass back here! You can do your nails later! Oh, dear lord. I should have known better than to strike a deal with the devil."

Morgan and Naomi held hands while holding the ancient book of incantations. It was glowing green while Morgan swept her hand over the perfect inscription. Her eighteen-year-old lips curled up in a devilish smile as she closed her eyes and forcefully said, "Tempus advenit pro nostra maxima pugna. Sorores ubique unite. Invocate spiritus sorores nostras et amicos nostros in natura ad oppugnandum maleficos et privandum eos horrida armamentis (The time has arrived for our greatest battle. Sisters everywhere unite. Call upon our spirit sisters and our friends in nature to attack the evildoers and deprive them of their horrid weaponry)". The message was received by strategically placed members of the Brigade of Persistence throughout the world. Millions of women lovingly held hands with one another, smiled, and echoed Morgan's incantation. "Tempus advenit pro nostra maxima pugna. Sorores ubique unite. Invocate spiritus sorores nostras et amicos nostros in natura ad oppugnandum maleficos et privandum eos horrida armamentis."

At every military base that was run by the Anglo Nationalist Society, dark silhouettes of women appeared on the horizon. The spirits cackled as they flew closer to their destination. Their cackling intensified as disoriented men began shooting randomly at the swift, foggy flying forms. Their bullets were greeted by a barrage of dagger emojis that flew out of the giddy spirit's mouths and into the flesh of howling men. The soulless male soldiers were cut down by the tiny, lethal cartoonish images while the female and kind-hearted male soldiers turned their arms against their former comrades. The shrieks of men wailing was overcome by the sound of huge tornadoes thundering through the buildings that contained the armaments of oppression. Huge, twisted metal shards that had once been tanks flew through the sky and crashed into the unforgiving earth.

Inside the missile silos, men frantically ran away from huge, fortified tree roots that had burst through the metal walls and wrapped themselves around the apocalyptic projectiles. Screaming men were crushed by tree roots the size of trucks against the exploding computers in their underground control centers.

Deep in the ocean, seaweed entangled submarines were being mangled by spiritually enhanced coral. The cries of drowning men went unheard as their metal coffins sank to their crypts on the floor of the ocean. Massive aircraft carriers and other aquatic vessels of war were turned over by monstrous tsunamis sending billions of dollars of machinery and thousands of men sinking into the watery abyss. Sharks and other aquatic carnivores were summoned by nearby witches to clean up whatever unfortunate survivors there might be.

Squadrons of planes scrambled to get off of the ground, only to be forced down in fiery crashes by torrential rain and wind. Those that remained grounded were disabled by fierce lightning strikes.

Summoned earthquakes swallowed up entire forts of weaponry causing sensational explosions to billow out of the enormous cracks in the ground. At military bases throughout the world, the pawns of the soulless were running. As was their blood. And it all happened in a blink of an eye. In the blink of an eye, the lethal toys of inhumane men were relegated to scrap by the unity of millions of humane women.

"W-what in the hell is happening?" Himler stuttered as drool and snot ran down his beleaguered face and onto his bright pink 'Daddy's Princess' T-shirt. He sat quivering on his throne as he heard the pained shrieks of his fellow elders echo throughout their complex. He heard a key frantically trying to open the door until a sweaty elder burst into the room. "Sire! It is all lost!" the panic-struck elder yelled out. "They have taken out all of our military installations! And they are here! The women are here! They areRRRRRRRR!"

His warnings were silenced as a perfectly aimed arrow pierced through his back and out his heart. The bloodied projectile landed in Himler's throne next to his right ear. Josephine Patricia Sommers Parker calmly strode into the room. She was wearing a skin-tight dark green vinyl cat suit and a wicked little smile upon her adolescent, freckled face. Her emerald eyes glowed as she said in a deep, menacing voice, "Okay, ladies. Time to take out the trash."

She was met with eerie silence and her confused green eyes began darting around the room. "I *said*, time to take out the trash!" she yelled out in an annoyed tone. "Hey! Where in the hell are you? I said, time to take out the trash! That's your cue!"

A young woman's voice yelled out from the hallway, "GAAAAAWD! Fine! Get off of our asses! I totally just broke a nail! What are you going to do about *that* Josie? Huh? I just got them done! It was like, fifty bucks or something! Are you gonna pay to get my nails done at the mall?"

"Yes," Josie responded through greeted teeth. "Fine. I'll take you to the mall to get your nails done. But first, it's time to take out the...

oh, screw it. This entire scene is toast. I feel like a complete idiot now. It was the perfect line, then you were supposed to come in looking all menacing and shit and haul his sorry ass off. Is that too much to ask for? Is it too much to ask for you to read the goddamned script?"

"What*ever*," an irritated Sparkles stated as she and her three BFFs strutted into the room. Their cheerleader uniforms were covered in sticky, bright red blood and the smell of iron permeated the room as a thick crimson liquid dripped from the ends of their razor-sharp pom-poms. Missy, Buffy, Sparkles, and Trish glared at the confused and trembling Himler. Josie stood there with her arms folded and rapidly tapped her size six left foot while impatiently waiting for the girls to complete their work.

"Okay," Buffy stated. "Like, you've gotta come with *us*, or *somethin'*, 'cause, like, Queen Zenobia is like *really* pissed at you or somethin'. I don't know. Just get your old ass up. I have a broken nail, and I need to get to the mall. We *are* still going to the mall, aren't we Josie? Like, you *totally* promised. And while we're there, we need some conditioner. And eye liner. And…oh! Where did you get your pink 'Daddy's Princess' T-shirt?"

"OMG it's soooo totally cute!" Missy agreed. "Oh! I just have to have one! Josie, can we, like, look for a 'Daddy's Princess' T-shirt when we go to the mall? *Pleeeease?* We'll *totally* be good and, like, *totally* do what you want. Okay? Go ahead. Like, do the line again. I *promise* we won't screw it up."

"Fine, let's try this again. It's really the perfect ending to this scene where I say something cool, then you four carry him off. Thank you, girls, for understanding how important this is to me. Okay, here it goes. This is going to be soooo cool," a delighted Josie replied as she unfolded her arms and shook her curly, copper head. She once again twisted her mauve lips into an evil little grin and said in a dark voice, "Okay, ladies. Time to take out the trash." She was once again met with silence. She looked behind her to find four mean-girl cheerleaders primping their blood-soaked hair and filing their bloody nails. "What the *hell*, guys? We *literally* just discussed this like thirty seconds ago."

"Oh, right," Trish answered. "Our cue. We totally, like, forgot. Soooooorrrry. But, like, can we *still* go to the mall?"

"Yes, we can still go to the mall," an infuriated Josie growled. "This is ridiculous. You girls are worse than dealing with my parents, and that's saying something. Just bag this douche up and throw him in the trunk of the van. Then we'll go to the goddamned mall. We may as well. This entire chapter is ruined anyway."

CHAPTER 21

WE INTERRUPT THIS BROADCAST FOR AN IMPORTANT MESSAGE

"Huh. Well, *that* was easy," the pajama-adorned Lori stated to her mother and daughter after blowing steam off of her freshly brewed coffee. "I mean, it seems *too* easy. If it was so easy to do this, then why in the hell didn't women rise up centuries ago? Why have we allowed ourselves to be ruled by hellish men? Have our rights stripped from us? Work for way less money? Not have dominion over our own bodies and health care choices? Why have so many of us allowed ourselves to be beaten and raped and humiliated? Why have we put up with the leering stares and inappropriate comments and pats on our asses in our workplaces? In some societies to be genitally mutilated? Be told who to marry? This world has been nothing but insanity for us for centuries! Why didn't we rise up before now?"

"Because this *hasn't* been easy," Sophia replied as she tightened the belt on her robe and took her place at the round Formica kitchen table. "None of this has been easy, dear. It was not easy for me to realize that witches were just as kind and valuable as I. It was not easy for me to embrace Victoria and truly love her. And it has not been easy for women throughout the world to unburden themselves of the indoctrination that other women were our competition and not to be trusted. Oh, I know there were plenty of women who were best friends and all of that. But deep down inside? They didn't trust their BFF any more than they would trust a common criminal. In the backs of our minds there was always the nagging thought that we should fear this woman sitting next to me. That she would tear me apart at the first opportunity if I had something that she desired. I should know. I held those exact same beliefs. Regardless of whether the woman was a witch or not.

"That was the design of the cruel men of the world. To keep us divided so that they were free to dominate us. They held the levers of power and used them to indoctrinate us into mistrust of one another. I mean, we even get blamed for all of the sin in the world because Eve ate some apple or some such bullshit. If the starting point is women being blamed for the sins of all humanity, well maybe we shouldn't be surprised at our systemic oppression. So, my dear daughter, this was *not* easy. It had been easy for many of us to get along on the surface. It was *not* easy to move past getting along and to genuinely trust and love and care for that other woman. That was not easy. It was especially difficult for those poor unfortunate women who became so brainwashed that they actually bought into their man's fascist bullshit. But even they were able to see the light. To see the truth about their persecution. To see the potential of their strength through their natural instincts of love and humanity. It all began with an example. The love between two friends. One, a medium. The other, a witch. Yes, our Morgan and Naomi were the example that allowed we women to unite. And then, to bring others along. Once we had cleared that hurdle, then everything else fell into place. *Then*, it became easy. Once women embraced one another in their hearts and trusted one another implicitly, they were ready to be evolved. They were ready to tap into their innate power as a medium or a witch."

"Or a Fabula," Morgan added as she munched on a glazed donut. "Yes, of course," a chuckling Sophia replied. "Or in those most rare cases, a Fabula. The rest of this was indeed easy. Man's weapons of war never had a chance against us. They never had a chance against the power that comes from unity. True unity that is born out of true love and regard for one another. It wasn't our powers that achieved these decisive victories. It was our unity. Because, without our unity we would not have had our powers to wield. United we stand, divided we fall, as the saying goes. This is the perfect example of it. Throughout history there are plenty of examples of sadistic regimes quickly falling to the united masses. Perhaps not *this* quickly and not on *this* scale, but it has happened many times over. So, this should not come as a surprise to any of us. This has always been possible. Our unity gave us power. And that power allowed us to topple tyranny. In other words, we kicked their goddamned asses and…oh, wait. Turn the TV up. I want to hear this."

Morgan picked up the remote and turned the volume up on the small television that was resting on the kitchen counter. A bubbly Black female anchor was saying, "And we are expecting an address from Queen Zenobia herself in just a few minutes. No matter what channel you are watching or listening to, her address will be simulcast everywhere throughout the world. And, because Queen Z is sooooo cool, she will be speaking to each of us individually in our native tongues."

"And speaking of tongues," the pale-skinned, brunette co-anchor added. "While we are waiting, I need to tell our audience about a new taste experience that will positively delight your tongue! It is called 'Agatha Cabot's Old-Timey Cobbler' and it is the best cobbler you will ever taste! I tried a sample last night at her Patriarchy Downfall Watch Party, and it was to die for! It is so rich and delicious. Available soon in supermarkets everywhere. So, try 'Agatha Cabot's Old-Timey Cobbler'. No matter what tongue you speak, it will surely melt on it."

"What the hell!" an infuriated Sophia bellowed. "Grandmother Agatha is mass producing her cobbler? She promised *me* that recipe! I was going to sell it exclusively at the diner! Oh, I'm going to have a little chat with that old bitch the next time I see her."

"So much for unity," Morgan whispered to her chuckling mother.

"And here she is now!" The ebony anchor announced. "Ladies and, um, a few gentlemen, may we present to you Queen Zenobia!" The picture turned to bright green static before the image of a woman wearing a gladiator helmet came into focus. She scowled at her audience while wearing a frightful grin. She opened her mouth to address her worldwide Brigade of Persistence.

"Yo, bitches! Wazzup! I just flew in from Eden, and boy are my wings tired! *Ba-dum-bum-ching*. It's so cool to address you all. Well, maybe not you," she stated while staring at a particular woman who was watching from Plymouth. "Maddy told me *all about* you. Wouldn't share your garlic bread, huh? Yeah, I'm keeping my eye on you. But to everybody else, it's a pleasure! Alright, let's get down to business. As you may have noticed, oh hell, as you all have participated in, the international male patriarchy has been defeated. Soundly. So, good game, ladies!"

"Ah shit, why did she have to say that," Lori muttered before being slapped on her backside. "Yeah! Good game, Lori!" Maddy exclaimed as she and Erick entered the kitchen. "What are we watching? Queen Z? Booooring. I've heard enough of her shit. Where's the remote? Let's see here. How's about a little murder show to start the day off right? Nope. Queen Z. Nope. Also Queen Z. What the hell? Is she on every damned channel?"

"Yes," Morgan answered. "Now sit down and shut up. We're trying to hear this." "Daaaamn, I guess *someone* took her bitch pill this morning," Maddy commented as she poured a cup of coffee for her laughing husband.

"Alrighty folks," Zenobia continued. "Let me tell you what is happening. All of societies' institutions have been taken over by women. The governments, the militaries, the corporations, the religions. Everything is controlled by women. So, what's next? So glad you asked! This is the exciting part! First, elections will be held all over the world for representatives to a newly formed Ministry of Humanity. Or MoH, for short."

"Moh?" Maddy exclaimed. "What in the hell is 'MoH? That's the dumbest Fu-uh-damned name I've ever heard! Gimme the phone. We need a cooler name than that."

"So, anyway, MoH is going to oversee and coordinate cooperation between all the nations of the world. We are going to share everything! You in a country that needs water? No problem! A neighboring country will help you out. Need grain? Look no further than to another hemisphere. Science and technology will be shared equally. Medical services. Education. Financial prosperity. Everything will be shared. All boats are going to be lifted by our new world order and...oh, sorry. That's my phone. I hate these things. Minnie, how do I answer this stupid thing? Oh, *that* button? Okay. Yes, hello. Z-String here. I'm kinda busy at the moment and...oh, hi Maddy. What is it? Not cool huh? Makes no sense? Sounds stupid? You got a better suggestion? Naw. I don't like 'Murder, Inc.' Because it's already been done and I don't want to steal someone else's idea! You got something else? Hey, I like that. Alright thanks. Yeah, good game to you too, kid.

"Okay, sorry about that folks. I've got breaking news for you. This just in, our international collaborative will no longer be called the Ministry of Humanity. Maddy didn't like it. From this point on it will be called the Parliament Of Women, or POW! Catchy right? So, for those of you taking notes, please just scratch out Ministry of Humanity and replace it with Parliament of Women. I'll wait for a moment."

During the brief pause, Minnie Marples appeared on the screen and whispered into Zenobia's ear. "Oh, great point M&M! Yeah, they probably do want to know about that. Yep, POW is our new collaborative. Which leads us to our male viewers out there. You see, POW can also stand for Prisoner of War. Which is what you are all about to become. Now, just calm down. I can feel your testosterone rising and you're getting all emotional and you want to crack open a beer and punch a wall. Just chill for a moment and let me explain. Now, many men have dark souls. They are self-absorbed and greedy and brutal against anyone that they perceive as a threat, which is pretty much everybody. And it has been largely *those* types of men who have been running everything through their patriarchies. That is why there has been endless war and bigotry and suffering and death.

Yep, it's been because of *those* assholes and *those* are the dicks we just overthrew. Um, literally.

"But that certainly isn't *all* men. Many men are kind-hearted and humane, and we got nothing against you. In fact, you will all be invited to join us in equality. Hell, we'll even let *you* decide what to do with your reproductive organs and will pay you equally. Pretty cool, huh? We don't *have* to do that, especially since none of *you* have any special connection to the spiritual realm or to nature, but we thought we'd be fair about this shit. Yes, women and men are going to work and live alongside one another in equality. But we do not want any dark souled men to slip through the cracks. I mean, they're everywhere, so I'm anticipating a few to come crawling out from under their rocks, but we sure as hell don't want them prancing around our new world order and screwing everything up.

"So, here's what's going to happen. Now, don't freak out. Just listen to me. Every man in the world is going to be rounded up and placed in holding cells. We have developed a system whereby every man will be processed. If you are a good soul, then no sweat. You will be immediately returned to your home without a scratch. You will be free to live your lives with the same rights and freedom as the women. Just a few days away, and everything will be okay. Shit, that's good. Hey, Minnie. Let's put that on billboards all over the world. You think that maybe you could conjure up some 'Painting' emojis and get that done? Yeah? Cool.

"Now, for those of you who are found to be *dark* souls...um... well let's just say that you might be staying with us for a bit longer. Or you might die. But listen, we're not going to kill *every* man that is a dark soul, as long as you behave. Um, probably. Now, we won't want you to breed, so castration is obviously going to happen. But we have a master surgeon who will perform the operation, and it won't be any big deal and...what's that Minnie? Alexander said that he and Melissa were going to make it as painful as possible? Well, shit. I don't want to tell them *that*. Ah screw it. I guess I already did. Okay gents, a slight correction. Yes, we do have a master surgeon but he's going to make it as painful as possible. But it won't last long and...*now* what? Alexander says he's also going to prolong their suffering for as long as possible? Well, sucks to be them, I guess. It would be nice if I could get these details in my intelligence briefings before I go on the air. I feel like a dumbass.

"Oh well, moving on. As I said, you're going to be castrated. We don't need your evil little seed being sprayed all over the place. Best to just clip your little hoses then it's no muss, no fuss. Now, we are still going to require a bunch of laborers, so that is what most of you will do. You'll work in the scorching hot fields and clean up after us and shit like that. Basically, you'll be our slaves and do all the shit that we don't want to do. Now, I want to make this perfectly clear. I'm not one to support abducting people and placing them into slavery, but *you* are the assholes who started this shit. *You* are the assholes who abduct people and make them slaves or send them off to concentration torture camps, so I don't want to hear any bitching! You started this shit and turnabout is fair play! We women have tried to be nice. Now we're gonna get naughty. So, tough shit. Cry me a damned river. You're lucky to still be alive.

"Okay, let's see here," Zenobia said as she reviewed her notes. "Uh, men taken to processing centers. Check. Good souls go home. Check. Castration. Check. Enslaved dark souled men. Check. I think that's everything, except, hey, Minnie! What is this Z,W,V at the bottom of this list?"

A giggling Minnie Marples appeared on-screen once again to whisper into Zenobia's ear. "Oh, right, I totally forgot that shit. Thanks, Minnie. And finally, *some* of you are going to be used as feed for zombies, vampires, and werewolves. I forgot that little detail. Okay gang! I think that's about it! Thanks everybody and looking forward to seeing all the men in the processing centers! Peace out!"

"Well, *that* sounds like a fun plan," Erick stated. "But we still get to feed the zombies, don't we?"

"Yes," Sophia answered. "Right after you feed my paying customers. Aren't you two scheduled to work the lunch shift at the diner today?"

"What?" Erick shouted. "You expect us to work at the diner with everything that's going on? This is ridiculous!"

"Yes, I do," Sophia sternly replied. "Now go get ready, you two. You need to get started on today's special. It's lobster bisque."

"No, it's not!" Maddy yelled as her size-six feet pounded up the stairs past the descending Connor. "I'm not making that smelly shit! Today's special is gonna be cheeseburger supreme! With my special sauce, heh, heh, heh. Oh, shit. I just thought of something. If there aren't going to be any asshole men in the world, whose food will I spit in? This is so disappointing."

"What's up *her* ass this morning?" Connor asked as he entered the kitchen. "What *isn't* up her ass *every* morning?" Lori answered before giving her fiancé a light peck on his rugged lips. The tender scene was interrupted by a knock on the door. "I'll get it," Connor stated before opening the front door.

"Well, good morning, Deputy Holloway. To what do we owe the pleasure?" he greeted. "Um, hi Detective. And maybe you haven't heard but it's *Chief* Gigi Hollway now. You know. Since the uprising and all. And that's why I'm here. I'm sorry, Detective, but I need to take you down to a processing center to get cleared."

"What?" Connor angrily responded. "I've already *been* cleared! Alexander already looked into my soul and said that I was one of the good ones! No! I'm not going! I have to call the florist and the photographer and then there's been a mix-up about our deposit for the venue! I have shit to do Depu...um...Chief!"

"Sorry, Detective, but I have my orders," Chief Holloway replied. "I know you've already been cleared, but that was before we developed the official paperwork. You need to be processed again and get your clearance papers. And make sure you don't lose them. You could be asked to present them at any time on the street."

"It's okay, Connor," Lori stated as she hugged her beau. "This shouldn't take long. It will just be a formality for you and Vince. You've got connections, remember? And I'll take care of all the wedding stuff today. Don't worry about it. Just go and have fun at the processing center, okay? I'll have dinner for you when you get back."

"Fine," Connor grumbled as vines from a houseplant that was under Chief Holloway's control stretched out and bound his hands. "But this better not take long. I hope to see you for dinner, dear."

The front door closed, and Lori turned to her family, "I feel really bad for the good men like Connor and Vince who are getting swept up in this. But at least we'll know which men are kind and trustworthy. And we know that *those* men will be treated fairly and have the exact rights as everyone else. Well, except for making sure to hang on to their clearance papers. This does make me wonder about the dark-souled men, though. I mean, where *exactly* do *their* souls go once they leave the Earth? I know we've just met Alexander and Melissa, but it *does* seem a bit far-fetched that all of those souls would go to an actual Hell. On the other hand, spirits and wind and plants just overthrew the entire world and freed us from those bastards, so what do I know? Maybe it's best if there *is* a Hell."

CHAPTER 22

I APPARENTLY MISS DOING SONG REFERENCES. AND OTHER STUFF HAPPENS TOO

"It's raining men!" Satan gleefully exclaimed as hundreds of thousands of dark souls plummeted into a fiery ocean of lava in hell. "Hallelujah, it's raining men! Just look at them all, Glen. All of these horrible, twisted little assholes who did nothing to contribute to humanity on Earth. All they did was abuse and torment and, in some cases, murder other people. Yeah, this is what I got into this business for. To see pricks like this get their comeuppance. Oh look! There's that asshole senator that stole Supreme Court nominees from a duly elected President! Wow, just listen to him squeal as his floppy skin fries in our lava ocean. And look! Here comes that dickhead who denied vaccines and caused way more deaths from infections and diseases than were necessary. And then, do you know where *those* souls go? Heaven, that's where! That dick is responsible for sending more souls to heaven before their time. And a lot of them are kids! That just pisses me off. Well, here he comes. Falling pretty fast. Let's see if he can stick the landing. Nope. Belly flop. I'll give it a 1.8. I think I know what I'm going to do with him too. He likes heroine? Well, how about an eternity of a needle stuck in your arm? How about an eternity of nightmares and psychological trauma? Yeah, I like that. Write that one down, Glen. I don't want to forget this shit.

Why didn't you bring a pencil and paper? I've told you a million times to always have a pencil and paper handy for when I get great ideas! Oh, Glen, you're the cutest demon in hell, but I swear you drive me nuts sometimes.

"And look at all of these soldiers who mindlessly followed their illegal orders and turned their weapons against innocent civilians. You thought following orders would get you out of this shit? Well, think again, assholes! Sinning is sinning. Just ask all these Gestapo dicks we have down here eternally being gassed and gasping for breath. Huh. I just noticed something Glen. No chicks. This is a total sausage fest. I mean, I knew Queen Zenobia could be persuasive, but I really thought that there would be *some* women who wouldn't make the cut. Women who were so down the fascist rabbit hole that there was no redemption for them. But no. Even *they* were able to see the light and become evolved into a witch or medium and join her Brigade of Persistence. Well, good for her, I guess. And I suppose I shouldn't look a gift horse in the mouth. I swing both ways anyway. And there are plenty of new assholes for me to rape. Literally and figuratively, heh, heh, heh. Like that one!

"Check out *that* pasty-faced, lying, worm of a man! Yeah, wrap yourself in the Bible while lying for your piece of shit dear leader. Support the kidnapping of innocent people. Take away emergency relief, and much-needed benefits, and health care. Be subservient to the Anti-Christ. And you're surprised that Jesus turned you away? Are you completely stupid as well as immoral and corrupt? Man, I'm gonna bang *you* harder than you bang your Bible. Oh, this is beautiful, Glen. All of these assholes who rose to power wrapped in their flag while spouting Bible verses are now realizing their true fate. And *that* is residing with me, Satan, in Hell, for all of eternity. I just love that shocked look on their face when they realize where they are. And, of course, all the screams from being tortured and shit. That always puts a smile on my face.

"But do you want to know why I'm *really* happy, Glen? Why today might be the most *glorious* day of my existence? Just listen for a moment. You hear that? Just the sounds of brimstone falling and explosions of fire and tortured souls screaming in agony. That's it. There's no insipid gossip. No back talk. And no goddamned gum snapping! They're gone, Glen! They're really gone! Those damned mean-girl cheerleaders Missy, Buffy, Sparkles, and Trish are finally out of my hair! Well, I don't actually have hair. Just calloused red skin, but you get my point. They are gone and it is time to rejoice in our peace and quiet and rainfall of horrible men! But there's so many of them that I'm afraid our intake processing system might get overwhelmed. Get me the phone Glen. I need to call Alexander and have him slow this shit down a little. I don't *know* where you put it, Glen! It's always supposed to be on the phone stand! Did you move it? Oh good, you found it. Under one of your throw pillows? Figures. You *always* just leave shit lying around. I swear Glen, if it wasn't for that cute, fanged smile of yours... just give me the phone."

"Of course, sire, I understand completely," Alexander was saying on his phone while seated in a dank interrogation room in Plymouth. "Yes, I can see how that may be quite taxing on your demons. No, no, we wouldn't want you to have to give out incentive bonuses so that they keep up. Not to worry, sire. Melissa and I and a delightful character from Morgan's book named Josie are in complete control now of the inflow to Hell. We are going from camp to camp, peering in men's souls, and determining which ones will be eventually sent to you. Yes, well, there are quite a number of them, but Melissa and I can provide due process to each man rather quickly, sire. Just a glance into their eyes and we are aware of all the atrocities that they have committed. Or haven't. It is always quite disappointing to us when we must let a man go free. But rules are rules, I suppose. No point in mistakenly sending the innocent to heaven before their time. Well, thank you sire. I am humbled that you are appreciative of our work. Yes, yes, I'll give Queen Zenobia your best and I'm *sure* she will be thrilled to be invited to your next poker game. Thank you again, sire, and feel free to call any time. Good day."

"Satan *again?*" a bored Melissa inquired as she filed her nails.

"What does he want *this* time? Couldn't find the ketchup in the convenience store or something?"

"No, no, nothing like that," Alexander answered as he wrapped his lanky arm around his beloved wife from hell. "I believe that I have finally got *that* little mix-up straightened out. I have no idea why he put that man in charge of my convenience store. For decades, I ran that shop with the utmost efficiency. And pride. And in just a few weeks, that dastardly man has destroyed all of my organizational systems. It really was quite a mess. In his interview, he kept going on about how he has the best brain and could get the best deals from suppliers and on and on and on. Despite his complete and utter incompetence at evil on Earth, Satan still gave him an opportunity. He, quite predictably, failed at that as well. He has been reassigned to a much more torturous eternal life, which is most appropriate if you ask me. And Satan now has some new perky, little demon running the shop. She seems to know what she's doing and everything seems to be running much more smoothly now."

"*Perky*, huh?" Melissa asked suspiciously. "I bet she's *cute too*, right?" "Oh, my darling Melissa," a chuckling Alexander answered. "What must I do to rid you of that little green devil in your soul? Perish the thought. No, Satan said that we need to slow down the process of sending him damned souls, that's all. Nothing important. And he wanted to invite Queen Zenobia to his next poker game. I doubt that she goes. She said that the last time she played with him, he cheated all evening. But that is in keeping with his character, I suppose. Now, shall we get back to work? We have millions of men all over the Earth to get through. Josie, would you please show our next contestant in?"

"You got it," Josie replied. She opened the door of the interrogation room and yelled out, "Next!" "Just get your ass in there or something," Trish ordered as she and her three BFFs shoved a quivering man into the dimly lit cell.

"Yes, hello there," Melissa greeted. "James, is it? This won't take but a moment James. Just look into my eyes." The sweating man stared into Melissa's pool of blue eyes then gasped as her pupils turned black. "Yep, that's what I thought. Guilty of wife beating, hit and runs, assault on police officers on January 6, and, um, jaywalking. Where do you want him assigned, Josie?"

"Um, let's put him in Group A and send him to El Salvador. We'll get him trained up for hard labor, work him until his arms fall off, then send him to hell."

"Come on you!" Buffy stated as she and the other cheerleaders removed the man from the room. "You voted to send innocent people to torture camps, huh? Like, how's *that* working out for *you* now? Dumbass. Get going. We got a lot of men to get through. And I need to get my nails done. And to take a shower. You damned souls are so, like, *gross*."

"Next!" Josie yelled out as another quivering man was placed on a hard metal chair in front of Alexander. He took one look into the man's eyes and said, "Oh dear, yes. Such perversions with this one. Child porn. Josie, would you please assign him to a group?"

"Oh, yeah," Josie gleefully snarled in response. "My parents *especially* love *you* assholes, so *you* get to go into *their* group. Group B. You'll be held until the last train to Galesburg. My parents will meet you at the station. You'll be there by 3:30. We've made your reservation. Then, um, you'll be fed to zombies in the mall. Next!"

Yet another sobbing man was forced onto the harsh metal chair. Melissa's eyes turned black, and she smiled at the man. "Oh good. I was hoping for one of *your* kind. Supposed men of God who use their power and influence to bilk naïve, innocent people out of their life savings. And what do you promise for that monthly stipend that they can't afford? Well, eternal bliss, of course. And *they* shall receive it. *You*, on the other hand, just punched *your* ticket to someplace else. Josie? Please tell this dick what he's just won."

"Well," a laughing Josie replied as she tried to mimic the voice of a game show announcer. "You sir have just won a one-way, all-expenses paid vacation to a luxurious retreat in scenic Transylvania! That's right! You and other contestants in Group C will be flown to Eastern Europe where you will reside in cramped, cold chambers until the festivities begin. Then, you will enjoy brisk exercise as you are hunted by werewolves in the dense forest. And finally, for being such a pompous, holier-than-thou creep, you will enjoy a lovely dining experience by being drained by blood-thirsty vampires. And all of this, because your sin was right! Now, get this asshole out of here. Next!"

The interrogation room door opened, and Sophia and Morgan entered followed by an angered Vince who stormed into the room, sat on the metal chair, and folded his arms in disgust. "Come on! Let's get this shit over with!" he bellowed while staring directly at Alexander.

"Hello, Vince," Alexander said. "Yes, you, of course, are cleared. Please just go out this door on the right and you shall receive your clearance paperwork. But do not go through the green door. You may be curious about what happens *behind* the green door, but you will *not* be pleased by what you will find there. Thank you for stopping by Vince. I may see you tonight at your fine establishment after I get off work. It has already been quite a long day, and I believe a small nip of gin might be in order."

"No, I'm not going," Vince replied in a determined voice. "I'm not going *anywhere* before I have my say. I'm all in favor of your overthrowing the patriarchy and torturing evil men and all that shit, but why are decent men like me and Connor and countless others forced into this indignity? Why must we sit here and prove ourselves to *you*? Lord knows, I'm not perfect. I've screwed up a few times. Hurt somebody's feelings. Maybe driven when I shouldn't have. Shit like that. But overall, I've lived a decent life. My actions have been mostly good, and I'm offended to have been rounded up and dragged here. I just wanted you to know that."

"I understand how you must feel, Vince," Sophia responded in an empathetic tone. "But we must be sure. Yes, you have done many good deeds as have *many* men in this world. But one's deeds are not the only determination of the purity of one's soul. No, it is not only one's deeds that determines one's final eternal destination, but the intent *behind* those deeds. For example, you could have two wealthy men each donate one-hundred-million-dollars to construct a children's hospital, which everyone can agree is a good deed. Exemplary, in fact. One of those men did it because he recognized the need for it in his community and genuinely wanted to help children and their families. He does not look for recognition. He wants nothing out of it except for the excellent treatment of ailing children.

"The other man, however, wants recognition. He wants his name emblazoned in big, gold letters all over the hospital. Perhaps he wants some investigation into his sordid business practices to go away. Or he wants the support of the community for his personal political aspirations so he can consolidate power and wealth. Two men with the exact same action. Two men with two very different intentions for performing that action. And two men who will meet two very different eternal fates. We must be careful, Vince. We must not judge men *only by their actions*. We must peer into their souls and understand the *intent behind those actions*. The truth of a man's character lies in their intent. Now, come on. This is over. Let's go home and help Lori and Connor with our wedding plans."

"Connor?" Vince asked. "I thought he was brought here too." "Oh, he was," Morgan answered. "I came down with him to check on how this process was working and to support him. He was pissed as hell, too. He was sent home an hour ago. See? Everything is working out fine. It's like Queen Z's billboards say, 'Just a few days away, and everything will be okay.'"

"Well, I still feel like a jackass, but fine. Let's go, Sophia. But I'm never going through this shit again," Vince grumbled as he and his fiancé left the room. "Ah, good, another satisfied customer," Alexander stated before getting back to business. "Josie, who is next?"

Josie opened the door and yelled out, "Next!" The four mean-girl cheerleaders dragged a struggling man into the room and threw him onto the floor. He leapt up and took a swing at Buffy who caught his fist in mid-air and crushed it. The pained man screamed then kicked at Sparkles. She casually moved to her left, then swung her pom-pom leaving several huge gashes in his face.

"I've seen enough," Melissa observed. "Just throw him behind the green door. He's in Group D. Going right to the Devil." Missy applauded, kicked her leg high into the air, and said as her friends fell into formation next to her, "Ready? Okay! Gimme a G! Gimme an R! Gimme an E! Gimme another E! Gimme an N! What does that spell? DEATH! YAAAAAAYYY! Go Team Green Door!" "You girls aren't terribly bright, are you?" Melissa stated as she unlocked the green door and opened it just before the four girls picked the bloodied man up and threw him into the blackened room.

"What in the hell do you guys *have* in there?" an astonished yet intrigued Morgan asked as she heard deep growls emanating from behind the green door. Her amazement increased when she heard a bubbly voice yell out, "Oh joy! Oh joy! He is all mine! I shall rip his spleen out in a matter of no time!" The joyous voice was followed by the sound of flesh being torn apart while a man let out his final shrieks of agony.

"Larry?" a shocked Morgan exclaimed. "Larry? Is that you?" She was greeted by the skulking form of a blood-soaked, bright yellow leopard strutting into the interrogation room. "Larry! What has happened to you? I wrote you to be kind and sweet and peace-loving! This can't be happening! Not to *you*!"

Larry pounced up onto his hind legs as his yellow tail curled into a curly-Q and his goo-goo-googly eyes rolled around in his bright-white sockets. "Why hello, Morgan!" he yelled out in his goofy voice. "I'm so glad to see you! Please, come see my bachelor pad which is completely new!" He turned back around, led Morgan to the entrance of his room, and turned the light on. Morgan cautiously went behind the green door and gasped at the sight.

There was the completely dismembered and disemboweled man bleeding all over thick, orange shag carpeting. A bright pink lava lamp illuminated a corner of the room above a zebra-printed futon. The walls were adorned with pin-ups taken from a variety of nature magazines. Larry went over to a small turntable and turned it on. As the thick, black vinyl rotated, safari-themed exotica music came pouring out of the tinny speakers.

"I have a new home now, can't you see?" Larry began explaining. "I believe that it is just perfect for me.

"The home of the Ladies Cabot is getting a bit tight, and I frequently dream of having Maddy for a bite.

"She does annoy me night and day, and I thought it best to just get out of her way."

"Can't blame him there," Josie muttered under her breath as she listened on.

"But, Larry," Morgan replied in a pleading tone. "Larry, you weren't written to do such *awful things!*"

"And what is so awful," Larry answered. "About doing bad men in? To send men to their deaths after they commit horrible sins?

"It is not my intent to disappoint you, my dear sweet friend. But it is time for my innocence to come to an end.

"I have seen the horrors that humans have wrought, and I think it's great that the evil men are being caught.

"I understand that peace is the best way to go, but when our survival is threatened, we must overthrow.

"And if violence is the only means, then violence it is. It is not at all our fault. These bastards started this.

"They have done this to themselves by pushing us to the brink. Payback is indeed a bitch, now don't you think?

"We are merely doing what we must to protect our own. In order for there to be peace, the evil must be overthrown.

"So yes, my friend, I have joined in the cause. Once I saw the tyranny, I gave it no pause.

"But my dream is that we shall now all thrive. Through love and unity and respect for one another's lives.

"I am sorry Morgan, but I must now go. Sruja has arranged a visitor for me, don't you know.

"She is a beautiful creation from another writer. With lush, pink fur and a cute figure to die for.

"So please excuse me while I prepare for my darling little doe. I want to look my best for when we give it a go.

"I may put on some antlers and dress as a buck. That should get her into the mood for a long, hard..." He was interrupted by an aghast Morgan yelling out, "Larry! Shut your mouth!"

A snickering Larry closed the green door as Morgan stood with her mouth agape. There was a knock at the interrogation room door and Josie went over to answer it. Standing in the doorway was a bright pink animated doe. She had ripped fishnet stockings on her furry legs, and a cigarette was dangling from her blistered lips. Alexander felt familiar violent urges creeping into his soul as he lasciviously stared at the cartoon prostitute. Melissa patted him on his clenched fist and whispered, "Calm down, dear. We promised. No more hookers. Well, maybe after Larry has had his fun. It's not like she's real and it *has* been a while after all. Besides, I didn't like the way she looked at you."

"Yeah," the doe said through her coughs in a raspy voice. "Hey there sweetheart. Listen, some chick named Sruja ordered me up out of an animated adult book for some leopard named Larry. You think you could be a sweetie and point me in his direction?"

Josie stood in shocked silence and pointed toward the green door. "Thanks, doll," the pink doe replied. "Say, you got a cute little figure on you, kid. And really nice curly red hair. You got potential. Well, for a human, that is," she said before disappearing behind the opening green door.

A dismayed Josie looked at Morgan and said, "You know what, Morgan? Maybe you need to take a break from writing. This shit's getting weird."

"Yeah, maybe you're right," an astonished Morgan replied. "I think I'll just go now. I promised Connor I'd pick up his tux. And Naomi and I need to get the spirits together for a wedding rehearsal. This is going to be the craziest party there could ever be."

CHAPTER 23

WHO INVITED YOU?

"Oh my, don't you two look absolutely beautiful," Agatha Cabot stated as she walked into the dressing room in the rear of a grand pavilion. "Sophia, I had my doubts about tie-dying that wedding gown, but I must say it turned out wonderfully. And the turquoise necklace, anklet, and bracelet accent it perfectly. I'm not so sure about the sandals, but you do have your own style, now, don't you? Even as a little girl, you shunned pretty dresses for ripped bellbottoms or some hippie-dippy dress. We all thought you would grow out of it. I'm so pleased that you didn't. I'm so glad this world did not beat the independence out of you as it did for so many other women. I'm so proud that my granddaughter turned out to be exactly as she wanted to be. Strong. Independent. And one hell of a medium to boot. And I'm also so happy that you raised a daughter and granddaughter who share your strength." Sophia had to turn her seventy-four-year-old face away from her grandmother to conceal the tears that were rolling down her weathered cheeks.

"And Lori," Agatha continued. "*Your* dress is simply stunning. The silver sequins underneath all of that bright white fringe makes you look like the celestial universe on Earth. It almost makes me homesick for my little bungalow in Eden. Almost. I wouldn't miss this wedding for all the worlds in the cosmos."

"The sequins and fringe was *my* idea, toots," Minnie Marples squeaked while her army of bright yellow hand emojis were meticulously working on Sophia's hair and Lori's makeup. "Makes her look like a real doll, don'tcha think?" "Absolutely," an assisting Sruja agreed while her come to life creations made out in the corner. "Larry. Darlene the Doe. Could you two maybe find a more appropriate time to do that?"

"Oh, but Sruja," Larry the Leopard countered in his cartoonish voice. "Can't you see? There is nobody but Darlene the Doe for me!" "It's alright baby," Darlene the Doe stated through her coughing fit. "I need a drink anyway. Where's the bar? And where can we smoke in this joint? Then we'll find a closet and I'm gonna bang those spots right offa-ya."

"Oh joy! Oh joy!" a bouncing Larry yelled out while his goo-goo-googly eyes rolled around in his sockets. "I'm getting laid! And since she's my girlfriend, she doesn't expect to be paid!"

"Oh, dear lord," a chuckling Lori said as the hand emojis applied rouge to her porcelain cheeks. "Sruja, you really did it when you brought *those* two characters to life out of books. I can't even *imagine* a more messed up pair."

"Really?" Sophia sneered. "You can't imagine a more messed up pair of book characters? Morgan sure as hell did."

"Oh, well, yes," Lori giggled in response. "*Them.* Yes, they *are* a bit, um, *high strung*, now aren't they? But I must admit that I've grown to love them, especially their daughter. She is so smart and sweet yet has the tenacity of her parents when needed. And I do love the other two as well. I almost feel guilty about sending them to Galesburg to feed the zombies the day before our wedding. Almost. We just couldn't take a chance on them ruining our day. You just never know when someone will upset them and then, before you know it, there's a carved-up corpse in the basement. Are you *sure* they won't make it back in time?"

"Oh, I'm sure," Sophia replied. "I made sure that the conductor would take his sweet ol' time on the return trip today. There's *no way* they'll make it in time. Not even for the reception, heh, heh, heh."

"Mom! Dad!" Josie yelled up the staircase of the home of the Ladies Cabot. "Would you two hurry up? We're going to be late for the wedding!"

"We're almost ready sweetie!" Erick shouted back before being interrupted by his frustrated wife. "Yeah, I'm almost ready! Erick, zip up my dress, wouldja? Just look at this stupid thing that they're making me wear. Where in the hell did they find this peach, puffy monstrosity? They did it on purpose. I know they did. Probably stupid Lori's idea. And I bet stupid Sophia was the one who scheduled the zombie feeding in Galesburg for yesterday. Hell, I had to hold a knife to that train conductor's throat all the way here just to get him to step on the gas! Or the coal. Or, oh, who cares. Let's just get going."

Maddy and Erick descended the staircase to find a flowered dressed Josie eating a hot dog. "Hey! Where in the hell didja get the hot dog?" Maddy roared. "I'm starving! Gimme a bite!" Maddy grabbed the sandwich from her dismayed daughter and took a huge bite. She immediately spit it out onto the floor. "BLECH! What the hell Josie? How many times have I told you that ketchup on hot dogs is doing it wrong!"

"Mother!" Josie yelled back. "I do *not* have to eat hot dogs the way that you do!" "Yes, you do!" Maddy angrily countered. "As long as you're living under *my* roof, ketchup on hot dogs is banned!" "We're not living under your roof!" Josie screamed back. "We are living with the Cabots! And another thing…"

She was cut off by Erick stepping between the combating pair. "Ladies. Is this really important right now? Can we just go? We're already late. And Josie, you can eat your hot dogs however you like." "You *always* take her side," a fuming Maddy stated as the trio exited the home.

"Oh, great, it's already started," Maddy said as the family opened the doors of the pavilion. Lori and Sophia had just begun their procession down the long red carpeted aisle while an orchestra softly played in the background. Giggling smiley emojis were tossing rose petals in front of them as the mother and daughter held hands while stepping towards their loving futures. At the front of the pavilion stood the tuxedo-clad and quite sweaty pair of grooms. Connor fought back tears while Vince nervously pulled at his soaked collar. They were flanked by the beaming faces of Naomi, Morgan, Victoria, and the entire Plymouth coven. And between the two anxious men stood a proud Queen Zenobia dressed in a bright purple gown. She gave the approaching ladies a reassuring smile. Her face then turned to one of horror.

"I can't see a damned thing from back here," Maddy whispered to her husband. "Hey! Look! I think there's a seat in the front row. I'm a dignitary! That's where *I'm* supposed to be!" Erick's pleas for her to stop went unheeded as Maddy strutted down the aisle behind the two brides. "Excuse me, ladies," Maddy stated as she walked through their clutched hands. "Sorry about this. Sorry we're a bit late. Gee, I wonder who's responsible for *that*? Doesn't matter. Wouldn't want to spoil your big day. Have no fear, for we are here! Sorry for the interruption everybody! Just getting' to my seat in the front row and…hey. Move your fat ass over. Aren't *you* the bitch who wouldn't share her garlic bread with me? What the hell, Queen Z? How in the hell did *this* bitch get a front row seat? I can tell by the look on your face Queenie that now isn't the time. Okay. I'm settled in. You may proceed with the wedding." She then turned around and shouted at a chatting couple, "Hey! I said they may proceed with the wedding so stop your yapping back there! My friends are getting married! Jesus, some people are so rude! There you go, Queen Z. I always got your back."

"Okay," a relieved Queen Zenobia said as Lori and Sophia took the hands of their respective grooms. "Let us begin. Yes, let today's union between Sophia and Vince, and Lori and Connor mark the dawn of a new day. A day where love and respect and kindness is embraced by all. A day where mindless hatred and evil is extinguished. A day when the souls of humanity can begin to come together and heal. A day when we turn away from the destruction of our beloved planet and allow *her* to heal as well. And heal we shall. Our Earth shall heal so that she may provide a home for humanity and all living creatures for millennia to come. And humanity shall heal as well. Humanity shall now come together as one. Regardless of our gender or age or culture or sexual identity or sexual orientation or race, we shall come together. Our souls shall bond, and we shall come together and provide for one another. We shall support one another. We shall love one another. And we shall all persist together."

"Uh, I gotta take issue with you on *that* one, Z-String," Maddy blurted out. "I mean, yeah, yeah, yeah, love and peace and happiness and all that shit. Great. I'm *totally* on board. But are you telling me that I have to love *everybody*? Even *this* fat bitch who wouldn't share her garlic bread? 'Cause *that* shit doesn't seem right. Oh, and one more question. Does this mean we can't murder anybody anymore? What the hell am *I* supposed to do? I'll be bored out of my mind and I'm sure as hell not working at the diner the rest of my life. And *another* thing..."

A large bouquet of flowers grew and wrapped themselves around Maddy's mouth as vines from a houseplant lifted her struggling body from her seat and planted it in the back row next to her laughing husband and daughter. "So sorry about that," Morgan sheepishly stated. "Please proceed. She won't be any more trouble."

"Riiiiiiight," Sophia scoffed. "She'll bust out of those vines in no time and ruin the rest of the wedding. Let's just get this shit over with. I think we've made our points in this book already. No need for any more long, drawn out speeches about the evil that lurks in some people's hearts. No need to talk once again about how we can all triumph over the forces of evil by unifying with one another and standing resolutely for our humanitarian principles. No need to talk about the urgent need to stand up to the bullies that ruled this world. To use peaceful means of protest. To be knowledgeable about the actual events of the world and cast our votes accordingly. No need to again talk about the need for revolution should our peaceful means be stripped away from us through their kidnapping us off of the streets and placing us in concentration camps. No need to talk about finally achieving justice against the cruel and the corrupt. No need to talk about how we may have love in our hearts for our fellow man but when our fellow man's heart is pure evil and threatens us with extinction, that we can be *just* as cruel and merciless as they are in order to protect our loved ones. Nope, we've made all of those points already, so there is no need for another big speech. This author tends to get a bit preachy anyway. Let's just get hitched and move on to the reception."

"Cool," Queen Zenobia stated. "There's nothing like brevity. Plus, I'm starving. And I need a drink. So, Lori and Connor. You two wanna be married to one another for eternity and support one another in sickness and in health and all of that shit or what?"

"Um, yeah, sure," a bewildered Lori answered. "Um, Connor?" "Well, yeah, sure. I've loved you since high school Lori. I remember the first time I saw you in the study hall. I think my eyes musta popped out of my head because..."

"Yeah, yeah, yeah," Queen Zenobia interrupted. "Save it for the honeymoon suite. We're on a schedule. Sophia and Vince. You wanna get hitched and love one another and blah, blah, blah?'

Sophia peered into her groom's tender eyes and thought back to the first time she had walked into his bar. She had been so taken by his brawny build and kind spirit. She secretly had always hoped that this day would arrive but was frightened at revealing her true nature to him. She was frightened that he would shun her if he understood who she truly was. She had to evolve in order to fully embrace the love and caring of this fine man. And now finally, she felt whole. Finally, she was able to...

"Sophia!" Queen Zenobia yelled. "What's the answer? We've got S'mores to make! We've got a sacrifice out back that's ready to be lit up to cook our little treats. What'll it be, sister?"

"Yes," Sophia eagerly answered. "Yes, I absolutely take this man as my husband." "Cool, cool, now it's your turn Vince," Queen Zenobia prodded. "Well, of course I do, but I've got something to say first!" "No, you don't," Queen Zenobia said. "Now, by the power invested in me by the universe I hereby declare you folks married. Let's get to the reception! Maestro, if you please."

"Let's boogie, bitches!" Papa Doc yelled into his microphone from behind his DJ stand. The entire congregation got up and started hugging and dancing as the pavilion became flooded by brilliant flashing lights and pounding rhythms. Everyone danced except one person. "And one *more* thing!" Maddy shouted over the thunderous bass as she pulled vines and leaves from her petite frame.

"Oh, dear," Lori said pitifully. "She's going to ruin the reception too." "No, she won't, Mom," Morgan reassured. "Don't worry about it. I know a way to keep her preoccupied. Just enjoy your reception. And congratulations. And Connor? Um, would it be weird if I called you 'Dad'? My real father was a complete asshole, and you've treated me like your very own daughter ever since you and mom started dating. So, would that be okay?"

Connor's eyes filled with tears as he embraced Morgan, lifted her up, and gleefully spun her around. "It would be my honor," he said in a choked-up voice before Queen Zenobia thrust herself between the pair and said, "Hellooooo! S'moooooores! That asshole isn't going to light *himself* on fire! Let's go!"

The four newlyweds were seated at a long table and surrounded by a tittering congregation while they unwrapped their wedding gifts. Sophia opened yet another toaster and Vince whispered to her, "Do these people think we're twenty or something? We're in our seventies. We've had all this shit for years."

"I'll take it," Connor stated as Lori and Sophia reached for another present. "I can use it at the station." "Um, what in the world could these big, long, hard things be?" a confused Lori asked. "You might want to rephrase that," a chuckling Sophia replied as the pair shred through the bright wrapping paper revealing two brand-new brooms. "Oh, I do hope you like them," Victoria said. "These aren't easy to come by. I had them specially made. And these brooms have a special feature. They contour perfectly to your ass which is really nice for long flights. And see here? It will vibrate and this light comes on if you swerve."

"Oh man, I totally need that!" Naomi yelled out. "Oh, wow. Those are really nice models, Victoria. I asked my mom and dad for one for my birthday but they said that they were on back order so they got me a bunch of games that I can play alone instead. Not that I don't like the games. They're really cool, and mom and dad say that it's nice to see me playing alone in my room quietly. They really emphasized the word 'quietly' for some reason. Don't know why. Anyway, if I had a broom like *that*, I'd never ever hit another tree. Or chimney. Or wall. Or flock of birds. Or Mrs. Anderson's mailbox. Or that picture window in the barber shop. Anyway, I'm totally jealous! You guys want me to teach you how to drive it?"

"No!" Lori and Sophia yelled out in unison before reaching for their final present that was addressed to them both. They lifted the large, heavy, square package and shook it before shrugging at one another and tearing the paper from it. Sitting on the table in front of them was an ancient book that was glowing red. It appeared to be bound by human flesh and slight wails were emanating from it. "That is from me," Agatha Cabot said.

"This is my ancient recipe book. All of my recipes are in here. Including my super-duper top-secret recipe for my cobbler. It is *not* the recipe that I'm selling in supermarkets everywhere, so pick yours up today. It is a *special* cobbler. Just as *every* recipe in this book is special. These recipes will guarantee you both a thriving diner and catering business. And, as an added bonus, any dark soul who eats one of these dishes will glow red so they will be easy to recognize and capture. Oh, and then there's an incantation in the back that you can use to summon a demon from hell to take the bastard out. You know. If you're busy running errands and don't have the time to take care of it yourself."

"Thank you, grandmother, this means the world to me," Sophia said as she teared up. "Yes, thank you, Grandmother Agatha," Lori echoed. "And thank you to everyone who has made this day so special for all four of us. Thank you for your attendance. Thank you for your gifts. And thank you for your love. This reception has been just wonderful." She then held a puzzled look on her face as she inquired, "Yes, it has been quite peaceful. Maybe *too* peaceful. Just where did Morgan take those three anyway?"

"Where in the *hell* are we going Morgan?" an annoyed Maddy asked as she, Erick, and Josie were being lead down a dark, stone hallway in the basement of the pavilion. "We're going to miss the entire reception! And the S'mores! And the dancing!" "Well," Erick said softly to his daughter, "Nobody's gonna miss watching *her* dance." "What did you just say?" Maddy asked the chortling pair. "Oh, whatevs. Let's just get this over with. I need to get my dancin' shoes on!"

"Well, I just thought you might enjoy..." Morgan paused before opening a heavy iron door. "This!" Maddy, Erick, and Josie squealed with delight as they saw what was behind the door. They began high fiving, jumping, and clapping while peering at the pathetic face of Elder Himler. He was naked, bound, and draped face first over a table that was covered by his tears, drool, and snot.

"Hello, Elder Himler," Morgan said as she put her cool sunglasses on. "I bet you've been frightened, haven't you? Confused? In pain? I bet you really don't like being confined down here, do you? Now I guess you know how it feels. You now know how it feels to be abducted and thrown into a hot cell. To be stripped of your clothes and of your dignity. To be tortured physically and emotionally. To not know when or if you will ever get to go home again. You now know how it feels to be treated worse than an animal. Just how *you* treated thousands of people. You now know how it feels to be taken from your loved ones and have your world turned into a perpetual nightmare. You now know how it feels to be completely and utterly hopeless. The people that you did this to didn't know why it was happening. They were just living their lives and then masked thugs came and took them away. And beat them. And laughed at them. And they did so under *your* orders.

"They didn't know what they did wrong. But you do, now don't you. You know what got you here. You know, it isn't just that your policies were cruel. There have been a lot of cruel policies that assholes like you have implemented over the years. No, it isn't just the policies that got you here. It's the fact that you took *joy* from your cruelty. You took *joy* from people's suffering. You *enjoyed* watching children cry as their parents were taken away in black vans. You *enjoyed* watching people starve to death or die from lack of medical care or from the beatings from your terrorist thugs. And that makes *you* a special kind of evil. That makes you the *worst fucking piece of shit to have ever walked this Earth.* Here Maddy, take this and have fun with it."

Maddy's eyes grew wide as she took the long, hard, wooden paddle that was imbedded with rusty jagged nails, shards of glass, and twisted pieces of sharp metal. Tears of joy began running out of her brilliant green eyes as she looked fondly at her creator and said, "Oh my God, Morgan. Thank you. Does this mean…. does this mean that I can say *(expletive)* now?"

"Nope," Morgan answered. "Only one time per book for this audience's age." "Well, that's not fair!" Maddy screamed out. Erick went over to Morgan and said, "Nicely played. That should *really* piss her off." "Yeah, well, I did create her after all," a chuckling Morgan replied.

"Oh, you twisted son of a bitch! I'm so pissed right now!" Maddy screamed before slapping Himler with the torturous paddle and yelling out, "Good game, Himler! Um. Aw shit. The nails and shit seem be stuck in his ass. It's really hard to pull out. Hey baby, help me pull the paddle from his ass, wouldja?" "Of course, dear," Erick answered. He gripped the handle of the paddle and tore it from Himler's body. Himler screamed in anguish as a huge bloody chunk of his ass went flying into a dark corner where a pale man's hand bent down and picked it up.

"Oh, you're here too, huh?" Maddy said to the dark figure. "You sure get off on watching don'tcha? Well, watch this shit! Good game, Himler! Sonofabitch! It's stuck again! Baby, couldja help me again? Cool. Thanks. Wow. Look at all that blood pouring out of his ass. And a few nails and pieces of glass are stuck in there. Oh well. Not that he's going to be sitting ever again. Let's try again. Good game, Himler! Oh, screw this. Stuck again. I'm not wasting my time with this shit anymore. I'm kinda tired of the whole 'good game' schtick anyway."

"Oh, thank God," Morgan and Josie muttered in unison. "Hey, I got an idea!" Erick excitedly exclaimed. "How about you start saying 'an idiot says what?'"

"I *love* that idea, baby!" Maddy squealed as she jumped into her loving husband's arms. "I could *totally* polish off *that* old chestnut! Yeah, that should annoy the *shit* out of stupid Lori and stupid Sophia for a while."

"Or" Josie chimed in. "You two *could* just grow up and not be assholes all the time." Maddy and Erick stared at one another with mischievous grins. They could feel their souls connecting once again. It was the same feeling for one another that they had felt when Morgan had written about their first meeting. Maddy's smile widened, she looked into her daughter's green eyes, and playfully said, "An idiot says what?"

"No, Mom, don't start with me," an annoyed Josie answered. "An idiot says what?" "I'm serious, Mom! Stop it!" "An idiot says what?" "Mom! Just stop it! And this isn't funny Dad!" "An idiot says what?" "Oh, screw this! I'm going back to the reception!" "An idiot says what?" Maddy said again as she and her laughing husband began following their perturbed daughter out the door. "Hey, Poindexter!" Maddy yelled out as she was leaving. "This asshole's all yours! Enjoy! Hey Josie! Say something to me! I want to say 'an idiot says what?' to you again!" "No, mom!" Josie's voice echoed down the cold, stone hallway. "I'm not saying another thing to you *ever again!*" "An idiot says what? Heh, heh, heh."

The sobbing Himler lifted his head and watched as two figures approached him from the dark corner. "Well, hello there Elder Himler," the man calmly said in his British accent. "It is so nice to finally meet you. This will take a while, so why don't we get acquainted? This is my lovely wife from hell, Melissa Bartlesworth and I am Alexander. Alexander Picklesbee. But in just a moment, you will know me as Jack. Jack the *Ripper*, heh, heh, heh."

Later that evening, an exhausted Ladies Cabot were drinking tea in their living room. "What a nice day," Lori observed. "Yes, perfect." Sophia agreed. "Well, almost perfect," Morgan stated. "I'm really sorry about Maddy. She means well, but she just can't help herself sometimes. I've tried to write her as being more mellow, but that only lasts a few pages, then her true nature comes out."

"It's okay dear," Lori said as she tussled her daughter's hair. "We'll just have to learn to love her." "Or chop her up," Sophia tersely said. "I swear, if she says, 'an idiot says what?' *one more time*, I'm going to make her into tomorrow's lunch special." "Yeah, well, that's easier said than done," Lori replied. "And at least she isn't slapping our asses anymore. Oh man, I'm beat. I need to get to sleep. Connor wants to leave early for Niagara Falls tomorrow. I'm just going to check my social media and hit the sack."

Lori opened her computer and began looking at all of the glowing posts from her wedding guests. "Awww, that's sweet. Oh, look at this cute picture. Their daughter is so adorable. Oh, here's a picture of a vampire and werewolf laughing with each other. The vampire is holding a silver bullet, and the werewolf is holding a wooden steak. I'm so glad they bathed before coming. Oh, here's one of Papa Doc dancing with the coven. Wait. Who's peering between them? Oh, goddammit. It's Maddy! Look! I didn't notice at first, but she's photobombed every single picture! Oh shit, my wedding photos!"

She opened a file on her computer and began looking at the proofs that the photographer had sent her. She turned the computer screen so that a reluctant Morgan could see the work of her creation. "Ah shit, I'm sorry, Mom," a regretful Morgan said. "Um, maybe she can be cropped out or something?"

At that moment, Lori's computer pinged. "All right. I'll deal with it tomorrow. I'm going to read this last post, then I'm going to bed." Lori turned her relaxed face to read the post. Her face reddened as the words pounded into her head and forced flashbacks of all of the abusive men that she and her beloved daughter had been subjected to in her life. "What is it dear?" Sophia inquired. "Listen to *this* shit," Lori answered in a dark voice.

Went to the wedding of the bitches Cabot today. Yep, I was right in the middle of it. Right in the middle of all of these leftist libtards. They were so stupid. They never caught me and never will. And there are more like me out there. More men like me who will take this country back and put women back in their place. So, hey Lori Cabot. If you ever read this, just know that pretty soon you're going to be cleaning my house and pleasuring me whenever I want. And that goes for all of your stupid witch bitch friends! And the cake was dry too!

"What are you going to do, Mom?" Morgan asked. "We knew that there would be a few who would slip between the cracks, but for one of them to be at your wedding is just awful. Plus, he insulted your cake." Lori stared at the screen for a moment in silence. She used her right hand to hover her cursor over the post. Her lips curled upward in a wicked little smile as she clicked her mouse and responded by posting an 'Angry' emoji. "I sure hope he gets a lot of 'Likes' on this one. Yeah, a lot of 'Likes' right up his evil fat ass. Minnie, do your thing. It's now time for the Ladies Cabot to be put to bed."

THE END